BATHING BEAUTY

Daniel was sitting some distance from the fire, staring broodingly into the flames, his brown eyes flecked with the reflection of red, orange and bronze sparks. He glanced up as Vanessa emerged, unclothed, from the trees. She saw his throat work, and then he averted his gaze.

"Enjoy your bath?" he asked gruffly, threading his fingers through hair still glossy and wet from his own bath earlier.

"Yes," Vanessa answered. "It was lovely."

With a crook of his finger, he beckoned her forward, "Come here, Vanessa."

She debated a moment, uncomfortable, uncertain. Yet she knew she wanted to be close to Daniel.

Inching over, he made room for her on the mat. As she seated herself at Daniel's side, she gave a subtle tilt to her head, sending her hair forward over her shoulder to partially obscure her breasts.

From beneath her lashes, she watched Daniel very slowly reach out and take a lock of her hair between his fingers, rubbing the strands back and forth.

"Vanessa," Daniel asked, "do you know the meaning of desire?"

JAGUAR EYES

CASEY CLAYBOURNE

LOVE SPELL BOOKS NEW YORK CITY

LOVE SPELL®

November 1998

Published by

Dorchester Publishing Co., Inc.
276 Fifth Avenue
New York, NY 10001

ISBN 0-505-52284-5

Printed in the United States of America.

Jaguar Eyes
is dedicated to
Daniel Hersh,
one of the few men I've known
worthy of an Amazon.

With extreme gratitude and endless thanks
to the amazing Shelley Blanton-Stroud,
without whom this book would never have been written.

JAGUAR EYES

Prologue

Lincolnshire, 1840

Damn the man! Damn him to hell and back again. He's gone too far this time, just too bloody far.

Daniel Heywood clenched his fingers until his hands ached with the desire to release their pent-up violence. The tendons in his wrists stood out like steel cords—strong as the unbreakable ties that bound him forever to the man he cursed: His father, the Earl Bretton.

Daniel's eyes narrowed as they scanned the familiar spareness of the Bretton Hall study; it was his father's lair, the den of one of England's most powerful men. It was a military man's workroom, practical and simple. The only concession to decor was a collection of antique armor displayed austerely along a far wall. None of Lady Bretton's fondness for the baroque could be seen here, no gilt-edged tables or Louis Quatorze fauteils. The mahogany floor lay bare, the windows stood unadorned, and the stiff-backed chairs were cushionless and uninviting. The room's sterility reminded Daniel of a laboratory—one in which he had been the unwitting experiment.

Similar to the monster in Mary Shelley's famous tale, Daniel had been crafted by his father's hand in this stark, cold laboratory. He had been molded and shaped, mercilessly tested and challenged until—as in the story—he had eventually risen up and turned against his creator.

Daniel flexed his fingers. How many times had he dreamed of wrapping them around his father's neck?

With slow deliberation, he relaxed his fists, recognizing that he would need every bit of self-control he possessed not to leap at his father when the man came into the room.

And yet, at the same time, Daniel knew with certainty that he would not give the manipulative bastard the satisfaction of seeing that he'd pierced Daniel's shell. That even now the creator still held the power to govern his beast.

Walking over to the window, Daniel pushed open the casement. Even so, the acrid stench of his father's pipe tobacco lingered in the air, a scent that at one time had made Daniel's gut kick with nausea. He'd long since trained himself not to react to that particular smell but, when he'd been younger, a summons to the earl's smoke-filled study had invariably meant a reprimand. Perhaps only an admonishment, sometimes a caning . . . But always the humiliation of knowing that he'd failed. Failure and the fragrance of Perique tobacco would forever be linked.

He glanced at the small German clock on the desk. He'd waited forty-five minutes. His father might make him wait another three-quarters of an hour, or perhaps the rest of the afternoon. The earl loved to play such games, but Daniel could play them, too. Perhaps not as well as his mother, he thought wryly, remembering how the halls would echo with her shrieks and his father's answering bellows; but then again Lady Bretton lived every day of her life with the earl. And while the entire family had learned to play these power games, Daniel felt that they seemed so futile and longed to end them once and for all.

Indeed, though Daniel despised his father for expecting so much and being so demanding, at least, he respected him. Unfortunately the same could not be said of his feelings for his mother. Emotionally absent daring his youth, she had been consumed by her interactions with high society. At least his father had made the effort—misguided and brutal as it had been.

Without warning the door to the study flew open, crashing against the wall with a *bang* that rattled the shields and armaments. Daniel didn't even blink. He was too familiar with his father's tactics. Everything that Thomas Heywood did, he did to impress. Even something as simple as entering a room.

Their gazes clashed and, for the thousandth time, Daniel cursed the irony of staring into a face he abhorred. A face that could have been his own. For all that he tried to forget it, there was no disputing that he was the Earl Bretton's son.

They shared the same chestnut hair, though his father's was now liberally threaded with silver. Their eyes were the same brown, their cheekbones severe slashes across angular features. No, neither man was particularly handsome. But what good was a pretty face? his father would say. All that mattered was strength. The power to drive a man to his knees with the force of your stare.

And, God knew, Thomas Heywood had driven dozens of men to their knees.

The earl was dressed for riding, his coat tailored to perfection across his youthfully broad shoulders. He held a crop in one hand, and Daniel wondered whether he had brought it along purposefully.

His father led with the first sally.

"I thought I taught you to be a man of your word," he drawled. "What of your vow never to return to Bretton Hall?"

Daniel matched his father's unfeeling smile. "An oath given to one undeserving of its honor is no oath."

Tapping the riding crop in time to his steps, the earl strode into the room, leaving the door ajar. "Oh, so now the boy speaks of *honor?*"

Daniel did not rise to the bait. "The only reason I've come is to inform you that this time you have failed, Father. Your plan did not succeed. In spite of your meddling, I have found other financing for my trip."

If he hadn't known him so well, Daniel might not have seen the spasm of surprise that jerked across his father's shoulders.

"For God's sake, who would lend you money for such a ludicrous venture? Those book-loving naturalists you're so fond of? Or was it your sickly scientist friend Darwin?"

Daniel's eyes slitted half-shut. "I'm sure you'll make it a point to find out who's backing the voyage, so I see no reason to tell you. Though I *will* have you know that your influence will be of no use this time. I won't let you sabotage me again."

"So you go?"

"I leave within the fortnight."

His father's poise began to crumble, his face flushing with anger. "You're a damned fool, Daniel! A bloody damned fool. All you are doing is chasing fame and fool's gold. And for what?" he scoffed. "Accolades from those bloodless academics? Election into the Royal Society?

Nothing but horseshit!" He spat onto the wood floor.

"I never expected you to understand my studies," Daniel said. "But I give you fair warning—do not dare to interfere again."

The earl raised his riding crop and pointed it at Daniel's chest. "You threaten me? Have you forgotten to whom you're speaking?"

Daniel let all of his loathing show in his expression. "I could never forget."

The air fairly crackled.

Then his father began to nod slowly, as if in realization, his lips twisting into a smirk. "You won't find it in South America."

Daniel stilled, knowing what was to come. And hating his father for it.

"Do you honestly believe that this will make a man of you? A jaunt through the wilds?" The earl stepped closer, the tip of the riding crop still hovering above Daniel's heart. "Do you run from your shame, is that it?"

Daniel clenched his fists at his sides as he met his father's taunting grin. "I run from nothing, old man."

Before the earl could answer, Daniel reached up and wrenched the riding crop from his grasp. In one sharp movement, he snapped the crop in two and tossed it aside.

Fury and determination pulsed through him and, in that moment, he vowed he would find what he sought in the Amazon . . . or never return.

Chapter One

South America, 1840

She stood at the edge of the cliff, her toes curling tightly around the rim of the precipice as if that grip alone could hold her earthbound. The wind swirled around her, plucking at the ends of her hair, cajoling, pleading. *Come,* it called, *come fly with me.* And, oh, how she wanted to.

Spreading her arms wide, she stretched out her fingers, reaching for something elusive and unknown—something that might ease her growing restlessness. But her hands filled only with the scent of cedar and the heat of the Mother's sun.

The wind soughed seductively again in her ear—*Come with me*—and she answered it with a throaty laugh. Alone on this ridgetop, Vanessa felt almost free. Almost.

Here she could laugh at will, weep when she needed to. She could shout and scream and wail, with only the macaws to scold her for her lack of restraint. Only here could she let loose her passions, the uncontrollable emotions that marked her as different from her stoic people.

Wrapping her arms about herself, Vanessa looked across the valley to where the Great River undulated through the forest like an immense copper serpent. On this particular day, the river's waters were serene, like the people who had taken its name: the Ama'zon.

But unlike Vanessa's people, the river's nature was as unpredictable as her own. The next sunrise might find the river raging and churning, angrily flooding its shores. And just as the riverbanks were incapable of withstanding the great Ama'zon, neither could Vanessa contain her fluid passions.

It was so that the Mother had made her.

Vanessa felt the sun's caress grow warmer upon her bare arms, and she knew that it was time to return to the village. She would be missed if she stayed away too long.

With a last lingering look across the emerald-swathed horizon, she turned and began the climb down the ridge's steep face. She moved easily, her pack bouncing as she leaped from one foothold to the next.

At the base of the cliff, she sought an opening

amid the dense brush and plunged into the forest. The jungle swallowed her up like the jaws of a hungry beast. But Vanessa had no fear of it. She knew each tree and each plant by name. She knew to look for the clump of slippery moss at the base of the *heve* tree; she knew where a knot of roots jutted from the earth in the shape of a giant mushroom. This was her home, as familiar to her as her own hearth.

She wound her way up and down the valley past waterfalls and sheer-edged cliffs. Sprays of orchids in colors so bright it almost hurt to gaze upon them arched above her like fragrant rainbows. The mud beneath her feet was cool as she followed the trail to a hollow tucked beneath a cluster of trees.

The area was shadowed, water dripping insistently from the overhead branches. An enormous flat, pink-streaked stone rose from the center of the basin and Vanessa climbed atop it. She looked out onto what seemed to be an impenetrable wall of vegetation, nothing but green rising up to the sky. But, as always in the Great Mother's forest, all was not as it appeared.

Tilting her head, she continued gazing into the thicket until a blinding beam of sunshine cut through the gloom. The radiant light illuminated a narrow pathway that had been completely hidden only moments earlier.

She jumped from the rock and strode onto the path, her pace hurried. The day's heat advanced, telling her that she had been gone longer than she'd realized.

She rounded the next bend and sighted the walls of Eldra'to. A soft sigh escaped her. She should be glad to be home—this was the only one she had ever known. But a vague melancholy washed over her as she approached the entrance to Eldra'to.

She did not belong here. She had never truly felt as if she did, not even as a child. Something called to her. Something pulled at her to go, to fly away with the wind. But to where?

Vanessa sighed, noting the position of the sun. There was little hope of her slipping back into the village unnoticed. Tucked into a large cavern, Eldra'to was bordered on three sides by cliffs, with only the fourth side accessible from the jungle. Even if she were to pass through the gates undetected, the village would not be quiet so late in the morning.

She crept around the open gateway and any hope she held of not being seen was lost. She had forgotten that the testing had begun.

In the main square, nearly three dozen of the youngest Ama'zons were competing, vying for the honor of commencing warrior training. Sparring, the youngsters were rolling about in the dust, the sounds of their scuffles only sporadically broken by a soft cry or a grunt of pain.

As Vanessa skirted the edge of the square, she could not repress the pang of envy that shot through her, watching the warriors put the candidates through their paces. At one time she had desperately longed to belong to their ranks, to find acceptance in the exalted role of warrior. But her "flaw" had made that dream impossible. Perhaps a teacher or a healer might be forgiven an occasional outburst of emotion, but not a warrior. Never an Ama'zon warrior.

Vanessa was pulled from her thoughts when she nearly collided with a small figure. She reached out to steady the child and her fingers grew wet with blood. A gash on the young girl's upper arm trickled scarlet, most likely a wound acquired during the testing. The child's face was white as she held her tiny fists clenched to her mouth.

"Helen." Vanessa crouched to her knees and took hold of the girl's shoulders. "Are you unwell?"

The child averted her face, but not before Vanessa saw the glimmer of tears rimming the youngster's eyes.

"Oh, little one." Without thinking, Vanessa wrapped her arms around the child, drawing her close. She ran her palms soothingly over Helen's back as her heart swelled. She knew how hard the girl must be struggling not to shed shameful tears. Shameful, at least, to the Ama'zon.

"Are you not doing well in the exercises?" Vanessa asked. The small body trembled in her embrace, then Helen shook her head "no" against Vanessa's breast.

Vanessa hugged her more tightly. The girl's disappointment must be keen. Tears were almost never seen in a child as old as this, who had already seen nine cycles of the seasons.

"Sweet one, you don't have to—"

"Vanessa." The cool-voiced interruption brought Vanessa to her feet at the same time that Helen was pulled from her arms.

"Camilla." Vanessa straightened her spine in an effort to equal the warrior chief's superior height.

But as she raised her chin to meet the other woman's gaze, Vanessa knew that she was no match for the great Camilla. This warrior's strength came from more than just her height or physical prowess. She was like the python who could paralyze its victims with simply a show of its power, with but a shift of its lethal and bone-crushing coils.

Camilla gestured for Helen to return to the drills and the child darted away, her head bowed. When the warrior turned back to Vanessa, her expression was impassive, although censure shone clearly in her hard black eyes.

"Vanessa, you should not encourage the child in her weakness."

"I did not—"

"As a teacher," Camilla tonelessly interrupted, "you must be careful to guard against your own frailty, Vanessa. Children learn by example. You would not wish to dishonor them with your . . . deficiencies."

Vanessa bit down on her tongue until she tasted blood. *I only embraced the child,* she wanted to protest. Instead, she stared down at her feet and watched the dust eddy around her toes, thankful that she'd made her trip to the windy ridgetop that sunrise. The emotions within her were not as keen; her impulses were under control.

She offered Camilla no response as the silence stretched between them. She had long ago stopped apologizing for her differences.

"Diana has been searching for you," the warrior said abruptly. "The Seer has fallen very ill. She has called for you."

Vanessa could not disguise her surprise as her head snapped up. "For me?"

Camilla nodded. "You should go at once. Diana says that her time is near."

Vanessa clamped her lips together to conceal their trembling. The aged Seer had been one of the few who had tolerated her "weakness," who had not labeled her inferior. She had been kind and sympathetic—as much as the stoic Ama'zon manner would allow.

"Yes, of course. I will go to her now."

Her heart pounding, Vanessa hurried across the village to the healing chambers. The heat of the day had risen in sinuous waves that pulsed from the earth, so that Vanessa was perspiring when she entered the coolness of the clay-domed huts.

She shivered, more from apprehension than

from chill. The Seer was the most holy of the Ama'zon, the oldest and most revered of all her people. That she would summon to her bedside Vanessa, a lowly teacher who had not yet even passed into womanhood . . . What could it mean?

The tunnel-like corridors were respectfully quiet, and Vanessa did not need to ask in which room the Seer lay. Four of the more senior healers lingered outside the chamber as Vanessa walked past them and tapped at the door.

A voice bade her enter. She pushed open the portal and paused on the threshold, awed by those who had gathered to witness the Seer's transition to the other world.

Diana, the Teacher Superior, was there, as well as the Healer Superior, Daphne. Cassandra, the most decorated warrior in Ama'zon history, stood at Penelope's right, and behind her were Ariadne and Leander, both high-ranking healers.

"You have arrived just in time," Diana said.

Like the movement of a wave upon the shore, the Elders stepped back from the veil-shrouded bed. They waited expectantly until, with hesitant steps, Vanessa crossed to the bed. She barely stifled a gasp when her gaze fell upon the Seer.

The old woman appeared to have aged a full generation during the past night. Her skin, already as thin as the wing of a moth, was stretched tautly across her cheeks. Her faded blue eyes had receded so deeply into their sockets that Vanessa could not make out their black pinpoint pupils. And her hair, once the color of sun-bleached sand, was now as white as the palest ivory.

"Sit down," the Seer rasped, feebly patting a spot by her side.

Vanessa obediently sank onto the bed, and the old woman reached out and clasped Vanessa's fingers in her own clawlike hand. "My child . . . you must wonder why I have summoned you here."

Vanessa nodded, feeling the gazes of the others burn into her back.

"During the night, the Mother sent me a vision. A very powerful one . . . very powerful." Her glazed eyes sharpened with the intensity of a bird of prey. "You, Vanessa. You will be our people's savior."

Vanessa stiffened, sensing the others' shock, though none made even the slightest sound behind her.

"Me?" she whispered. "How am I to do this?"

The mystic's brow furrowed into a pattern of fine wrinkles as she turned her gaze inward. "I wish I knew, my child," she said softly. "My time is nearly upon me and I do not see as clearly as I once did. The Great Mother has shown me that Eldra'to will cease to exist in the generations to come."

At Vanessa's gasp, the Seer squeezed her fingers. "No, child. I no longer battle the horror of this vision but have accepted it as one of the Mother's truths. The future of the Ama'zon lies with you, Vanessa, and yet I cannot be certain how."

For a brief second, Vanessa glanced over her shoulder to those standing behind her. Surely anyone present could more competently carry out this quest for salvation, she thought. Cassandra or Diana—

"I must leave you with some guidance to confront your destiny," the Seer said in a featherlight voice.

Her destiny. A shiver ran up Vanessa's spine.

"I have spent the last of my life's breath in supplication to our Mother. She has shared but a small wisdom with her dying servant."

"Yes?" Vanessa asked, her palm growing damp in the Seer's grip.

"You—" A fit of coughing overtook her and Penelope rushed forward, waving a smoking dish of herbs beneath the old woman's nose. The Seer's coughs subsided.

"You will"—the old woman paused, and Vanessa could hear how each word had become an effort—"will have to make a choice."

"What choice?"

A skeletal hand fluttered over the sheet. "A difficult choice, my child."

Vanessa's frustration mounted. "But *how* shall I choose?"

The Seer's eyes closed on a sigh. Unconsciously, Vanessa clenched her free hand around a wad of sheeting. *No,* she cried mutely, *not yet.* Infinitely slowly, the transparent lids raised again.

"You must follow your heart," the old woman whispered. "The Great Mother will speak to you."

"But . . . but the Mother has never spoken to me before."

The Seer's hand drifted across the coverlet to rest in the center of her concave chest. "Follow your heart," she counseled, then breathed her final breath.

Chapter Two

It called to him. Hypnotic and timeless, the rhythm of the Amazon night: shrill birdcalls and rumbling animal cries, wind whispering in the tree fronds and gurgling streams. The sounds of the night came together to form a relentless cadence that pulsed through his veins, echoing the beat of his heart. The primitive song beckoned to Daniel as he leaned over the ship's railing, staring into the moonless night.

Brushing his hair from his forehead, he tilted his head back to allow the breeze to float over his throat and neck. The cool air felt like silk against his sunburned flesh, as he took a deep breath, filling his lungs with the fecund aroma of the tropics. Beneath his feet, the ship swayed in a slow, seductive rhythm.

Daniel lowered his gaze again to the stand of trees across the water's expanse, squinting as he tried to pierce the darkness and see into the mysteries concealed behind the thick foliage. His muscles twitched with impatience.

He was drawing closer. He could feel it.

A shadow shifted to his right as MacDougal, the first mate, joined him at the railing.

Unlike any other crewman aboard the *Angela,* the navy veteran had earned Daniel's trust these past months—a trust not easily won.

"I'd damn these cursed bloodsuckers to hell if I didna believe we was already there," the first mate muttered, waving a hand through the buzzing clouds of mosquitoes and gnats.

"Hell?" Daniel allowed himself the hint of a smile. "It could be that, I guess. The Amazon's a river like no other in the world, Mac. A giant. 'The Freshwater Sea.' A man could spend his entire life sailing her and never reach the end."

MacDougal slapped at a mosquito on the side of his neck. "Well, if it's all the same to ye, m'lord, I dinna much care to spend my life in these funny-colored waters. Give me the blue of the ocean any day. Not this strange red-brown, the color of old blood."

In the milky light of the ship's lantern, Daniel saw the shudder that ran through the Scotsman and suppressed a mocking retort. Sailors were a notoriously superstitious lot, and the *Angela*'s first sighting of the bronze-hued river had set the crew on edge. "The River of Death," they'd called it. And rightly so.

"Yes, she's seen her share of blood," Daniel agreed, "but I don't intend to offer her any more."

"How's that, m'lord?"

"Captain," Daniel reminded him.

"Oh, sorry, Cap'n. I keep forgettin'."

The first mate said nothing more, but shifted his weight so that the planking creaked a protest. Daniel knew what question lay unspoken in the silence that hung between them.

Four heat-soaked months of sailing the Amazon had taken their toll on the crew. Although they had replenished supplies in Belém and were well-stocked with water and rations, Daniel had seen the question that lay behind the face of each weary crew member: Just how far up the river did he plan to take them?

A bat swooped low over their heads, the rush of its wings stirring the night air. MacDougal muttered an oath as he jerked his head to the side, and Daniel's gaze followed the animal until it vanished into the darkness.

"I've decided to continue on foot," Daniel said. "These short forays onto the coastline have been interesting, but they are not enough. I need to press farther, deeper, into the heart of the jungle."

MacDougal's surprise was palpable.

"I will leave the ship in your care," Daniel went on. "If you receive no word from me in a month's time, you may turn around and return to England."

"But . . . but ye canna go into that jungle on your own! 'Twould be suicide, pure and simple."

Daniel's mouth thinned. "I'll offer double wages to any man willing to accompany me, but if I have to, I *will* go in alone."

"Double wages?" The first mate shook his head. "Only the greediest lads'll take you up on that offer, and I dinna know if you want that lot at your back. Especially with the talk of mutiny I been hearin'."

"Exactly."

MacDougal sputtered and coughed. "Are you sayin', Cap'n, that you want to bring the likes of Phipps and Reeves with ye?"

"If there is going to be trouble, I want to be the one to handle it. I don't want to leave any malcontents on the ship for you to take care of, Mac."

Although Daniel had carefully selected the sixty men who comprised the *Angela*'s crew, he had anticipated that the Amazon's harsh conditions would expose the weakest among them. It was just as he and Darwin had discussed: "survival of the fittest." The strong endured where the feeble faltered.

"I know you well enough by now to know I canna talk you out of this," the Scotsman said mournfully.

"That's right, you cannot." Daniel turned back

to the railing. "Why don't you go below, Mac? I am going to stay on deck for a while yet."

He felt the first mate's curious regard rest on him for a long moment before MacDougal finally went below.

Daniel's knuckles shone white on the railing. He knew that he could never explain to Mac—just as he had been unable to explain to his father—the compulsion that gripped him to head off for these Amazon wilds. Yes, he knew from his friend, Charles Darwin, that the dangers were many, but Daniel felt pulled here inexorably; it was as if the secret of his destiny thrummed in the jungle's primal melody.

Even now, the prospect of entering that mysterious labyrinth of vines and overgrown trees caused Daniel's pulse to accelerate in anticipation. Something was out there—something meant only for him.

Against the ship's side, the waters of the Amazon lapped rhythmically like the call of a siren's song.

The machete ploughed through the undergrowth in a steady meter of slashing and slicing, its lethal edge cutting through vines as thick as Daniel's forearm. That same forearm glistened with sweat as Daniel paused to shift the machete from his right hand to his left.

After seven days of hacking their way through the sea of vegetation that choked the forest floor, Daniel and his men knew a fatigue that reached deep into their bones. Muscles burned from the constant swinging of machetes, blisters bled on even the most calloused palms. The suffocating heat billowed about them in waves, sapping their strength as quickly as the voracious mosquitoes sapped their blood.

Only six of the *Angela*'s men had volunteered to join him in the exploration, all of them dangerous men motivated by avarice. It was for coin that they braved exhaustion, disease and the constant threat of predators, but Daniel could not condemn them for their greed. While it was the lure of gold that kept them trudging by his side, something infinitely less reasonable motivated him.

The promise of redemption.

He could not explain his reasons, but he knew it was here. Here in the Amazon.

Wiping his brow with the hem of his linen shirt, Daniel glanced up to the canopy of trees stretched a hundred feet above them. The foliage of cedars, laurels, palms and balsa spread so densely across the sky that no blue was visible among the green, and only the thinnest rays of sunlight penetrated to the forest floor. Even without the benefit of the sun, the heat was punishing.

In the lead position, Daniel pushed a feathery palm frond from his face, admiring the delicacy of its fringed leaves. Amazing how such a fragile plant—

He froze. On the ground before him, a gaudily

striped coral snake had risen up. Black, red and yellow bands blurred momentarily before his eyes as he fought to bring the deadly serpent into focus. The *Micrurus fulvius.* One of the most venomous vipers known to man. So close that Daniel could count its brightly shimmering scales.

He felt the men behind him go still, hoping that none would be so foolish as to rush forward. The slightest movement might spur the snake into action, and its bite would assuredly prove fatal. Daniel's machete was in his left hand while the snake hovered to his right. He didn't dare risk the time it would take to swing the machete across his body. . . .

He counted silently, *One, two, three—*

His right hand whipped out and gripped the snake directly behind its eyes, squeezing hard to immobilize its jaws.

"Dear God," someone breathed in awe behind him, as Daniel concentrated on the angry viper whipping and twisting around his wrist.

The serpent wrapped its rainbow-hued length up Daniel's forearm. His knuckles felt as if they would burst through his skin, his grip was so tight. Daniel raised his arm and pivoted to present the reptile to his men.

The two sailors closest fell back a few steps.

"Beautiful, isn't it?" he murmured. "Too bad it must die, but I see no other way to extricate myself."

With his right hand, Daniel unwound the

snake, then held it outstretched in front of him.

"Brown." He gestured to the nearest crewman. "Here. At the base of its head. A clean cut, if you please, leaving my fingers intact."

The sailor inched forward, positioning himself. His fear-widened eyes met Daniel's before he lifted his machete and sliced neatly through the spot indicated. Blood spurted in all directions and Daniel flung the still squirming body and lifeless head into the bushes.

He glanced down and noted the dark, wet spots speckling his trousers. When he looked up, he saw that Brown's gaze was also trained on the bloody droplets. The sailor raised his eyes.

"Gor, Cap'n," he breathed. "Were it poisonous?"

"Aye, Brown, it was." Daniel's gaze swerved to the other men. "Let's move on," he directed. "It's getting late and we need to find a campsite for tonight."

Disregarding the murmurs behind him, Daniel transferred the machete back to his right hand and continued carving a path through the thick bamboo.

Although he regretted the fact that the snake's life had been sacrificed, he could not help but think its death had served his cause. The men who followed him were vultures; they would seize upon any weakness he might inadvertently display. His brief battle with the hapless snake might have given the hardened crew members something to think about. Something to consider before they thought to mutiny against him in this pitiless no man's land.

Nearly an hour later, Daniel and his crew emerged in a clearing adjacent to a narrow stream.

"We'll camp here," he called back. Groans of relief met his announcement.

The crew fell to work in pairs, efficiently setting up camp. Daniel had matched the men into teams of two, dividing the supplies between each pair. If for any reason the group became separated, each man was to remain with his partner.

Odd man out, Daniel was not paired, although the arrangement suited him. Fiercely independent, he preferred to rely on his own resources rather than to depend on another for his survival.

Shrugging out of his pack, he laid out his tent, staking the poles into a site slightly removed from the main camp. Within a few minutes, his modest shelter in place, he began to organize his company. With limited food supplies, they needed to start drawing on the river's bounty.

"Reeves, you and Brown, see if you can't catch something in the creek." He hesitated. "But use caution, understand?"

"What should we be on the lookout fer?" Reeves called back.

Daniel squinted toward the water. Dammit, there was no point in pretending.

He strode over to the stream's edge and looked down into the slow-moving waters. The creek ran only about twelve feet wide and was lightly dotted with sandbars and miniature islands.

He slid a glance to the two men awaiting his response.

"You ask what to watch for? Let's start with stingrays, alligators, electric eels, piranha."

"Peer-anha, Cap'n?"

"Aye, Reeves. Piranha. A small, deep-bodied fish whose razor-sharp teeth and powerful jaws can bite off your toe with a single snap. A hungry school can pick a man apart in less than half an hour."

He saw Reeves and Brown exchange an uncomfortable look. Brown tossed out his half of the net. "Is that the worst of it, Cap'n?"

Daniel folded his arms across his chest. "Depends how you look at it, Brown. While an encounter with the piranha or stingray might be fatal, many a man would sooner die than fall victim to the candiru."

Both sailors stopped in their tracks.

"The candiru is a quill-backed fish no longer than your eyelash. It takes refuge in a natural orifice of the human body, preferring . . . a man's most private parts. The removal of the candiru is said to be excruciatingly painful."

Reeves blanched and dropped his end of the net.

"Look alive, man!" Daniel barked, hastily

stepping up to grab the net's corner before their haul escaped.

With muttered apologies, the sailor rushed forward to assist. After Daniel had inspected the net's contents, the fish were gathered and the two sailors dispatched to prepare the meal.

Daniel watched their departure, his expression tight. Although his lecture had unsettled the men, Daniel understood too well the costliness of ignorance, especially here in the Amazon. This treacherous jungle offered no mercy to the foolish or fainthearted.

Their first evening ashore, Daniel and his crew had learned a valuable lesson about retiring to their tents before the sun fully set. Once dusk fell in the jungle, jiggers, mosquitoes and vampire bats descended on the land like a biblical plague, preying on any warm-blooded creature reckless enough to expose itself to the Amazon night.

So before the final rays of light faded into the sky, the men had cleared the meal and disappeared into their canvas tents. Beneath his own tarpaulin, Daniel worked by the light of an oil lamp, scrawling page after page into his notebook. The occasional *hiss* and *ping* of an insect flying into the tent's canvas wall punctuated the stillness as he wrote. It amazed him that despite the many years that men like von Humboldt and d'Orbigny had spent exploring this country, so much of it remained a mystery.

A bead of perspiration dripped from his brow

to smear the last word inked onto the paper. Daniel checked his pocket watch. Midnight approached. He laid aside the pen, closing his eyes to the now familiar rhythm of the tropics. His back ached from the hours spent hunched over the notebook and he stretched languorously, ears attuned to the distant roar of a roaming jaguar.

He removed his boots, extinguished the lamp and rolled over onto the pallet. By all rights he should have been senseless with fatigue, but anticipation acted like a stimulant on his nerves. He felt as if each day that passed brought him nearer to his destiny. He could almost smell it in the moldering scent of marsh grasses and algae. In the blistering wind. In the steaming earth.

On the edge of sleep, Daniel jerked awake. A muffled sound broke the evening's quiet. Although the forest buzzed constantly with life, the faint noise had raised the hairs on Daniel's nape in an instinctive warning. He held his breath, straining to hear. All was silent—unnaturally so.

In one smooth motion, he rolled off the cot and reached for his pistol. Noiselessly, he groped in the dark at the tent flap's ties until they fell open.

Crouched low at the front of his tent, he gazed into the black void of the Amazon night, his senses tuned to a fever pitch.

Then . . . pandemonium exploded around him.

The high-pitched whistles of arrows lanced through the darkness, accompanied by the ominous patter of footsteps racing across the ground. A man's hoarse shout came from the far side of camp.

"Attack!" Daniel bellowed. "We're under attack!"

He dropped to his stomach and levered up on his elbows, struggling to focus on the figures sprinting by. He aimed his gun and pulled off a shot. A dark shape plunged to the earth.

Indians!

A curse escaped him. What chance did they stand against the natives' blowguns and bows? A daytime attack would have been difficult enough to withstand, but hampered as they were by the dark . . .

Gunshots and inhuman screams collided in the chaos while ghostly silhouettes raced across the clearing. A figure reared up beside Daniel and he plunged his knife dead-center into the man's chest.

Even as the savage fell, a sharp sting jabbed Daniel's thigh. Fire burned a swift path up and down his leg. The pain spread higher into his groin, but he ignored it as best he could, slaying another native who raced too near the tent.

By God, he had to see to his crew. Turning toward the central core of camp, he placed his weight upon the injured leg. Nausea spiked through him like a harpoon. A groan tore from his chest and he spun around, clutching at his tent pole. His vision began to grow cloudy.

The dart. *Dammit, it must have been poison-tipped.*

His limbs started to grow heavy. Weakness pulled at him. He fought it, muttering oath after vile oath in an effort to keep his brain functioning. *Blast it, I will not die without a fight,* he cursed. *I will not die.*

Suddenly a piercing war cry sounded from behind his tent. He forced open his eyelids to see at least ten more figures step from the bushes into the clearing. He knew that his pistol lay somewhere on the ground nearby, but his muscles would not cooperate in retrieving it. The best he could do was keep on his feet by digging his fingernails into the wooden tent pole.

The new contingent dashed past him and, as they did, a realization pierced his drug-dulled thoughts. These shadowy silhouettes were much taller than the natives who had attacked the encampment. Broad-shouldered. Different.

Daniel watched as they hurled themselves into the conflict, attacking the natives with a fierceness that was awesome to witness. Shrieks rent the air. Weaponry clattered. Within what seemed minutes—or could it have been hours?—the Indians fled back into the forest.

Weak with relief and poison, Daniel slid drunkenly down the pole, unable to support himself any longer. His head cracked onto the ground with a thump. He barely felt it, he was so numb from the agony in his leg. One part of his brain labored to remain conscious. Who were the warriors who had rescued them from certain death? Guardian angels armed with spears and crossbows?

A torch flared to life and Daniel sluggishly rolled his head toward the flickering light. One of the tall victors walked across the clearing, waving the torch in a semicircle in an apparent search for survivors. *Thank God,* he whispered, then wondered if he had cause to be thankful. Had this second band of natives only saved him for a worse fate? Many of the South American tribes practiced cannibalism—

Daniel's stomach lurched.

However, as his breath grew more shallow and pain pounded through his temples, he recognized that death was his only alternative. He opened his mouth to call out, but his tongue lay thick and heavy in his mouth. He must have moaned or made some discernible noise, for abruptly the torch turned toward him.

The light expanded as it neared and Daniel made out the outline of a person bending over him. His last thought as he tumbled into unconsciousness was that he must have already died. The face above him was surely not of this world.

Chapter Three

The sun had not yet crested the horizon when Vanessa left her hearth the following morning. The sorrowful cry of the howler monkeys wailed in the distance, as if they too mourned the passing of the great Ama'zon prophet.

Vanessa's thoughts were with the Seer as she descended the twisting path and gazed out over the fog-shrouded valley. At first glance, the dim light and mist revealed only the jungle as it appeared outside Eldra'to's gates. Rocks, trees, earth and leaves blended together in a neutral palette of grays, browns and greens.

But if one looked more closely along the base of the ridge, one could see lodges, carved generations earlier, hidden among the walls of rock. Blending seamlessly into the silvery stone, the cavelike compartments housed food, weaponry and supplies. In the other direction, clustered at the base of a *heve* tree stand, the healing chambers' clay roofs were almost undetectable against the red-brown tree trunks. And there, jutting against a sheer bluff, the Ama'zon arena appeared to be nothing more than a mound of boulders that had tumbled from the precipice above.

Their people had taken great care not to disturb the land, to merge the village peacefully with the jungle and its inhabitants. Nonetheless, Vanessa did not feel as free here as she did in the open jungle. Often she felt like an outsider among her people, an outsider in her home. . . . But never as much as she did this morning.

She had not slept well last night, pondering the enormous responsibility that had been laid upon her shoulders. She, a savior to her people? Vanessa, the weak one, who felt more emotion than any Ama'zon was expected to feel? Why, the idea would be laughable if not for the memory of the Seer's raven-sharp eyes, the urgency with which she had clung to Vanessa's hand.

Follow your heart.

The more Vanessa thought, the more peculiar she found the Seer's counsel to be. An Ama'zon was not trained to follow her heart—quite the opposite. She was taught to think logically and analytically, not instinctively and emotionally, as was Vanessa's nature. Was it perhaps for these very differences that she had been singled out by the Seer?

Vanessa bit down on the inside of her cheek, thinking back to the mystic's death. No one had spoken to her afterward; no one had commented on the Seer's remarkable vision. With typical Ama'zon stoicism, the healers had begun to prepare the Seer's body while the others discussed the upcoming Rites of Womanhood.

Vanessa had been too shocked to heed their conversation, but now she wondered how the Seer's death would affect the Rites. The hunting party had already been away three nights; what if it did not return with its quarry? Would the Rites continue? In spite of the Seer's death?

As if her thoughts had summoned it, a cry suddenly rang out from the central gate.

"It returns; the hunting party returns!"

Vanessa's heart jumped in her chest. She hurried down the path, arriving at the far end of the central square just as the warriors passed through the gates. A crowd had gathered. She could not tell if the mission had been successful, but neither did she wish to fight her way toward the party of warriors to find out.

She did not have to. Ariadne separated from the crowd and approached.

"Vanessa, you are to go to the healing chambers," Ariadne told her. "They need someone who speaks the language of the English."

Vanessa's mouth went instantly dry. So the Rites would proceed, after all.

* * *

A healer sat to the side of the curtained bed, methodically crushing herbs with a mortar and pestle. Vanessa saluted the guard posted outside the sickroom and shut the door behind her. Initially she had been surprised to see the warrior in the healing chambers but had not questioned it. It was not her place.

From behind the bed's protective netting came a deep groan. It was the voice of a man.

Daphne, the healer, raised her gaze from her work and saw Vanessa at the door. She beckoned Vanessa forward. They dipped their fingers from their brows in mutual greeting and Vanessa darted a glance at the bed.

"An Englishman?" she asked.

"Two Englishmen," Daphne corrected. "The other is being tended in the far wing." She tossed her floor-length braid over her shoulder. "Do you speak English?"

Vanessa shrugged. "I speak it better than any other Ama'zon, but many seasons have passed since I first learned this language."

"Damn you, Father! You've gone too far this time," the man cursed, his voice raspy.

"Is he very ill?"

Daphne nodded. "He took a Moxo poisoned dart in his thigh, but he will live. He is strong," she added admiringly.

Vanessa's gaze followed that of the healer to the figure thrashing about atop the woven coverlet. Her nostrils quivered as a foreign scent wafted toward her. Rich, musky, tangy—it bore no resemblance to the scent of her fellow tribeswomen. It was the smell of man, and it acted upon her with a strange potency.

Vanessa could not restrain her curiosity any longer. She took a few steps forward and peered through the netting. Her breath caught. This one was nothing like the Englishman she had known as a child.

Sprawled naked across the coverlet, his bronzed body stretched from one end of the grass-filled mattress to the other. He was younger and leaner; infinitely more handsome than Harold, who had taught her to speak English ten cycles ago. Harold had been a kind and intelligent man, though much older and without much hair covering his head. Heavy chestnut locks fell over this one's brow, and similarly colored curls tufted his sun-browned chest.

Vanessa's gaze followed the path of those curls and her eyes widened. Since she had been only a child and not ready for a woman's rites, she had never seen Harold without his breeches.

"He's very different from us, is he not?" From behind her, Daphne vocalized Vanessa's thoughts.

She turned around to face the healer. "Had you known before?" she questioned, feeling foolish for asking. Daphne was of her generation, so she, too, would be experiencing her Rites of Womanhood soon.

The healer shook her head, setting her thick braid in motion. "No, it was a mystery to me before the senior healers disrobed him. Since they have all known the wonders of motherhood, I was the only one unfamiliar with his . . . with him," she finished.

"Aagh," the man groaned, and both young women turned toward the bed again. "She seduces me, this damn jungle!" he muttered, rolling fitfully onto his side.

"What does he say?" Daphne asked.

"He curses the jungle," Vanessa answered, unable to pull her gaze from his long muscled back.

The healer swung around and moved over to the worktable, where she added another pinch of herbs to her remedy. "No wonder, for I overheard a member of the hunting party describe the savagery of the Moxo attack. Only this man and the other survived the assault."

"Have you seen the other Englishman?" Vanessa asked, absently observing as a bead of sweat wound its way across the man's brown shoulders.

"No, but he fares much better than this one, I hear." She approached the bed again to stand at Vanessa's side. "However, the Elders instructed that he not be told about the other man until . . ."

A stab of remorse shot through Vanessa as she silently completed Daphne's unfinished sentence. *Until.*

"You are to watch over him," Daphne continued, "and learn what brought him to this part of the jungle. Reassure him when he awakens."

"And what of the other man?"

"Penelope has been called to translate for him."

Vanessa nodded. Penelope had also learned English from Harold, but she was more proficient in the language of the Portuguese.

"Here," Daphne said, "help me pour this into him." She drew aside the filigree curtain, gesturing for Vanessa to pull the patient into a sitting position.

Placing a knee upon the bed, Vanessa leaned over, grabbing the man by his bare shoulders and turning him toward Daphne. He was heavier than she anticipated and she allowed him to sink against her, bracing some of his weight against her chest.

His skin burned beneath her fingertips, setting them to tingling in a strange way. His hair brushed along her shoulder as his head fell back, and Vanessa marveled at its silky texture. She had expected the dark brown hair to be coarse and stiff to the touch.

Daphne spooned the concoction past the man's lips and Vanessa watched, mesmerized, as he unconsciously swallowed the liquid. She studied his profile, the arrow-straight nose, the square jaw, the broad forehead. Although she had only Harold as a comparison, Vanessa sensed that this man was attractive. Her body told her so. Where his back pressed against her, her breasts swelled to his touch, and her abdomen tightened in an unfamiliar pulling sensation.

"There," Daphne said, shoveling the last drop into her patient. "He should awaken soon."

The healer rose and went to the worktable, where she gathered together the contents of her medicine bag. "I have to replenish my herbs for the evening remedy," she explained. "I will not be long. He might be thirsty when he awakens, so you may give him water, but nothing else. If he does awake, you should know that his thoughts will not be clear."

Vanessa nodded and pulled a stool alongside the bed while Daphne, with one last lingering glance at the man, let herself out. Vanessa watched her go, aware that the healer was as captivated as she by the stranger in their midst. How could they not be? He might very well be the *one.*

The man lay on his back and Vanessa's gaze skipped down his chest, hastily passing over his manhood to the wound on his leg. Swollen and fiery red, a lump about the size of an egret's egg rose from the center of his thigh, marring the beautiful symmetry of his limbs.

Vanessa had a sudden impulsive desire to see the man healed. *He must not die.*

But Harold had died, an inner voice whispered. Poor, gentle Harold, whom Vanessa had felt was more like her than even her own people. Harold had never reproached her. He had understood her, been kind to her. Might this Englishman understand her as well?

Only a child, Vanessa had been too young to prevent Harold's death. But this man . . .

She studied the Englishman, trying to judge his age. Although she knew that other peoples were not necessarily separated by generational intervals as the Ama'zon were, she guessed that the man might be three generations old. The strength of his body attested to youth, while his face revealed a maturity beyond her own twenty-one cycles.

Her gaze lingered on his features. Even in sleep, they seemed taut with purpose—the tense set of his jaw, the sharp crevices beneath his cheekbones. She wondered what sorrow in his past had carved the lines of sadness around his mouth.

He mumbled something and Vanessa leaned forward, hoping to catch his words. Her face hovered only a hand's width above his, when his eyelids trembled and then flickered open.

A jaguar. He was staring into the eyes of a jaguar. The hypnotic yellow eyes loomed directly above him, holding him spellbound.

Buried beneath an exhaustion beyond any he had ever known before, Daniel felt the instinct for flight wing along his nerves. But his limbs would not respond. God, he was exhausted. His eyelids wanted to flutter shut, but his gaze was snared. His vision slowly began to clear and he realized that he was mistaken. Jaguars did not have eyelashes or brown brows.

He blinked, and his lids felt as if they were weighted with lead when he reopened them. He was staring into the face of a woman.

Then it all came tumbling together in a rush of raw-edged memories. The midnight massacre, the agonized screams, the maddening feeling of helplessness. For the space of a heartbeat, Daniel wondered if he had indeed died, for certainly no earthly woman could possess eyes of such an unnatural color.

But as Jaguar Eyes drew back from him, he saw that she wore neither halo nor wings. In truth, she wore little at all. Draped from one shoulder, a meager animal skin reached only mid-thigh on her bare legs. Firm, brown legs that had to be about a mile long.

Daniel felt his naked body jerk in reaction. Dammit, he was too bloody tired for his body to show interest in . . .

With stiff fingers, he fumbled clumsily at the sheet to cover himself. It was the blanket's silky texture between his fingers that finally snapped him into total awareness of his surroundings.

Dear God, where am I? Daniel struggled for cohesive thought but found it difficult to concentrate over the pain searing his thigh. The wound had to still be fresh; had he been ill for only a few days? Or could weeks have possibly passed?

He grimaced, wondering if any of his crew had survived the nightmarish attack. By God, who knew how many days he might have lain here senseless with fever while his men struggled for their lives? Were they even now lying half-dead along that embankment?

The woman stepped forward and placed her palm against the slickness of his damp forehead. The gesture only served to underscore his frailty. He tried to jerk his head aside but could not muster the strength. She withdrew her hand, and Daniel's gaze fastened to her yellow eyes.

He had to admit that she was a strikingly beautiful woman. And tall. He estimated her to be perhaps only an inch shy of six feet. Far from gangly, her muscles were firm and defined, as only physical exertion could make them, and her skin was nearly as bronzed as his own. In startling contrast to the pale yellow-green of her eyes, brown hair fell like a seamless curtain to her waist.

"Water?"

The single word interrupted his inspection of her.

"You speak English?" he asked, his voice dry and cracked from lack of use.

"I speak a little," she answered in the clipped syllables of an upper-crust British accent. "Water?" she asked again, pointing to a pitcher resting atop a roughly crafted table.

He frowned and nodded, although the movement cost him and he forcibly bit back a grimace of pain.

As she swung away, one side of her wrap gaped open and Daniel caught a glimpse of her naked hip. His brows drew together. How could someone so obviously primitive—at least in her dress—have learned the Queen's English?

She poured the water, then turned and walked back to him. He accepted it, irritated by the heaviness in his arm as he reached for the cup.

He drank thirstily. A droplet of water hung on his lips, and when he backhanded it away, his hand scratched against newly sprouted beard. He ran his fingers across his stubbled chin, attempting to gauge the number of days since he had last shaved. Five or six, perhaps.

Struggling to make sense of his situation, he watched her refill the cup. His brain felt sluggish, as if his thoughts were mired in mud. Was it the fever, the poisoned dart or perhaps some drug they had been giving him that left him feeling so muddled?

The woman returned to the bed and, as Daniel made to accept the water, the door to the room swung open. He strained sideways to see through the netting. The cup's contents spilled from his hand. *Holy Mother of—*

A giant strode into the room, a hemp bag swinging from her shoulder. Her blue eyes widened as they met his, and she issued a flurry of indecipherable words, apparently directed to Jaguar Eyes.

Damn. She had to be six-foot-four if she was an inch. Daniel had the momentary delusion that he'd fallen into a Jonathan Swift novel.

He scowled, forcing his deadened wits to focus. He was a scientist, for God's sake, an educated man. He had read everything available on South American natives, and he could not remember any tribes being noted for their unusual size. Of course, that was assuming he was still in South America.

"Where am I?" he asked abruptly, interrupting their melodic chatter. "And where are my men?"

Jaguar Eyes turned to him, her expression questioning.

"My men. My crew," he repeated, worry making his tone irritable and sharp. "Was anyone else rescued with me?"

She turned to the side, her hair casting a curtain about her profile. "The Moxo were fierce fighters," she said sadly. "You should be grateful you are alive. Give thanks."

Give thanks? For what? For leading six men to their deaths? Remorse flooded him in sickening waves, compounding his nausea. *If only I weren't so damned obsessed. . . .*

"Where am I?"

She didn't seem offended by his gruffness. "You are in Eldra'to."

"El-what?" Daniel searched his sluggish memory for the unfamiliar word.

"Eldra'to," she said again. "Land of the Ama'zon."

Daniel's stomach pitched. Although she had pronounced it as if it were two words, it had damn sure sounded to him like she'd just said *Amazon.*

"What? Are you talking about the river?" he asked. "We're near the river?"

"Near?" Jaguar Eyes repeated the word in evident confusion. Apparently her English wasn't as good as he'd first thought.

"The big river"—with effort, he spread his arms wide—"is it far?"

"Ah, far." She nodded in understanding. "No. Not very far."

"How far? How many days?" He heard the urgency in his voice but could not contain it. To think that an undiscovered people might dwell in the recesses of this jungle . . .

"The *big* river," she emphasized, evidently to distinguish it from its hundreds of tributaries, "is three sun-passings from Eldra'to."

Sun-passings? Passes of the sun. Days.

"Bloody—" Daniel could not believe it. He must be mistaken. Perhaps his yellow-eyed jungle woman referred to a different river, he thought. After all, how could he be certain he was in the Amazon?

The room was cool—too cool. After the heat he and his crew had suffered, he could not believe such comfort could be found in the heart of the jungle. His gaze scanned the room, taking note of the painted clay walls, the slatted shutters over the window, the leather-hinged wooden door. And the bed. It was primitive, but it was an honest-to-God bed.

No. It wasn't possible.

He had studied drawings of native shelters, and none were even close to being as sophisticated as this.

But . . . But if it *were* possible, could this be the discovery he sought? Had Eldra'to called to him from the jungle depths?

Daniel abruptly shoved aside the blanket and tried to push himself up.

Hell.

His breath caught as his head spun in three different directions. Still he struggled to rise, refusing to give in. Just as he'd managed to lever himself up on one arm, Jaguar Eyes placed her palm on his bare chest and pushed him back onto the bed.

"What the—"

Daniel glared up at her, galled at the evidence of his weakness.

"You must rest," she said evenly, although he saw something spark in her eyes. For a brief moment, he thought it might be amusement. She damned well better not have been laughing at him.

"Look here, Jaguar Eyes, I don't know what makes you believe that you are in charge here, but I'm starting to grow annoyed—"

"Vanessa," she interrupted. "My name is Vanessa."

She thrust back her shoulders in a proud gesture that caused Daniel's gaze to linger on the full swell of her breasts.

"Vanessa." Distracted, he tried to recall what he'd been saying, but fatigue was flooding through him like rain on the plains. "My name is Heywood," he offered, his thoughts rambling. "Daniel Heywood."

He knew that there was something urgent he needed to ask her. The Amazon; that was it. He needed to find out where he was. . . .

He jerked awake as Jaguar Eyes said something to the other woman in their strange tongue. The taller one stepped over to the table and he tried to follow her movements as she tossed ingredients into a mortar, but his eyelids kept sinking closed. He fought the weakness with every bit of strength he possessed, laboring to hang on to consciousness. Yet it wasn't enough.

"Drink this," Vanessa ordered, pressing a cup to his lips.

"What is it?" he asked groggily, surprised to hear how his words slurred together.

"A healing drink."

She tipped the potion to his lips and, suspicious, he tried to sniff its contents. His senses, however, had dulled to the point of uselessness. He automatically swallowed the thick, sweet potion that was poured into his mouth while his head swam with unfocused images.

The river. The jungle. Sinuous curves.

As sleep claimed him, Daniel's last thought was that he was drowning. Drowning in a pair of glowing liquid gold eyes.

Chapter Four

There she was.

Daniel had almost convinced himself that his fevered delirium had invented the woman, Jaguar Eyes. Visions of her strangely knowing amber gaze had fueled his dreams, merging with fiery images of the jungle. Those yellow eyes had become the hot sting of an afternoon breeze or the steam that rose from the coppery Amazon waters. They had seemed unreal, as had she.

But there she stood at the window, peering through the slats of the wooden shutters, her profile etched starkly against the reddish clay walls. Cloaked in the soft light of morning, she stood perfectly still, her flesh golden and polished like the mellowed ivory of an ancient statue. Although she moved not at all, Daniel could actually see the energy pulsing beneath her muscles; the sleek cords of her legs and arms stretched taut, poised for action. Or for attack.

"What's out there?"

Her body sprang to life at his words and he saw how quickly she masked her surprise.

"You sleep long," she commented, turning to walk toward him.

She moved with the grace of a wild creature, in a flowing, limb-rolling movement that was so far from being a *walk* that Daniel had to search for the right word. She prowled. That was the only term that seemed to fit. She moved with an awareness of her body and motion that was so primitive, so basic, that it appeared to him animalistic.

Again she was dressed in an animal hide—he thought it to be that of a black panther. Despite the fact that it covered only the most intimate parts of her figure, she seemed totally unselfconscious. As unselfconscious as the pelt's original owner would have been in its own skin. Vaguely unsettled, Daniel wondered at his response.

"Do you want a drink, Daniel?"

He nodded, evaluating her accent, thinking it belonged on a corsetted and furbelowed London debutante, not a half-naked savage. He found the contradiction jarring, begging an explanation. But not one, however, he was in a position to push for. Yet.

Wordlessly, he accepted the cup, continuing his inspection of her. She allowed him to look his fill as she stood beside the bed, returning his gaze with equanimity. She was every bit as beautiful as his fevered dreams had imagined her—with a slight difference.

The gleam in those catlike eyes was not feral, as he had supposed, but, instead, oddly innocent. Guileless. He felt hard-pressed at first to define it, but then it occurred to him. The eyes staring back at him were those of a wild creature, pure and untainted by man's vice.

He had read of such a naïveté among primitive peoples who had never been exposed to the avarice and selfishness of modern man, but he had not truly understood the concept until now. The prospect fascinated him—on a personal level, as well as a scientific one. When had he ever been as open or as trusting? He couldn't remember ever being so—even as a very young child.

He continued to hold her gaze, her regard clear and direct. Not threatening or defiant, but curious, innocent. Compelling. For some reason, Daniel could not pull his gaze from hers.

"How is your wound, Daniel?"

Her question broke the odd connection between them.

He glanced at his leg. Hell, he'd almost forgotten what had brought him here. The attack.

His stomach spasmed with guilt as the horror of that night replayed in his mind.

"Do you hurt?"

He did not answer her, his thoughts with his lost crew.

"Your leg?" she persisted. "Does it hurt you?"

Drawn back to the present, he scowled and tested his thigh muscle by raising the injured leg from the bed. Immediately a burning ache radiated from the center of the wound.

"It feels wonderful. Now, if you'll get me my trousers, I'd like to get up and take a look around."

She blinked, staring at him as if he had asked for the moon instead of his pants.

"Why do your words have one meaning," she asked, "and your face another?"

"What?"

"You say your wound does not hurt, but I see"—she pointed to her right eye—"the pain in your face."

"Can it be these people don't even know what a lie is?" he muttered beneath his breath.

"Lie?"

Daniel narrowed his eyes, nonplussed by the keenness of her hearing. "A lie," he explained. "Not telling the truth."

She drew herself up stiffly. "My people do not lie. It would mean losing one's honor. Worse than death."

Daniel couldn't help but be intrigued by the idea of such virtuousness. Hadn't Rousseau argued the existence of such a noble savage?

"Why have you come to the jungle, Daniel? Are you a seer?"

"A seer?"

"One who studies the spirit world."

"A priest?" He barked a harsh laugh. He'd been called many things in his day, but a man of God sure as hell wasn't one of them.

"No, I am a naturalist. I study the sciences."

"Ah." Her pale golden eyes lit up. "You are teacher?"

"More or less."

"I too am teacher." She tapped her chest.

For some inexplicable reason, Daniel suddenly pictured Raddison, a sallow-faced, beady-eyed, irascible son-of-a-bitch who'd instructed him in physics while at Cambridge.

His gaze followed the curve of her pelt. This society certainly had one up on Cambridge.

A breeze whistled through the shuttered window and Daniel glanced out to the filtered sunlight. Another day had dawned, and he knew not which.

"How long have I been here?" he asked abruptly.

"They brought you yestermorn."

"They?"

She nodded. "Our people."

And who were her people?

Vaguely he remembered having spoken with her before during a moment of consciousness, but he had been disoriented, his thoughts muddled. Testing his memory, he tried to bring that earlier conversation into focus.

"Your name is Vanessa?"

"Yes. I am daughter of Marta."

He recalled that she had introduced herself previously in this same manner. Interesting.

"Is yours a matriarchal society?"

"Mate-arcal? I am sorry. Much time passes since I speak your English."

"You trace your lineage through your mother's family?" Daniel tried to clarify.

"Yes. We are of the Mother."

Evidently she did not understand his question.

"See here, Jaguar Eyes, I don't mean to slight your abilities, but is there someone who speaks English more fluently? I have more than a few questions I'd like answered."

She smiled faintly. "I speak English best of my people, man named Daniel."

Man named Daniel, she called him. Was that a subtle rebuke for not addressing her properly? To be truthful, he thought the exotic "Jaguar Eyes" suited her better than *Vanessa.*

"Who taught you English?"

"Harold, an Englishman."

Judging by the accent Harold had imparted to his student, her teacher must be of the upper classes, Daniel thought. Another naturalist? Or a well-born adventurer?

"Is Harold around? Can I speak with him?"

Emotion flashed across Vanessa's face before

her expression smoothed into one of calm. "Harold is gone many cycles of the seasons now."

Cycles of the seasons . . . Sun-passings.

"Yes," Daniel murmured to himself. She had spoken of "sun-passings." Hadn't she said that the main river lay only three days—or three "sun-passings"—from this place? At the time, he had not been thinking clearly, but now he had to wonder. . . . Was it possible? Could these unusually tall natives live so near the great Amazon without already having been studied? Yet Daniel could think of no reference to such a people in any of his readings. And certainly no reference to a native settlement as developed as this one.

"You have said that Eldra'to was the land of the Amazon. What did you mean?"

"Eldra'to," she pronounced succinctly. "Land of the Ama'zon."

"Yes, yes," he said, with an impatient wave of his hand. "But by Amazon do you mean the big river? Or are we talking about a tributary?"

She sucked in her lower lip, apparently perplexed. "Ama'zon," she repeated. "We *are* the Ama'zon."

Comprehension burst through him in an exhilarating rush. Dear God, she referred not to the river—but to her people!

Inconceivable. Preposterous. Yet even as his logic rebelled at the possibility, Daniel took a deep breath, his head spinning with the prospect. By God, to have discovered the mythical Amazons! What greater coup could he have hoped for?

He had read the stories. Through the centuries, men like the sixteenth-century Dominican friar, Gaspar de Carvajal, had written tales of fierce female warriors encountered in their South American travels. Even Sir Walter Raleigh had professed to visit the cities of the Amazon, going so far as to describe the Amazon kingdom as an Eden revisited.

Naturally, learned men had later debunked the myth, citing native South American tribes whose women fought by their men's sides in battle. But those scientists had referred to Indians—not white women.

Daniel tried to contain his enthusiasm. He had seen nothing more than two unusually tall women and the walls of this room; he would need more hard evidence to substantiate such an extraordinary theory. Tangible, precise evidence.

A pen. His journal—

Daniel swung himself up out of bed. Instantly, pain knifed through his thigh. His leg crumpled under his weight and he started to fall.

Fast as quicksilver, Vanessa lunged forward and caught him, her hands strong around his ribs. In his haste, Daniel had forgotten that he was naked. He could hardly forget now.

Breasts, firm and full, pressed into his shoulder blades, and the backs of his legs were cradled intimately against her thighs. Only her thin, satiny animal pelt lay between them, separating her flesh, her warmth, from his.

She smelled smoky and sweet, of sandalwood. And her hair—Jesus, her hair had spilled over his shoulder, across his bare chest and down to his hips. Down to his awakening manhood.

The feel of the silken mane caressing him tore a faint groan from his throat, a sound that he could no more have restrained than he could have stopped his body from responding to her touch, her smell . . . her nearness.

Fire surged in his loins. He glanced down to find himself hard and pulsing with need, tangled in her tresses.

Damn!

Gritting his teeth, Daniel pulled free from her arms and lunged toward the bed. As he tumbled onto the mattress, he felt Vanessa's eyes upon him. She made no effort to assist him. She only watched in silence as he dragged himself awkwardly into a sitting position and tugged the sheet up to his chest like some wedding-night virgin.

He felt faint with dizziness. He also felt angry and embarrassed.

He avoided her gaze while debating whether or not he ought to apologize. *But apologize for what?* he thought irritably. For reacting like any warm-blooded male? After all, it wasn't as if she had swooned at the sight of his erection. Hell, if anyone was in imminent danger of swooning it was him. He had almost passed out from the pain in his leg.

Before he could decide what to say, a woman walked in, the same exceedingly tall woman he remembered having seen before. Earlier, in his half-conscious state, he had actually wondered if he had fallen into a land of giants. *Not giants,* he now understood. *Amazons.*

Vanessa spoke to the nurse while Daniel focused on their strange foreign chatter. The language was unlike any other he knew. The sound was musical, lilting, totally unrecognizable. What could be its origins? What could be its people's?

The chirping ended and both women turned toward the bed. Daniel forced himself to sit up straight, his eyes narrowing. Like Vanessa, the nurse was well-muscled, athletic yet curvaceous. Though rounder and prettier of face, she did not have the same effect on him that Vanessa did. Her gaze was not as . . . compelling. As guileless. Vanessa's eyes held an understanding, an unspoken empathy that he didn't truly know how to describe.

Daniel allowed the nurse to push aside the sheet just far enough to expose his injury. Gently, she traced the swollen and inflamed wound with the pads of her fingers, then singsonged a message to Vanessa.

"Daphne says you heal well," Vanessa translated. "You are strong."

Daniel grunted. "How soon until I can walk?"

Vanessa posed the question to the nurse. "Perhaps a sun-passing, perhaps two."

Sun-passings again. Daniel squeezed his eyes shut, then reopened them. God, if only he had his journal. He ought to be taking notes. Copious, detailed notes.

"Vanessa, I need a writing implement. Do you know what a pen is?"

"Pen?"

"You know. Write." He jerked his hand in a hasty, scribbling motion. "Do your people make any markings? Art? Decoration?"

She gave him a blank look before reaching for a large square of woven fabric that had been lying next to the herbs at his bedside.

"Decorate this?" she asked.

"Forget it," he said, taking the cloth from her. "Just tell your friend here to concoct one of her magic potions so I can get out of this damned bed. I'll go stark raving mad just lying here. I need to see where I am. I want to talk to someone in charge."

She flipped a strand of brown hair away from her face in a smooth, effortless motion. "I will speak to the Elders," she finally offered.

"Fine." Although uncertain who the Elders were, Daniel thought the proposition sounded promising, especially if it meant he could speak to someone in authority.

Vanessa exchanged a few more words with the healer, then turned back to him, nodding a farewell. With that same mesmerizing animal grace, she crossed the room, her footsteps padding silently on the rush matting. Her hips swayed, not in a deliberately seductive movement, but like the supple roll of a cat's haunches.

She let herself out the door and Daniel watched her go with regret. His only link to communication had been severed, and he was left to ponder the significance of their conversation. He replayed every word in his head—analyzing and evaluating—trying to hold the rush of excitement at bay but not succeeding.

Good God, could it be true? His fingers balled into fists, clutching the fabric square, as he stared toward the shuttered window. It seemed incredible, unbelievable, but he felt as if reality had been suspended from the moment he set foot in this fantastic jungle. Had he entered another world? The magnitude of the discovery was almost too great for him to perceive. To locate a civilization unknown until the middle of the nineteenth century . . . By God, his name would be on a par with those of Galileo and Cook!

While the promise of such fame tantalized him, Daniel knew in his gut that more lay at stake here. He had needed this. He had needed it for himself; not for the Royal Society and not for his father, but for his own self-worth.

Casey Claybourne

For a man whose life was focused on achieving concrete goals, it was not enough to draft treatises and to lecture on the scientific circuit. He could have drowned himself in esoteric academia for the remainder of his days and still not felt satisfied. He had needed to accomplish something tangible. The medal, the cup, the trophy . . . the legacy. He had yearned for it, spent sleepless nights searching for it, but that elusive prize had always dangled frustratingly out of his reach. He had been unable to grasp it because before now he had not known what it was.

Now he did.

Chapter Five

Damn that cat woman for leaving me trapped here, a prisoner in my own bedsheets!

Daniel had had enough. Jaguar Eyes had been gone for over twenty-four hours and he'd nearly gone mad waiting for her return. Patience was a fickle mistress, and she too had deserted him. All night and morning Daniel had listed the questions for which he required answers. Who were these people? Where had they come from? And above all—was it, in fact, possible—were they actually the lost race of Amazons?

Lord, no normal man could stand this uncertainty. . . .

"All right, dammit, off with the manacles," Daniel muttered, shoving off a double layer of sleek animal pelts. Even if it cost him the use of his leg, he was determined to get out of bed. He could no longer tolerate this waiting.

Glancing down, he realized that he could not go far without clothes. These women might not be shocked by nudity, but he could scarcely imagine chopping his way through the forest's thick brush in this state. *Clothes. I've got to find my clothes.*

As he swung his legs over the side of his pallet, traitorous nerve endings sent a fiery message up from his thigh to his eyeballs. Legs dangling, head spinning, one hand clutching a pelt, Daniel focused on the doorway mere steps away from his bed. He could do this.

Relying on momentum, he pointed his body toward the door, lurched forward and fell right through the opening and into the less-than-welcoming arms of what looked to be a medieval foot soldier.

Garbed in a breastplate of thick hide, a quiver of arrows at her back, the warrior—or guard—was the most savage-looking female Daniel could ever have envisioned. Bare legs widespread, she gripped a six-foot-long spear before her with an ease that told Daniel she knew how to wield it. Her helmet's nose piece bisected her face, shadowing her eyes, hiding whatever humanity might reside within. She looked displeased to see him, but Daniel had not been raised to avoid confrontation.

"My clothes," he ground out, shoving away

from her to lean against the wall. *"Clothes!"*

The sentry's fingers lowered to hover threateningly above the knife at her waist, but she said nothing.

"Dammit, doesn't anyone speak English around here?"

He received only a flinty stare. Furious, he stepped forward, his nose mere inches from the sentry's own. "Where is the catwoman? Jaguar Eyes? Vanessa?"

"Daniel!"

The warning hiss came from his back and he whirled around, scowling.

"Where have you been?" he demanded of a frowning Vanessa.

She ignored him and laid her hand on the sentry's arm, seeming to indicate that she would take over from here. The warrior's displeasure was palpable, but the woman gave an abbreviated nod and moved aside.

Vanessa turned to Daniel, her frown still in place. "You must not speak so to an Ama'zon. You do not understand the danger you invite."

She stepped back to fully view him. "And why are you not in bed? Does your leg no longer pain you?"

Daniel shot a defiant look at the warrior who stood but a few feet away. "I'll live," he said gruffly.

"Yes, you will," Vanessa agreed. "But Daphne says you must rest." Pushing open the door to his chamber, she beckoned him to follow.

"Daniel?"

"No." His gaze was hard as stone. "I'm not going back into that bed or that room until I first have a look around. I want my clothes, Vanessa. I want them *now.*"

Vanessa stared back, her expression as subtly mutable as sand. For a full minute, as she looked into his eyes, Daniel felt as if she were reaching inside him, searching. For what, though?

Taking a deep breath, Vanessa turned slowly toward the sentry and said something in their odd chitter-chatter language. Although Daniel could not understand her words, he sensed that the guard was not cooperating. The sentry responded. Though Vanessa was the smaller by four inches and perhaps forty pounds, she stepped closer until she and the guard stood only a hand's breadth apart. Tension charged the air. Daniel's heartbeat seemed to slow to nothing as he waited.

At last, the guard turned away and headed down the hall. Vanessa's shoulders eased with relief.

"What was that all about?"

Vanessa did not immediately answer him as her gaze continued to follow the movement of the sentry. "She goes for your clothes."

Daniel's eyes flickered. "Thank you," he offered a bit reluctantly, although he was glad to have confirmed at least one ally in this unfamiliar place. "However, I would sure as hell like an explanation as to why there is a guard posted outside my sickroom."

Vanessa's cat eyes were veiled, unreadable. "She protects you."

"Protects me?" In other circumstances, Daniel might have been tempted to laugh. "Protects me from what?"

At the end of the hall, the guard reappeared with a bundle of clothes in one hand, her spear in the other. Warily, Daniel watched her approach, waiting with half an ear for Vanessa's response.

"From what you do not understand," she answered softly.

Before he could question her meaning, the guard joined them, stiffly passing the clothes to Vanessa who, in turn, handed them to Daniel. He hesitated only a moment, then spun around, dropping the pelt he had been clutching as a makeshift loincloth. Modesty be damned, he told himself. Let them gawk at his bare ass. He sure as blazes wasn't going to go back into that room until he'd gathered the information he sought.

Even if it meant dressing in the open hallway.

Swiftly, he pulled on his trousers and shirt, ignoring the aching throb in his leg. Already his thigh was killing him, but he wasn't going to surrender to the pain now. Not when he had this opportunity. With his shirt hanging open at the neck, he left the fur bedding on the pressed-clay floor and, without a word, started down the hall.

He'd taken no more than two steps when a hand grabbed hold of his upper arm. Daniel pulled up short, gazing down at Vanessa's tanned fingers wrapped around the top of his biceps.

"I go with you," she said.

Suspicion tightened his jaw.

Her jaw tensed as well. "You must have an escort."

Knowing that the guard stood just behind his shoulder, Daniel did not think it prudent to argue.

"Fine," he muttered. "Let's go."

She released him and he started down the hall again, Vanessa at his side. He was about to turn toward the entrance when Vanessa called, "This way," waving in the opposite direction, to the other end of the corridor.

He paused, using the opportunity to rest his leg.

"Come," Vanessa called.

Gritting his teeth, he joined her, their shoulders brushing in the narrow, tunnel-like hallway.

"Are the men of your tribe as tall as the women?" he asked.

With plenty of time to think during this last day or so, Daniel had prepared a list of questions he wanted to ask about this intriguing, apparently female-dominated culture. He only wished that he were more familiar with the myth surrounding the Amazons to compare the fact to fiction.

Vanessa looped her hair behind her ear. "All Ama'zon are tall."

"Really? I ask because the women appear to hold the positions of authority in your culture. I assumed this role reversal was due to the female possessing the greater size and strength."

Vanessa did not comment. Daniel, however, was undeterred.

"You talked about a Englishman named Harold," he persisted. "What did he do?"

"Do?" Vanessa kept walking, her gaze fixed straight ahead.

"You said he taught you English. Did he live here in Eldra'to? Like a visiting professor?"

Her pace increased. "He came to the jungle to teach people about his God."

"A missionary?"

Vanessa stopped in front of a closed door, inviting him to proceed.

Daniel hung back. "Where are we going?"

"We see Eldra'to." She reached out and opened the door to reveal a tall, winding staircase.

"A tower?"

"Yes. Are you strong enough to walk stairs?"

"Of course," he replied, though his leg was already starting to weaken.

As she moved ahead of him to lead the way upstairs, he took the opportunity to study her further. Though both of them were barefoot, only his steps could be heard on the wooden stairs. Hers were virtually silent. She moved with a litheness that, to his mind, was simply not human. It was feline. And strangely provocative.

In their slow progress up the staircase, Vanessa's short pelt swayed back and forth, repeatedly revealing to Daniel a glimpse of smooth thigh, a tantalizing curve of rounded hip. He felt his loins grow heavy with sudden desire, and he hurriedly, angrily, wrenched away his gaze. Although many long months had passed since he'd last enjoyed a woman, he knew he had to keep his baser instincts under control. He sure as hell could not risk offending perhaps his only friend here in Eldra'to. Especially since he was not entirely sure that he could find out what he needed to know and then return to his ship without Vanessa's help.

But above all, he could not forget that he was a scientist. A scientist who might be on the verge of making one of the most momentous discoveries of the nineteenth century. Whatever else happened, Daniel knew that he had to stay focused on his mission: collect and record evidence . . . and see that he brought that evidence home.

With renewed determination, he concentrated on pulling himself up the last steps to the landing. His leg ached, but he ignored the discomfort.

Vanessa pushed open the turret's door. Suffocating waves of heat rushed through, causing him to squint against the singeing wind. His nostrils burned as he inhaled, but he gathered his breath and walked through the door that she held open.

Dear God!

His feet took root on the wood plank floor. He felt Vanessa move behind him, but his mind wholly dismissed her presence. What lay before him overwhelmed his senses. His head whipped to the left and then to the right, his eyes trying to take in everything that the three-hundred-and-sixty-degree view afforded him.

Spread before him was a city, awe-inspiring in its immense simplicity. Buildings of pale gray rock huddled against a slight cliff running along one edge of the village, while directly beneath him he saw a honeycombed network of domed clay huts. So deftly was the village incorporated into the jungle that he had to keep searching for other evidence of their dwellings. Even this tower had been built around a tree, so that the branches above them sheltered them from the direct sun. A timber wall encircled the town and beyond . . .

Goosebumps rose on his arms at the sight of the endless green landscape rolling away from the village; a mantle of emerald treetops stretched uninterrupted into the horizon until broken off in a snakelike line. The river.

In the far distance, the bronze width of the

Amazon wound its way across the jungle like a glittering, sun-kissed serpent. Its waters shimmered in the glaring morning light, taunting Daniel to deny its people's existence. He could not. It was true. He had discovered the lost civilization of the mythical Amazons.

Damn you, Father. I found it!

"It's true." His voice rasped softly. "You are the Amazon."

Vanessa's brow furrowed. Had Daniel not believed her until now? Had she not told him that her people did not lie?

"Ama'zon," she repeated. "As I told you before."

Daniel swiveled around, impaling her with his feverish gaze. "Why do you pronounce it like that? What does it mean?"

"Ama'zon means *children of the Mother.*"

Like heat off the jungle floor, energy seemed to emanate from him, pulsing in almost visible waves.

"I have to know more, Vanessa. I have to know everything!"

Confused, Vanessa tilted her head, her eyes narrowing. *Know everything? Did Daniel believe such a thing possible?*

Reaching out, he clutched each of her shoulders in a warm, callused palm. "Will you help me?" he demanded roughly.

Never before had Vanessa been deliberately touched by a man—certainly never by Harold—

and the intensity of her body's response shocked her. Frightened her, even.

The previous day, when she had saved Daniel from falling, she had known a similar reaction, a similar stirring or awakening within her. Those sensations had not left her, but had followed her back to her hearth, tormenting her during the warm hush of night. She had wondered as she lay sleepless in her bed if any young Ama'zon approaching womanhood would react so to his touch. Or was her response uncommon—as she herself was different?

Yet the sensations she was experiencing now were even more potent, more unsettling. Daniel's touch was sizzling along her bare skin like the sun's fire, his eyes blazing so brightly Vanessa feared she would be consumed within them. Instinctively, she pulled away.

She backed up a step. "I . . . I will help you learn as much as I am able."

He searched her face for a long moment. "Do you understand the significance of my coming here, Vanessa?"

By the Mother, she understood far better than he. And she wished to the very core of her being that she did not.

"This discovery is exactly what I have been looking for," he said. "The mystery that lured me halfway across the world to this jungle."

His voice vibrated with a grasping, desperate

emotion; an emotion that troubled Vanessa more than she could say.

"Tell me," he asked, "how long have the Amazon lived here? Decades? Centuries?"

"Eldra'to has always been our home."

"But how?" he demanded, raking a hand through his hair. "How did you come here? And how have your people managed to remain hidden from the rest of the world?"

Vanessa shrugged lightly. "The entrance to Eldra'to is not open to any but our people. It is concealed, a secret."

"It could not be discovered by chance?"

"No. The Mother keeps it hidden."

"Hidden," he repeated. "How then did this Englishman—Harold—find you?"

Vanessa resisted the urge to wince. She should never have mentioned Harold to Daniel. That had been a mistake. "Harold was brought here, like you."

"And he never left? He died before he had a chance to return to England?"

She nodded mutely, stabbing her fingernails into her palms to keep her expression smooth.

"So no one else has seen your village? No one else but Harold has learned of the Amazons' existence?"

"In my lifetime, Harold was the only one from the outside ever to have come here," she said quietly. "Until you."

"My God," he muttered. "This is amazing. To think that in this day and age—in the year

1840—your people have managed to remain secluded, untouched."

"Nearly so," she whispered.

"Yes. Except for Harold." He pivoted to stare out upon the horizon again, as if he could not get enough of the sight. "So the Amazon do not associate with the native Indians?"

She shook her head. "Our contact is slight."

"No commerce or fraternization?" he persisted. "Your people never mate with local tribes?"

She took refuge in the simplicity of her answer. "No."

"Extraordinary," Daniel breathed. "Completely autonomous, cut off from the outside world. Your population must then be fairly large?"

Before she could answer, he brushed aside his own question with a derisive laugh. "What foolishness. What would you have to compare it with?"

He dipped his head to the side, his hair lank and dark with sweat. His cocoa-colored eyes pinned her in place as surely as if he'd taken hold of her again. "So you have never left Eldra'to, Vanessa? You've seen nothing of what lies beyond these walls?"

The familiar ache of longing pulled at her. The need to fly away across the green expanse. She pushed it back and answered calmly. "Like all Ama'zon, I have ventured no farther than the boundaries of the surrounding jungle."

"Incredible." Then something flashed in his expression. "But if the Amazon deliberately avoid all contact with outsiders . . . why did your warriors rescue me?"

"Would you rather they had left you, Daniel?"

"No, of course not. This is precisely what I have searched for. But, dammit, I have so much to learn, to understand."

He wiped his sleeve across his brow, speckling the light linen with beads of sweat. "Come," he said, suddenly impatient. "I must see more."

He took a hasty step toward the door, then, without warning, pitched forward with a low groan, catching himself on a wooden post.

Vanessa started to reach out to him, then snatched back her hand. His touch would make her weak and overheated again. And while the sensation was not unpleasant, its strangeness disturbed her greatly.

"Blast it," he muttered. "Blast this bloody leg." He continued to cling to the post, his face so pale that Vanessa felt concern.

"Daniel, you must rest. I fear that the sun leeches away your newfound strength."

He jerked up his head, his mouth tight with frustration. "For God's sake, I can't simply lie abed when the discovery of a lifetime is out there waiting for me!"

But he had to regain his strength, she thought. And soon. Before the next rising of the full moon. . . .

Daniel straightened and tried to push away from the post.

Vanessa recognized that she had no choice. Not only must he be healthy for the upcoming Rites, she could not allow him to endanger himself by trying to leave the healing chambers again.

With a faint sound of regret, Vanessa stepped forward and struck a carefully controlled blow to the back of Daniel's neck. He crumpled like a fallen leaf.

Chapter Six

The drums woke him. Disoriented, Daniel tried to get his bearings in the shadow-filled room. Wrenched from his heavy slumber, it took a few moments for the lingering fragments of his dreams to fade as he reoriented himself to the physical world.

Anxiously, he peered into the darkness, assuring himself that he was still in Eldra'to. Devil take it, he would have gone absolutely berserk had he woken to find that he'd been returned to the jungle, cast out before he could learn the Amazons' secrets. Hell, he could almost picture it—him, a crazed and gnarled old man, having spent the remainder of his days in a futile search for the gateway to the hidden Amazon city.

He rolled his shoulders. His neck ached. Why? He last remembered standing with Vanessa on the viewing tower. Had he passed out and struck his head?

The drums echoed again more loudly. *Thump-thump-da-thump,* the rhythm repeated, uncomplicated yet wholly compelling.

Through the shutters, moonlight slitted in zebralike bands striped the floor a ghostly gray-white. The moonbeams wavered and weaved, appearing to dance to the drums' hypnotic tempo.

Daniel shoved aside the sheet, levering himself off the grass-filled mattress ever so slowly to muffle the dry crackle; he had not forgotten the oversized Valkyrie posted outside his door. He tiptoed toward the window.

The drumbeat's primitive cadence was disturbingly familiar. It seemed the song of the wilds; the pulse of the Amazon's lifeblood. Primal and mesmerizing, the drums sang of mystery and shadows—and passion.

Running his fingers along the uneven wood paneling, he found the window latch and gingerly unhooked it. The shutters folded noiselessly back upon themselves as the night air floated into the room. Daniel leaned forward over the sill, gauging the short drop to the ground below: two body lengths, perhaps less.

With a cautious glance toward the door, he crawled over the sill, perching atop it for a moment. All was quiet, but for the call of the drums.

He shoved away from the window and dropped, his knees cracking as they absorbed the impact of the jump. His toes curled into the firmly packed earth, releasing the sharp green scent of moist dirt. He waited for a moment, gritting his teeth against the slight pain of his almost healed thigh. The relative coolness of the night surprised him, and a gentle wind carried to him the Amazon forest's unique perfume. As the breeze touched him, Daniel realized that while he slept someone had removed his shirt but had left him his trousers. He was grateful for that.

Careful to keep out of the direct moonlight, he used it to light his progress as he crept along the perimeter of the clay huts. From what he had seen from the viewing tower, he judged the center of the village to be to the west, in the direction of the steep gray cliffs.

Limping from shadow to shadow, he slipped through the Amazon village, amazed by how seamlessly the huts and buildings blended into the jungle. The silence was preternatural. As if, during his sleep, the encampment had been abandoned. Abandoned but for the drums beating in the distance.

Daniel crept through the darkness, feeling as if he was in a dream. It was all surreal—the primitive jungle setting, the unearthly quiet . . . the bone-chilling sense of destiny awaiting him.

The land grew rockier, sloping upward, when Daniel suddenly spied the glow of torches above him. Flickering in delicate tones of orange and yellow, the torchlight came from the upper end of the valley: from the same area as the drums.

As he approached, he could make out a large structure looming at the edge of the village. It was some type of stadium, crude yet vaguely similar to a Grecian amphitheater. Its skillful construction made it first appear as if the building was a natural projection of the cliffs to the north.

As Daniel circled around, searching for an entrance, the drumbeat approached a frenzied crescendo. Tension coiled within him. Some type of pagan Amazon ritual was taking place in that stadium, and he could be the first outsider ever to witness the ceremony. He quickened his pace as voices now rose in a mournful chant from within the amphitheater. Slipping through a narrow portico, he hugged the stone wall against his bare back. His chest rose and fell, perspiration trickling down its length to soak the waistband of his trousers.

He'd made it.

He inched toward the stairs, crouching low, then peeked out into the stadium. He felt the hairs at his nape stiffen like quills.

At the center of the arena, a dozen women gyrated about a body—a body laid out on an unlit funeral pyre. The dirge swelled about them as the women dipped and spun in a heathen dance of despair and celebration. Brown hair whipped around one of the women and he recognized Vanessa. She had never looked more like a wild creature to him than she did at that moment. Arching and twirling, she contorted her body like a snake caught on the end of a blade, her expression mirroring her torment.

The chanting ceased and the dancers fell to the ground on their knees, their foreheads pressed into the dirt of the arena's floor. It had to be some manner of burial ritual, Daniel realized, raising his gaze to the tiered steps of the stadium to observe the audience. He frowned, his gaze leaping from section to section. Foreboding pricked uneasily at the base of his spine.

They were all women. *There were no men.*

His gaze flew back to the center of the arena, where two women had risen from the ground. An older woman with gray-streaked hair struck a flint, igniting a torch, which she passed to Vanessa. Holding the flame far above her head, his only link to this odd culture advanced to the pyre. Humming began from the spectators and Vanessa thrust her head back, crying out in her foreign tongue.

Daniel could not have moved had he desired to. He was captivated, enthralled—attempting to commit each and every detail to memory. Suddenly Vanessa's head turned and her golden eyes fixed upon him. At first, he thought his imagination was to blame; how could she see him lurking in the darkness when hundreds of people filled the torchlit stadium?

But as their gazes locked and held for one . . . two . . . three long heartbeats, he knew. She saw him. Defying nature, she had pierced the shadows to find him.

Before he could consider what his detection might mean, Vanessa's eyes sent him a message—a message so unmistakable that it was as if she had voiced it aloud. *Flee,* her gaze pleaded. *Flee before it is too late.*

Daniel went utterly still. The devil knew that he would have bartered his very soul to have remained, to have watched the rest of the ceremony, to be able to include a description of this fascinating ritual in his report to the Naturalists Society. . . .

But only a fool would ignore what he'd read in Vanessa's gaze. She *feared* for him. And Daniel suddenly believed that she had reason to do so.

Cursing beneath his breath, he slowly backed out of the stairwell. The more he seemed to learn of this strange culture, the less he understood. Always more questions and no answers.

For instance, what of the Amazon men? Why had he not seen any at the stadium? And why, for God's sake, would Vanessa fear for him? Why was he in danger?

As he slipped away from the arena, retracing his steps toward the clay huts, Daniel found himself struggling to remember what he knew of the different Amazonian legends. According to Greek mythology, hadn't the Amazons lived near the Black Sea? Fierce fighters, they had supposedly battled different Greek heroes like Hercules and Theseus.

And their society was supposed to have excluded men.

Could it be? Were there no men in Eldra'to? Yet, just now, he had seen young girls, as young as ten or eleven, among those observing the burial ritual. They must have fathers, Daniel reasoned. But where were they?

As he questioned how he was going to slip past the guard to his room, the arch of his foot came down hard on a sharp object. Swallowing an oath, Daniel hopped a step before reaching down to remove a piece of charred wood that was clinging to his sole. He was about to toss the wood aside, before he reconsidered, slipping the sooty scrap into his trousers' pocket. Perhaps he could use the wood as a primitive sort of pencil.

It was at that moment that he heard a noise. The faintest scrape of a footfall.

I am being followed.

Without hesitation, he darted to the side, pressing himself against the thick trunk of a tree. The melodious buzz of cicadas was the only sound now audible. The drums had long since ceased. He held his breath but heard no one behind him.

Nonetheless he lingered, his instincts urging caution. Seconds later, a silhouette appeared only a foot or two from where he stood, moving in the direction of the healing chambers. He reached out to grab the person, to identify his pursuer—

The figure whirled on him, arm raised as if either to deflect him or to strike. Their fingers tangled. Recognition.

"Daniel," Vanessa gasped.

"Daniel, you—You startled me."

Vanessa's tense muscles went slack, the air slowly easing from her lungs.

Great Mother, that had been close. Too close for her peace of mind. Surprised and caught off guard, she might well have snapped Daniel's arm in two if she had not instantly recognized his touch. Recognized its odd and compelling effect on her.

Their fingers were still intertwined as Daniel dragged her forward, out of the moonlight.

"Why are you following me?"

"I was worried. I feared you might be discovered."

She tugged slightly at her hand, but he did not release her, instead pressing their joined fists to the center of his chest. The wiry hairs there tickled at her knuckles, his scent flooding her senses.

"And why should you worry? What would happen to me if I were to be discovered?"

Vanessa cast a watchful glance over her shoulder. Not even the wind stirred. "It is not permitted for an outsider to witness the Rites of Passage."

"So I *am* a prisoner, then?" he demanded harshly. "Expected to stay in that room?"

"You . . ." Vanessa jerked her head to the side, tossing her hair back from her face. "You are a stranger, Daniel," she said, choosing her words with care. "And thereby not free to roam Eldra'to as you wish. If you had been seen, you might have been punished."

He was silent for a moment. "Why does it matter to *you* if I am punished, Vanessa?"

She bit at the inside of her cheek. "I am not sure. I only know that you have become important to me."

"Important?"

His voice, deep and rich, had assumed a huskiness that made Vanessa's heart beat like the wings of a hummingbird.

"Yes. You make me feel . . . better. I know that you do not understand—"

His fingers tightened around hers. "Make me."

She dropped her gaze, searching in his language for words she seldom used.

"All Ama'zon are taught at an early age to think and to act with logic and reason. We are taught to channel our strength; the need for self-control. In our culture, powerful emotion is viewed as a weakness, you see. It is not permitted for an Ama'zon to weep or to let loose her temper or to allow passion of any kind to cloud her judgment. Emotions are dangerous and discouraged. Frowned upon. And because I am shaped by emotion, because I am sensitive to people's feelings, I . . . I have been frowned upon."

Beneath her hand, she felt the planes of his chest stiffen.

"In you, Daniel, I see the same—How do you say it? Intensity. The same intensity of feeling that I have always battled within myself. For the first time ever, I feel as if I am not alone. As if there is another who feels as much as I do."

Her voice faded into the night as she lifted her gaze to Daniel's deeply shadowed features. An owl hooted from a nearby branch.

"No," he said quietly. "You are not alone."

Then something pressed against her mouth, something warm and moist and fragrant. Daniel's mouth.

His lips molded to hers, playing with them, sucking gently at the corners. Timidly she allowed her eyes to flutter shut, surrendering to the sensations swirling within her. Sensations wondrous and magical. Sensations like none she'd ever known or imagined.

She felt his arm encircle her waist, and he pulled her closer. As his hardness, his *maleness,* pushed insistently against her hips, warmth flooded her, pooling in the pit of her stomach. The warmth became a burning when his tongue slipped past her lips, stroking the interior of her mouth with bold and exciting caresses. Caresses that stole away her breath, that touched her soul.

Lost in the fire that was Daniel's passion, Vanessa almost did not hear the snap of a twig, the warning that someone approached. But she did hear it. Heard it in the farthest corner of her mind, hazy and indistinct.

With difficulty, she made herself focus, dragging her thoughts back from their sensation-drugged state. She wrenched her lips from Daniel's and quickly lay her palm against his mouth before he could utter a sound. As his lips throbbed against her hand, she gave a slight shake of her head. He seemed to understand.

Both as still as statues, they stood in the shadows beneath the tree, waiting, their breathing too fast, too loud. Vanessa wondered what she would say if they were sighted. She could not speak falsely. She could not. An Ama'zon did not lie. But neither could she stand by and watch Daniel be disciplined when she knew that she was to blame.

If she'd been thinking clearly—as an Ama'zon should—she would have hurried him back to the healing chambers the moment she'd found him. To tarry in the darkness, to lose herself in that delightful mouth play, was foolishness when she knew that Daniel's life might be in peril.

And yet, she reminded herself unhappily, his life *was* in peril. Great peril. In but two nights, the moon would be full and the Rites would commence. A shudder rippled through her. What was she to do? The thought of Daniel entering that arena . . .

The footsteps had receded into the distance. They were safe. She removed her hand from Daniel's mouth.

"You must return to the healing chambers. Now," she whispered, "before you are discovered. Tell me, how did you slip past the guard?"

"I went out through the window."

Vanessa nodded. She should have known that he would find a way. "Come."

She took his hand and led him through the village, pleased that he could follow her in relative silence. His tread was light and he moved well, like one accustomed to the night.

She led them around the perimeter of Eldra'to's walls, then through the dense brush that grew at the base of the *heve* trees. She stopped when they reached the cluster of huts.

"What are you doing?" he asked.

Vanessa gestured to the window. "Returning you to your room."

Daniel looked straight up, the moonlight casting his features into striking relief. "But that window is almost ten feet from the ground. How am I supposed to climb up?"

"I will lift you."

He snorted lightly. "Right." Glancing around, he narrowed his eyes as he surveyed the nearby tree. "If only that branch was a little closer—"

"Daniel, come. We have not time to waste."

Vanessa braced her legs apart, twining the fingers of her hands together to accept his foot.

He only stared at her.

"You must be joking."

"Joking?" She did not know that word.

"Vanessa, do you realize that for me to reach that window, you would have to hoist my body weight virtually above your head?" He looped his arms across his bare chest, drawing her attention to the bulging strength of his upper arms. "I know of very few men who could manage such a feat, and certainly no woman."

Vanessa straightened from her half-crouch. "Daniel," she reminded him simply, "I am an Ama'zon."

His brows hitched together. She could tell he was considering what that might mean. She bent her knee again, urging him forward with a jerk of her chin.

With obvious reluctance, he approached.

"Hell," he muttered before placing the foot of his healthy leg in her hands.

"Steady yourself against the wall," she said. Then, with a deep, empowering breath, she lifted.

She heard Daniel scrape along the clay as he scrambled toward the window. His other foot rose and came to rest on her shoulder, and she continued to lift, the muscles along her upper back straining with effort.

"I've got it," he called to her at the same time his heel pulled out of her hand. She glanced up to see him dragging himself over the window ledge.

"Quiet," she urged, darting a glance in the direction of the entrance. She looked up to find Daniel peering over the ledge at her, his expression confused, wary, his hair tumbling over his forehead.

"Thank you," he whispered haltingly, as if unfamiliar with the words.

She nodded and waved good night. But as she slipped into the brush, she murmured in a sad, quiet voice, "Do not thank me yet, Daniel. Please, not yet."

Chapter Seven

"Take care, Vanessa. He is a man. His ways are foreign to us, particularly to you. You must act wisely. Cautiously."

Vanessa lowered her head, unable to meet the Senior Teacher's eyes. "Yes. I must act wisely."

As the sunrise sent pink-gold rays floating through her window, Vanessa knew that she had not been wise last night. She and Daniel had almost been discovered when she had lost herself in the wonderful caress of his lips.

When Diana had come knocking at her door early that morning, Vanessa's heart had leaped with fear. Had they been found out, after all? Had Daniel been apprehended returning to his room? No. The teacher only sought a report on the Englishman's progress.

"You are troubled?" Diana asked abruptly.

Vanessa's toe scuffed along the clay tile floor. "I merely wonder whether the man will be strong enough for tomorrow night's ceremonies."

"All will be as it should," Diana assured her calmly. "The Seer had prophesied it so."

"And what of the other man?" Vanessa asked, trying to mask the depth of her interest. "Has he recovered?"

"He does well, although it is difficult to understand him. He says this is because he speaks the dialect 'Cockney.' "

"Is he strong?" Vanessa's stomach twisted with nerves.

"Yes. Very. He suffered only from an arrow through the forearm and it has healed cleanly."

"Oh."

Vanessa wanted to ask more, but she knew that Diana would question her motives, question her concern for Daniel.

As if divining her thoughts, the older woman said, "I think it best that you not spend too much time with the Englishman, Vanessa. It would not be appropriate for you to draw . . . close to him."

Vanessa nodded, knowing that the teacher's warning came too late. Far, far too late.

Poised to leave, Diana hesitated as she stood in the doorway.

"Remember, Vanessa, that the Ama'zon have prospered because we have learned to take advantage of our strength. We use the maleness in us to our advantage, yet seclude ourselves in order to protect our people from *his* destructive influence. Long ago, our people saw that man's aggression and love of war were harming our society's development. So we chose to protect ourselves."

"What of our future?" Vanessa asked. "What of the Seer's vision?"

"Only you have the answer to that question, Vanessa. We must hope that the Great Mother guides you."

Alone in her home, Vanessa walked to the window, pressing her cheek against the smooth, rounded clay of the opening. She let the gentle dawn wind wash over her face like Daniel's sweet breath of last night.

"Oh, Mother," she whispered, "how am I to help my people when it is Daniel I long to help? Daniel for whom I worry?"

Vanessa felt trapped, caught in the middle between her love for her people and her feelings for Daniel. She did love her kinswomen, she did; she was simply different from them. She respected their mores. She admired their discipline. She took pride in their collective strength.

Yet all of those sentiments combined were not stronger than the bond she had developed with Daniel. In Daniel, she believed she had found someone whose emotions ran as closely to the surface as her own did, whose feelings were genuine and unrestrained. Granted, his passions were more fiery than hers—and he did appear to try to control those heated emotions—but, to her mind, Daniel was more like her than any other person she had ever known. She sensed a connection between them, a feeling that he had come to Eldra'to for her and her alone. He needed her.

He needed her to save him. To save him from her sister Ama'zon. But how could she? How could she help Daniel when helping him would mean obstructing the upcoming rites? But if she did not help him, would she be able to live with herself?

If only she did not feel this dilemma so deeply. As she felt everything. So deeply.

Always before Vanessa had been able to bear this difference between herself and the other Ama'zon by imagining that, with more work, with more discipline, she might become more like them. Yet now, now she understood she had been wrong. Because now she knew Daniel.

Turning her back to the wall, she slid down to crouch on the floor of her home. Time was running out for decisions. Time was running out for Daniel. The moon would be full tomorrow night and the Rites would proceed.

With an anguished sigh, Vanessa clapped her face into her hands, wishing that she had someone to speak with, someone whom she could trust to tell her what action to take. But there was no one. She might have sought out the Seer for counsel if the old woman had still been alive. And perhaps if her mother, Marta, had survived childbirth, she could have been someone with whom Vanessa would have been able to share her feelings without fear of condemnation. But, in reality, there was no one Vanessa felt she could talk to. No one except—oddly enough—the stranger in their midst. Daniel.

So Vanessa prayed. She prayed through that day and into the night, going without sleep or nourishment. The Seer had said that the Great Mother would lead her, and Vanessa needed to be led. She needed to know what path to take. She needed to know whom to put first: Daniel or her sisters.

After endless hours at prayer, when her knees and back ached with fatigue and the night sat thickly upon her, Vanessa set out into the jungle. She walked and ran and climbed through the darkness, seeking an answer, thinking that surely the Mother would come to her now in the open spaces of the great forest.

"Speak to me," she called out, her voice echoing into the emerald vastness. "Tell me what to do."

But at sunrise, exhausted and disheartened, Vanessa returned to Eldra'to and collapsed onto her pallet, still not knowing what course the Great Mother wished her to take. When next she awoke, the moon had risen in the sky as a swollen, milky orb, and drums were beating in the distance. The Rites had begun.

"Where the hell is she?" Daniel bellowed. "Where is Vanessa?"

Held by a long, thickly woven rope, bound in an impossible knot to his wrist at one end and a metal eye in the wall at the other, Daniel lunged toward the sentry. Lunged as far as his tether would allow him to go.

"Tell her," he yelled furiously into the woman's expressionless face. "Tell her I want to see her."

The sentry stepped forward, placed her large palm on his bare chest and sent Daniel sprawling onto the mattress. As he struggled to right himself, she turned on her heel and walked from the room, slamming the door shut behind her. An ominous metallic clink suggested that a latch had been dropped into its cradle.

"Damn," he gritted between his teeth. "Damn, damn, damn."

Yesterday, furious and impatient, he'd waited all day for Vanessa to come to him. Waited and paced, sketched a bit with his piece of charcoaled wood, then paced some more. He'd barely stopped short of climbing the walls. When dusk had fallen and Vanessa still had not appeared, Daniel had decided to take action. He wasn't the kind of man who could wait for tomorrow to unfold. He had to grab his future by the horns and ride it to his destiny. So he'd waited until nightfall to leap from his window again. And had been caught immediately.

Escorted back to his room by a pair of giantesses, he'd then been tethered to the wall like some sort of savage beast, as he'd fought and kicked and screamed with every ounce of his strength. He'd even managed to land a solid blow or two—might even have loosened a tooth on one of the Amazons. But ultimately they had prevailed and had left him shackled to the wall. A prisoner.

He had passed the rest of the night in agony. Mental agony. Although his instincts were telling him he must try to escape at the very first opportunity, he shunned the idea of having to abandon this amazing discovery. Truly, it was the find of a lifetime.

If only he knew why he was not allowed to leave his sickroom. Were these Amazons merely secretive, attempting to limit what he learned of their culture? Or were they keeping him captive for a reason?

He stomped back to the door and shouted, "I want to speak to someone! Anyone in authority! Now!" He pounded his foot on the floor a number of times for emphasis.

Silence from the other side. Daniel squeezed shut his eyes, battling to hold on to his sanity. *Another tactic,* he told himself, remembering the old adage about honey and vinegar. Personally, he'd never been disposed to "honeying" his words, but if ever there was a time to exercise diplomacy . . .

He lowered his voice, attempting a tone of reason. "Now, I acknowledge that you are an able soldier and Amazon," he said, hoping that, though the woman on the other side of the door could not understand his words, she could appreciate his meaning. "And I acknowledge that you have been assigned to hold me to this room. However—"

He jumped back as a club, or perhaps the blunt end of a spear, was struck against the door in warning.

"Blast it." So much for diplomacy.

He marched over to the window, glancing through the shutters, to find the same two guards posted below. He marched back to the door, knowing he would never be able to break it down and, even if he could, he'd not be able to overpower the heavily weaponed guard.

"Perhaps they mean me no harm," he said to himself. "Perhaps the Amazons only wish to safeguard the privacy of their world."

But if that was the case, then why had Vanessa not come to see him? At least if she were here, he could get some answers to the questions plaguing him. At least if she were here, he could gather information about the Amazons to take home with him, to document his discovery.

Two days chained in this cell. He felt as if he was going mad. Stark, raving mad.

Trailing the rope behind him, he moved to

the window again and placed his lips right up to the shutters.

"Vanessa!"

He bellowed her name again, his throat scratchy with the force of his cry.

"Vaness—"

When he came to, he was no longer at the window, but back in his bed. This time, with both hands bound behind his back and a coarse scrap of fabric tied around his mouth. *Damn.*

Screwing his face into every possible distortion, and repeatedly pushing his tongue into the fabric, Daniel managed to dislodge the offensive gag, but not before he'd reached new heights of fury. And concern.

"Where are you?" he muttered. As the time stretched on, he began to wonder if some ill had befallen Vanessa. Had those in charge somehow learned that she had assisted him and so were punishing her? Holding her captive as he was being held?

Daniel had believed Vanessa to be an ally. More than an ally, really. He knew that she was not indifferent to him. Her kiss two nights past had told him as much quite clearly, quite memorably. So where in blazes was she?

He jerked as the door to his room flew open. It was not Vanessa who entered, but two Amazon warriors and a third woman who was older and unfamiliar to him.

The older woman approached and studied

him as he might inspect a piece of horseflesh he was considering purchasing. Like all the others he'd seen here, she was tall and beautiful. But, also like all the others—save Vanessa—her eyes were cold and unfeeling. Devoid of any emotion.

"Where is Vanessa?" he demanded.

To his surprise, the woman responded in English. "Why do you ask?"

"Is she injured? In trouble?"

The woman's green eyes narrowed. "Not at all. When last I saw her, she was most comfortable in her home."

Perfidious cat-eyed witch. Why had she not come to him?

Daniel wrestled against his bonds, though his wrists were raw. The woman watched his struggles with a detached interest, saying nothing until he finally lay still, panting with his exertions.

"Take him," she ordered.

Chapter Eight

For the space of a heartbeat, Daniel imagined that he'd been thrown back in time. Back to the days of Caligula and Claudius, when gladiators fought for their lives as entertainment for bloodthirsty emperors, and Christians and lions did battle to amuse the bored Roman masses. There was an unreal element to the scene, a sense of being caught up in a web of illusions, a fevered dream. Or perhaps not a dream, Daniel thought to himself. *But a nightmare.*

He squinted into the acrid, smoke-filled air, the glare of the torches harsh in his eyes. Beneath his bare feet, the red clay dust of the arena floor swirled around his ankles, as if the earth itself wished to consume him, to suck him down into its fiery depths. The heat was unbearable tonight. Oppressive. Thick waves of it washed over the arena floor.

Defiantly Daniel looked up into the crowd, his fists curling at his sides. Through the filmy haze of smoke and light, he was not able to make out individual faces or expressions. But it did not matter. All the faces seemed to blur together into one: A lone deceptively lovely face whose treacherous yellow-green eyes mocked him. Mocked him and betrayed him.

Damn her, where was she? Where was Vanessa?

At the opposite end of the stadium, a door slid open like a monster's gaping maw. From out of the darkness appeared a pair of Amazon warriors escorting a third person onto the arena floor. A man—

"Reeves," Daniel whispered.

Blast it, Vanessa had deceived him in this as well. He had *not* been the only one saved by the Amazons that night. His crewman had survived and had been brought here just as he himself had been . . . but for what purpose?

Across the stadium, Daniel saw Reeves nod twice, as if responding to a question or instructions. Yet how was that possible? Had Vanessa not told him that she was the only Amazon who spoke English? Or had he made that assumption on his own?

A scuff of feet warned of someone approaching at his back. Daniel whirled around to face one of the Amazon warriors, the same warrior who had stood guard outside his door. The woman, her features empty of emotion, stopped before him and lowered her spear. Warily Daniel eyed the weapon, noting how its lethal point glittered in the torchlight. With a curt bob of her head, she held out the spear, gesturing for him to take it.

Daniel tensed, an abhorrent suspicion occurring to him. Again the Amazon thrust forward the lance. Still uncertain, Daniel decided that, in any case, he would be better off with a weapon than without one. Slowly he reached out and took the spear, the wooden shaft warm and weighty in his hand. In the next instant, the warrior disappeared behind a panel in the wall.

Suspicions mounting, Daniel turned around. At the other end of the arena a lone figure stood. Reeves. And he, too, now held in his grip a long, thick lance.

"Hell," Daniel muttered softly. An eerie quiet had settled over the stadium, a quiet that caused goosebumps to prickle Daniel's flesh. He knew that at that moment hundreds, if not thousands, of eyes were upon him, watching him as if he were some insect under a microscope. Watching . . . and waiting.

Then Reeves charged, kicking up a flurry of ochre dust.

Stunned, Daniel did not leap aside until the man's footsteps were almost pounding in his ear; until he realized that the tip of Reeves's spear was targeted for his heart.

"Good God, Reeves, what are you doing?" Daniel yelled as he spun away from the attack.

His crewman did not answer. Instead the man turned, his weapon raised, and lunged again.

Daniel deflected the thrust with the side of his spear, and the sound of their weapons' colliding echoed into the night.

"Reeves!"

The crewman's small eyes shone dark with malicious intent. "They say only one of us can leave 'ere alive, Cap'n. And I figure it's bloody well goin' to be me."

"Don't be a fool, man," Daniel hissed, his gaze pinned to the lance's steely point. "They're using us as pawns, as toys in a game. We don't have to play by their rules. We can outwit them, Reeves. And both leave here alive."

"I don't think so, Cap'n."

The sailor rushed forward and Daniel rolled to his knees to avoid the strike.

"I'm not going to do this, dammit! I will not fight you as entertainment for these savages."

"Then, Cap'n . . . ye'll die."

Reeves lunged, the point of his spear grazing the top of Daniel's right shoulder.

Daniel cursed as he felt the skin scraped from his bone, felt the blood begin to spill from the wound and onto his chest. He scrambled to his feet before Reeves could come at him again.

"Reeves, no!"

But already the other man's spear was upon

him and, with effort, Daniel parried the thrust. He darted to his left. Reeves jabbed the spear, just missing Daniel's arm. Daniel leaped to the right, feeling the muscle in his leg cramp. Reeves jabbed again.

"I won't do this," Daniel muttered to himself. He would not slay his own crewman. As it was, he carried the weight of the other sailors' lives on his conscience; he refused to take on another. Yet, years of his father's training resonated within him. *Be strong. Prevail. Survive at all costs.*

But Daniel refused to prevail at the expense of another man's life.

As he feinted and parried again and again, Reeves continued to pursue him relentlessly, the crash of their lances punctuating the night like small explosions of summer thunder. The dust now swirled around them waist-high, a hellish red cloud of heat and sand. Reeves was panting. Tiring. If only he could keep one step ahead, Daniel thought, he might be able to bring Reeves to the point of exhaustion. Exhaustion and surrender.

Yet Daniel, too, was tiring. The injury to his leg had taken its toll; he was slow on his feet, not as fast as he should have been. His eyes burned with perspiration and grit.

With both hands, Reeves made a downward thrust with his spear toward Daniel's stomach. Daniel absorbed the shock of the blow with the shank of his own weapon, but the force of the attack toppled him backward. As he tumbled head over heels, he could hear Reeves's breath catch in anticipated triumph.

Daniel kept rolling and glanced over his shoulder. Reeves was bearing down on him at a near run. Awkwardly, Daniel lifted his lance with the hope of parrying the thrust that he knew was coming at his exposed back. Then Reeves tripped.

The moment was still.

At the back of his mind, Daniel took note of the crowd's utter silence. Reeves tumbled forward, twisting, his mouth opening in pained astonishment as he impaled himself on the point of Daniel's spear. Defeated, Daniel let the lance fall from his grip. The *Angela*'s crewman sank to the ground, clutching at the instrument of his death as if he might yet pull it from his chest and save his dwindling life.

Daniel sat on the arena floor and stared at the fallen crewman, watching as Reeves's blood stained the clay earth a deeper, ghastly shade of red. And as he stared, a rage began to fill him. A fury as dark and dangerous as the Amazon itself.

He rose slowly to his feet. A pair of warriors emerged from a doorway and came toward him. One started to reach for him, but he snarled a warning. Surprisingly, his warning was heeded.

They led him from the stadium through the hot, hushed night. Daniel tried to think as he walked—to think of a plan. But his rage-clouded thoughts kept returning to the terrible silence that had hung over the stadium as Reeves lay dying. It had been so emotionless, that quiet. So cold-blooded.

The guards ushered him back into the same chamber he'd occupied these last five days and Daniel entered its coolness without a struggle, without a word. He was too shaken. He needed time to gather his thoughts. To accept what he'd just done.

He'd taken no more than three or four shaky steps toward the shuttered window when the door behind him opened. He ducked his head to the side, peering from the corner of his eye. He had known it would be her.

She did not come alone, however. The tall nurse, Daphne, followed Vanessa across the threshold, the light from a wooden candelabra she held flooding the room with a sickly yellowish glow.

"Daniel." Vanessa's voice wafted softly. "Daphne has come to see to your wound."

He turned back toward the window, swallowing a sardonic laugh. Like a prized bantam who has won his cockfight, was he now to be kept alive in order to fight again? Was that their strategy?

His lip curled as he stared blindly at the uneven wood slats of the shutters. "Like hell."

"Daniel—"

"Send the nurse away."

"But your wound might—"

"Send her away."

Angrily, he yanked open the shutters to admit the moonlight and the smell of all things green and alive. *Alive. At least I am still alive,* he conceded, although the admission left a foul taste in his mouth. He hated to recognize that, in addition to his gut-twisting guilt, he was also secretly relieved *he* had been the one to walk away from the arena. Apparently, he was not so very different from the boy his father had raised.

Whispers rose and fell behind him, and then the door clicked shut. He turned, fighting to keep hold of his rage. Damn her, she looked lovely. Her hair, her skin . . . her mesmerizing cat's eyes. God, those eyes. The moonlight sank into them, making them shimmer and shine as if lit from within. Or was it the threat of tears that glistened in her gaze? Did she dare weep after what she'd done to him?

"Daniel, I—"

"You lied to me."

"No—"

"You did. You lied to me, you deceived me. You knew all along what they had planned, didn't you?"

She nodded, her face downcast.

"Why didn't you tell me, Vanessa?"

"I could not."

"You could not spoil the fun? Tell me, Vanessa, who is next? Who must I kill next to amuse you and your friends?"

She glanced up, confused. "Amuse?"

"That's what it's about, isn't it? Sport?"

"Oh, no, Daniel. No." She shook her head, sending her silken hair sliding across her shoulders. "You do not understand."

"I do not *understand.*" He clenched his hands behind his back to keep them from wrapping around her sweet neck. "My humblest apologies. Perhaps you would care to explain it to me, then?"

She bit into her lip as she slowly approached him. "You are angry."

He couldn't believe it. Couldn't believe her. Hadn't she enough sense to see that she ought to keep her distance? That he was on the verge of losing complete control and throttling the very life from her?

" 'Angry' doesn't do my feelings justice. Now tell me—if it wasn't for sport—why the hell was I forced to murder my own crewman?"

She made an uncertain, fluttering motion with her fingers. "We had to know which of you was stronger."

Daniel's gaze flickered. "Why?"

"So that our children will be strong."

"Chil—" His breath stalled in his lungs. His hand sought the bedpost and curled around it, needing the feel of something solid and real.

"You see," Vanessa explained haltingly, "the Ama'zon are women. Only women. So in order to thrive, every ten years, we must . . ."

"Regenerate?"

"Yes, regenerate. Our hunting party goes out and selects a man. Two men. And the stronger of the two, who survives the contest, is chosen to father the next generation of Ama'zon."

"Oh, my God." Daniel gave a weak laugh and held more tightly to the bedpost. It felt as if the floor had just fallen out from under his feet.

"It is our way," Vanessa said, her tone pleading. "It is and has always been the way of the Ama'zon."

Daniel looked at her, thinking that one of them had to be thoroughly mad. He prayed it was her. "So I've been brought here to serve as a . . . stud?" He laughed again, a bit wildly this time, and leaned his forehead against the wooden bedpost. "Unbelievable. Bloody unbelievable."

Vanessa twined her fingers together. "I feared you would not understand."

"Understand?" Daniel squeezed shut his eyes as mounting rage overwhelmed shock. "Well, hell, I suppose some men would consider this a fantasy realized, wouldn't they?" he asked, his words dripping with sarcasm. "To be forced to play sex slave to every woman in town."

"Not every woman."

Daniel pivoted his head to stare at her, his expression icily blank.

"Only those entering womanhood," Vanessa said, averting her gaze. "Those of my generation."

"Your generation? My, my, why, that's even

better. The cream of the crop." His eyes narrowed as he scanned her up and down, his gaze contemptuous. "So you would be in line, Vanessa? In line to be . . . serviced?"

She nodded, color washing into her cheeks. The sight of her maidenly blush caused Daniel's groin to tighten unexpectedly, which only infuriated him further. He shoved away from the bed, roughly dragging both hands through his hair until his scalp began to throb.

"I know you are displeased, Daniel, but eventually Harold came to—"

His head shot up. "Harold? The missionary? Lord, don't tell me that *he* was your last victim?"

Vanessa lifted her shoulders in a diffident gesture. "Harold accepted his fate. He told me that it was the will of his God."

Suddenly Daniel was across the room, Vanessa's warm shoulders in his hands, and he was shaking her. Shaking her hard and shouting, "Well, I am not going to accept my fate, do you hear? To hell with 'God's will'! My will is all that matters and I will not do it!" His voice dropped to a low, aching rumble as he released her and stepped back. "I *cannot* do it."

Vanessa studied him, her eyes wide. "Cannot?"

"Cannot," he repeated bitterly. "And therein, Vanessa, lies the cursed irony of it all. You see, my dear jungle woman, I am sterile. I am incapable of fathering even one child, much less a village of them."

He turned to stare out the window, realizing that his father had been right after all, dammit. There was no escaping. Even here, a half a world away from home, he had to confront his secret.

"But how—How can you be certain?"

"I'm certain."

"Can you not . . ." she asked tentatively at his back. "The act?"

Daniel released an ugly half-laugh. "I can perform 'the act,' as you so delicately put it. But produce nothing. A disease in my youth left me infertile."

Frowning, he tried to remember himself at sixteen, but his memories swam before him vague and muddy. A gangly young man, eager to please . . .

"I was too young to appreciate the meaning of the loss, but not so my father. He was furious to learn that the family name would die out and blamed me for being so stupid as to fall ill. I'd failed him. Failed the family.

"So, like a fool, I spent the next five years trying to prove both him and the doctors wrong. From Dover to Dublin, I tumbled every skirt I could find, spreading my seed indiscriminately from tavern wenches to titled ladies. But my seed bore no fruit. Eventually I had to accept the truth. When I leave this earth, I shall leave no son, no daughter, no legacy. I will leave nothing."

With a wry, self-disgusted smile, Daniel

turned and spread his arms wide. "So, you see, Vanessa, Reeves could have helped you out, but not me. I'm useless to the Amazon. Completely useless."

Vanessa made a faint sound, either of sorrow or surprise, as she lifted a hand to her mouth.

"What?" Daniel mocked. "Are you worried that your friends will kill me once they realize I'm no good for breeding purposes?"

Pressed against her lips, Vanessa's fingers gave a guilty tremor. Daniel nodded. He had expected as much.

"Ah, I see. I would have been slain anyway once my work was done, is that it? Once I'd impregnated a sufficient number of women, then—?" He drew his hand across his neck in a sharp slicing motion.

"Six cycles of the moon," Vanessa answered in an unhappy whisper. "Then you are put to death."

Daniel nodded again. Calmly. Cynically. "And so it was with Harold? Six months?"

"Yes."

"But Harold was a good sport about the whole business, hmm? Not like me." Daniel glanced at the fine hairs on his wrist, matted with blood, and felt a peculiar sense of detachment. As if he would soon wake from this nightmare and think it particularly odd.

"Although," he said, "I do confess to a certain curiosity. I suppose it's the scientist in me. If you allow no men here in Eldra'to, what do the

Amazon do with the male offspring? Are they exterminated as well? Or do you simply leave them out in the jungle to die?"

He took a step forward, causing the shadows to shift so that a stray moonbeam caught and held the single tear clinging to Vanessa's cheek. Daniel knew he was being deliberately cruel, but, dammit, he didn't much care at this point. Not when Reeves's blood still soiled his hands.

"Well?" Daniel goaded.

Lifting her chin, she swiftly wiped away the tear. "We have no male children. Our people left the Old Land to escape man's aggression, the violent passions our people find to be destructive and dangerous. Over time, we simply ceased to bear sons."

"Natural selection?" Daniel wagged his head, huffing in amazement. "Darwin isn't going to know what to make of this."

"D-Darwin?"

"A friend."

A friend, Daniel realized, whom he would never see again if he did not find a way to leave Eldra'to alive.

"Vanessa," he said, leveling on her a fierce and determined stare, "you must help me."

She sent a nervous glance to the door behind her. "How?"

Daniel took another step closer. "You must help me escape."

Her brows beetled in an anxious frown. "But if I help you escape, the rites will not proceed.

A generation of our people will be lost."

"But you are forgetting that a generation is already lost," Daniel argued. "I am of no use to you. At least if I disappear, perhaps your warriors can still hunt down some other poor bastard to meet your barbaric needs."

Vanessa's teeth tugged at her lower lip. "You are asking me to betray my people."

"I am asking you *not* to betray *me*."

"No one has ever left Eldra'to—"

"Dammit, Vanessa!" He grabbed her wrist, hauling her forward until she was pressed up against him, supple and soft. "Do you really want to see me die?"

Chapter Nine

Vanessa sat in the quiet of her home and prayed. She prayed to the Great Mother until her voice rasped, until her shoulders sagged wearily with frustration and fatigue. She prayed into the small, deepest hours of the night as the bull caiman's call echoed through the valley, a guttural plaint that brought prickly goose-bumps to Vanessa's arms.

But no answer came to her. No simple answer, that was.

The Seer had prophesied this. She had warned Vanessa that someday soon she would be confronted with a difficult and painful choice, one that would affect the future survival of her people. And what had been the old woman's counsel?

Follow your heart.

But Vanessa's heart was torn. Torn in two. These were her sisters, her people, the only family she had ever known. If she was to do as Daniel asked and guide him back to his ship, she would most likely return to Eldra' to a traitor, an outcast. She would be scorned and punished—perhaps even banished. Could she bear it?

In her lifetime, she could recall no other incident in which an Ama'zon had committed a transgression as grave as the one she was contemplating. None. Yet, she knew that if she did not take the risk . . . Daniel would die.

From the outset, Vanessa had known that Daniel's death was predetermined, yet never had the realization sat easily with her. She had hoped that when the time came, Daniel—like Harold—would make peace with his God and accept his fate. That hope had vaporized like morning dew once she had come to know Daniel. He was not one who knew how to yield or relent. He was a fighter, a warrior. *A man.*

Vanessa's fingers wandered up to her lips, tracing their outline, remembering the feel of Daniel's mouth pressed to hers. How could it be that though he'd touched her here, on the outside, she felt that he had touched her inside as well? Touched her very heart.

Vanessa's breath quickened, her eyes opening slowly in wonder. *The answer.* This had to be it. After days of indecision and torment, she had to believe that this was the answer she had sought.

Quickly, she scrambled up from her knees and grabbed her sack from its hook, tossing into it what she thought she'd need for a short journey through the jungle: knife, cord, hammock, hides. Then she hesitated, scanning the cool stone walls of the chamber, asking herself what else they might need. Only once or twice had she passed the night outside Eldra'to's gates, and then she'd not been traveling alone. Food could be hunted, water found. . . .

As she surveyed the room, an unwelcome thought came upon her, causing her to shiver as if with a premonition. Would she ever again return to this place she called home? Or was she about to cross over a threshold from which there would be no turning back?

With an annoyed frown and a firm shake of her sack, she shoved the question to the back of her mind. She could not say what consequences she might have to pay for her actions, nor could she forecast the future. But she knew what she had to do. Her course was set.

As she crept from her room, she looked to the stars. The moon still held possession of the sky but, on the horizon, a faint whisper of gray hinted of dawn. Fearful that she'd been too long arriving at her decision, Vanessa hurried through the village on silent feet. She knew that if she and Daniel were not well away from the village by the time the sun rose, they'd stand little chance of eluding pursuit. Time was of the essence.

Outside the healing chambers, Vanessa stopped to conceal her sack behind an arrowroot bush.

"Mother, be with me," she whispered. With a calm, confident stride, she entered the clay huts and made her way down the hall to Daniel's room.

The guard posted outside his door gave a brief nod of recognition as Vanessa approached.

"I have been sent to relieve you," Vanessa said, pleased that she did not stutter too badly over the "English" lie.

The warrior's brow wrinkled, but she had no reason to doubt her—the speaking of falsehoods was completely foreign to the Ama'zon. With a slight shrug, the guard shouldered her spear and headed down the corridor. Vanessa waited until she heard the gentle thud of the central doors closing before she pulled the candle from the wall sconce and entered Daniel's room.

He was standing in front of the worktable. He glanced up as she entered but showed no signs of surprise.

"I'm ready," he said.

Vanessa stiffened. Had he been so convinced she'd come?

Dropping to all fours, Daniel reached under the bed and pulled out a bundle wrapped in a torn section of the bedding. He tucked the parcel under his arm and strode toward her.

"How do we get out?"

As he drew closer, Vanessa noted that his wound had been covered with a strip of cloth, again taken from the bedding. After refusing her help, he must have bound the injury himself.

"We walk," she answered simply. "Stay close to me."

She opened the door a crack and peeked out. The halls were empty. Motioning for Daniel to wait, she slipped from the room and replaced the candle in its sconce. But for the odor of warm wax, the air smelled empty as well. She waved for Daniel to join her.

Within minutes, they were filing along the timbered wall, keeping to the deepest tree-covered shadows.

"Can you see where you're going?" Daniel asked from behind.

She started to answer, then felt his palm slam against her spine as he tripped and muttered an oath. Apparently his vision was not as keen as hers.

"Rest a hand upon my shoulder," she told him.

His fingers closed around the curve between her shoulder and neck, causing an odd heat to spill into her stomach.

"Where are we going?"

"There is a narrow breach in the wall at the

southern corner," she whispered. "I think it safer than trying to leave near the gates."

He murmured an assent.

Gray continued to filter into the eastern sky as they hurried along, matching their steps stride for stride.

"Here," Vanessa said, pulling up in front of the gap a mere second before Daniel walked directly into her, flattening himself awkwardly against her back. She started to turn around as he tried to steady himself, and his palm settled atop her breast.

She'd never known a like sensation. The warmth in her stomach spiked low. Deep.

His fingers lingered, cupping her, gently squeezing, and she thought she heard him moan something beneath his breath. Then, suddenly, his hand was gone and she felt inexplicably cold.

"This is it?" he asked, his voice rough.

"Y-yes." She resisted the urge to warm her arms. "I'll go first."

Fortunately, the logs had shifted since Vanessa had last used this particular escape route, and she crawled through the crack without much effort.

Daniel, however, was just large enough to make his passage more difficult. As he wedged his body back and forth, he released a sharp hiss.

"What is it?"

"Nothing," he muttered. "Just this damned shoulder."

"Shall I look at it?" she offered, when he finally emerged from the opening. Her hand reached for him, but he brushed her aside.

"I'm fine."

Vanessa tucked her hair behind her ears, watching as he tugged the loosened bandage into place. Never would she understand Daniel's constant need to lie.

While the Ama'zon had practiced restraint to the point where, over time, all emotion had been extinguished within them, Vanessa knew that Daniel *did* feel. She knew that he did. Yet even last night, when his fury had been a terrible, raging thing, he'd insisted on keeping his anger leashed. Did he not trust himself with his emotions? Or, she wondered, did he fear them?

"Let's go," Daniel said, with one last careless tug on his bandage. "I think there's enough light for me to follow you now."

Vanessa sent a wary glance to his bloodstained wrap. "Are you able to run?"

"Of course."

"Let me carry that, then," she said, pointing to his mysterious bundle.

"I can carr—"

"Daniel, please, we don't have time to waste," she interrupted. "I assure you it will be far easier for me to carry it in my bag."

He wavered before reluctantly handing her the parcel. She quickly stuffed it into the sack slung over her shoulder, then turned and broke into an easy, ground-eating lope. He followed, his step heavier yet swift.

The sky lightened; the trail sped under their feet. An ear-jarring cacophony of squawks and trills and chirps filled the forest as the birds launched into their daybreak song. As they reached the end of the path to Eldra'to, a brilliant flash of orange signaled sunrise. There the jungle greeted them, forcing them to slow their pace slightly as they wove their way in and out of tree stands, dodging marshes and ducking under webs of grasping liana.

The sun inched higher. Heat began to rise from the earth, sending steam spiraling into the air from the moist, hidden places beneath palm fronds and broad leaves. Daniel's tread became sluggish, his breathing ragged; but he did not falter.

The morning grew warm. Perspiration began to stream down Vanessa's arms to drip from her fingertips. Upon her back, her hair hung like a weight.

"We'll stop soon," she called to Daniel. "I think I hear a spring ahead."

A circle of hummingbirds flitted away as Vanessa shoved through the rushes, veering toward the sound of bubbling water. She pushed aside the grasses and there, within a shaded grove, beckoned a crystal-clear pond, offering fresh water and a cool haven within which to rest. Vanessa sent thanks to the Mother. She crouched beside the pool, shoving her hair from her face, and scooped water into her hands. Its chill tingled her wrists.

As she drank, Daniel came to stand beside her. He bent forward, leaning his elbows on his knees.

"Damn," he said, his words thin from lack of breath. "I'd wager we've been running close to three hours or more."

Though unfamiliar with the term *hour,* Vanessa nodded and scooped up another drink. "We've done well."

Daniel continued to lean onto his knees, his lungs heaving, his breath harsh. He tilted his head toward her, and Vanessa remarked on the ruddiness of his complexion. "Do you train?" he asked.

"Train?" Twisting her hair into a rope, Vanessa piled it atop her head so that the breeze could wash over her nape. "What do you mean?"

Daniel pushed himself upright. "Do you work to condition yourself? For strength? Endurance?"

"No more than any other Ama'zon."

"Huh." With two fingers, Daniel plucked at the front of his sweat-soaked shirt. "Amazing," he murmured, before wading into the spring.

He sank into the waist-high water until his head was completely submerged, then resurfaced with a tired sigh. After gulping a few handfuls from the spring, he raked his hair back from his forehead and turned a brooding, speculative gaze upon her.

"Do you think they'll come after us?"

Vanessa splashed water onto her neck. "I do not know," she answered. "No one has ever escaped before."

Daniel's eyes narrowed thoughtfully and he waded toward the marshy bank. At the water's edge, he sat down, bending his leg into his lap to study the sole of his foot.

"Oh, Daniel!" Vanessa gasped. The bottom of his foot was raw and blistered, as if burnt by the sun. Without thinking, Vanessa knelt beside his other leg, took hold of the ankle and inspected the sole of that foot. Like its mate, it, too, was covered with torn and ragged blisters.

Daniel made an attempt to pull his leg from her grasp, but the muscles in his thigh quivered with the effort. "I'll be fine once they callus over," he said gruffly. "Unlike you, I'm not accustomed to running through the jungle barefoot."

"You must be in pain."

"I've known worse."

She frowned, convinced that he *had* known worse. Much worse. Would he share it with her? Share his pain?

"Daniel—"

"How do you propose to locate the *Angela*?" he asked brusquely as he pushed himself to a stand.

Still crouched at his feet, Vanessa glanced up,

noticing how his brown eyes had become shuttered and unapproachable. Did he loathe so very much the idea that he could feel pain? Did he see it as a sign of weakness, frailty?

Vanessa rinsed her arms in the water before answering. "We will first seek the river, then follow it until we find the ship."

"How many days, do you think?"

She arched a brow, pointing out, "Daniel, I do not know where your ship might be."

His forehead wrinkled. "Of course."

Placing his hands on the top of his hips, he gazed into the forest, a familiar expression settling over his features. An expression Vanessa recognized. One that, to her mind, had come to characterize this Englishman, Daniel Heywood.

Impatience.

"Shall we continue?" he asked.

She hid a smile and pushed to her feet. "As you wish."

Chapter Ten

If Daniel had believed his first trip through the Amazon to be arduous, this journey alongside Vanessa was the closest thing to hell he'd ever experienced.

For the first two days of their travel, he and Vanessa did not walk, but run. They ran miles and miles and miles in scorching heat and air so humid it weighted his lungs with suffocating moisture. At night, they took turns sleeping in the hammock she'd brought, while the other stood guard against hostile Indians or pursuing Ama'zon warriors.

Run. Drink. Eat. Sleep. There was no room for anything else. Those first forty-eight hours were a test of stamina and strength that pushed Daniel to the very limits of his abilities. And made him view his traveling companion in a new and significantly more respectful light.

As a guide, Vanessa was without peer. She could sniff out fresh water more keenly than a bloodhound, and her knowledge of the jungle's plants and herbs was a naturalist's dream. She knew which leaves to rub on their bodies to keep the chiggers and mosquitoes away, and where to search for the banana trees and sugarcane that provided their only nourishment those first two days. Like him, she continually pushed herself, asking her body to do what seemed impossible, to keep moving when exhaustion burned in every muscle. Yet she never uttered a word of complaint. Not one. When Daniel insisted that they push onward after each of their short resting periods, Vanessa would merely nod, toss back that glorious mane of hers and trudge on.

She was remarkable. One of a kind.

Early the morning of the third day, as storm-threatening clouds gathered in the sky, they reached the marshy banks of the Amazon River.

"I've only seen it from afar," Vanessa said quietly, as they stood beside the broad expanse of water that, even this far inland, stretched miles across.

"She's awesome, isn't she?"

"She?" Vanessa asked, smiling slightly.

Daniel gave a self-conscious shrug. For him, the Amazon would always be a woman: beautiful, unpredictable and the giver of life here in the jungle.

Vanessa removed her pack from her shoulder and looped it over a low, mossy branch.

"Do you need to relieve yourself?" Daniel asked bluntly. He had learned that modesty was not a trait with which Vanessa was at all familiar.

"No."

"Then why have we stopped?"

Linking her fingers together, Vanessa stretched her arms behind her, arching her back. The jaguar-skin dress she wore pulled across her chest as the hem rose to breath-stealing heights.

"We have stopped because we are safe now," she said.

Daniel swiftly lowered his gaze to his feet, pretending that his eyes had not lingered a moment too long on thighs shapely and sleek.

"The Ama'zon warriors would never venture this far," Vanessa explained.

He sent a skeptical look into the thicket. "What makes you so certain?"

Vanessa dug into the pack and withdrew a papaya. She rubbed it against her hip, explaining, "It is forbidden to journey to the river. Many people travel along its waters, making the risk of discovery too great. Only by remaining secluded and sheltered have the Ama'zon survived all these years."

"I see. And to ensure that your culture remains properly secluded and sheltered, you kill off interlopers like me and Harold, right?"

No sooner had the bitter words left his tongue than Daniel regretted them. He watched as Vanessa's eyes clouded, her gaze lowering to the papaya in her hand.

"I, uh, I didn't mean—"

Dammit, why was he stuttering over an apology? He shouldn't be the one begging pardon, now should he? If not for the Ama'zon, he would not be tearing through the jungle, running for his very life like a hunted animal. And if not for the Ama'zon, he would not be sentenced to living out the rest of his days with Reeves's death weighing on his conscience, eating away at his soul.

No, Daniel reminded himself with brutal clarity, Vanessa's people had brought him to Eldra'to with one thought and one thought alone. To kill him. To kill him only after they had used him in the vilest of fashions, stealing his manhood, his seed.

"To hell with it," he muttered. To hell with apologies and to hell with regrets. He needed to stay focused on his mission, to remember what had driven him to come to the jungle.

By God, in a matter of days—if luck was with him—he would be sailing for home on the *Angela.* And what would he have to show for his expedition? What proof would he have that he had actually discovered an ancient society hidden in the heart of the Amazon? A society that most believed to be no more than myth?

Granted he carried with him a few drawings, a few trinkets he'd taken from his room—but what would they evidence? Little. Very little indeed.

No, what he needed was to bring back to England substantive proof, something solid and tangible. *Or* . . . His pulse accelerated as an idea came to him. A wickedly brilliant idea.

Or he could bring home some*one* tangible.

Through slitted eyes, he glanced at Vanessa, who was solemnly paring the papaya with her knife. *She is an excellent model,* he thought to himself, *a splendid illustration of Ama'zon strength and beauty.* And as a teacher, she was supremely knowledgeable about her people's history and customs, their mores and religious beliefs. What better proof of his discovery could he possibly present?

"Vanessa, what will happen to you when you return to Eldra'to?"

She did not look up from her task of peeling. "I do not know. I doubt that I will escape some form of censure from the Elders."

"Mmm." Daniel's lips thinned. "I would hate to think that you will be disciplined on my account."

She took a wide-mouthed bite of the papaya. Its fragrant juices spilled onto her chin, glistening like drops of dew. Calmly, she wiped her mouth with the back of her wrist before answering. "My actions have consequences, Daniel. I accept that."

He frowned. Her lips looked sticky and sweet. "So you anticipate that you will be punished?"

She shrugged easily and took another bite of fruit. As perverse as it seemed, Vanessa's docile acceptance of her fate irritated him. After all, it was he who had convinced her to break the laws of her people. What had he expected? That she'd be honored upon her return?

"Vanessa, have you never wondered about the world outside Eldra'to's walls? Have you never thought of traveling to other lands? Of meeting other kinds of people?"

A light flickered at the back of her yellow-green eyes. A light of unmistakable interest.

"You do not have to return to Eldra'to right away, you know. In fact, it might be best to put some time between your transgression and your return. After a few months, the Elders's wrath will have cooled, and they might overlook your crime in assisting me."

"What are you suggesting, Daniel?"

"I am suggesting . . . that you come back to England with me."

A faraway look came over her, and she wordlessly offered him the rest of the papaya. When he shook his head, she tossed the remains into the brush.

"England?" she repeated.

"Yes," he said in a seductive whisper. "A world unlike anything you've seen here in the jungle. A world of carriages and books and gas lighting. A world where men and women live together side by side."

A ridge formed between her brows. "But the Seer has told me that I must save my people," she said, speaking more to herself than to him. "I cannot abandon them."

A spurt of annoyance jolted through him. He'd half-expected that Vanessa would leap at the opportunity to go home with him. What was keeping her here? Some deranged old prophet? "Seer?"

Vanessa gave a pensive nod. "Before she passed, she had a vision from the Great Mother. The vision told her that I was destined to save the Ama'zon."

Daniel thought quickly. "Well, perhaps you have already saved them," he suggested. "By helping me escape, you may have forced them to find another capable of spawning the next generation of Ama'zon."

Vanessa's lashes fluttered as she considered his argument. "But I feel," she said quietly, "that there is more that I must do. . . ."

An abrupt rustling startled them, jerking them both around. Up the trunk of a jubati palm, a long, fat lizard was chasing a smaller companion in a reptilian game of tag.

"A *jacuara,*" Vanessa identified.

"Are they tasty?" Daniel asked, his stomach demanding something more substantial than fruit. Slowly, he reached for the knife Vanessa had set on a nearby rock.

"Not particularly."

"Oh." He let his fingers fall to his side.

"But you are right in that we should seek a meal for this evening. Tonight we will be able to have a fire without worry." She rolled her neck on her shoulders, smiling faintly. "And frankly, I, for one, would not mind making camp early. I am beginning to tire from the pace we've set these last two days and could do with some rest."

Amen, Daniel thought to himself, and grabbed the pack from the tree limb. *Amen.*

Vanessa sighed and floated on her back, allowing the pale blue water to slide across her stomach and pool in her navel, soft and cool. The sensation was delightful—soothing yet oddly stimulating as well.

Above her, the stars shone as violent white dots in a royal blue canopy, and Vanessa imagined she could hear those beacons of light popping and crackling as they sparkled. In truth, it was the fire on the other side of the trees that sizzled and snapped, the sounds broken every few minutes by Daniel's muttered curses as he labored to shave himself with the knife.

Sand tickled Vanessa's feet as she stood, wringing water from her hair. Lifting her face skyward, she idly wondered if one could see stars from England. Daniel had said that there was no jungle in his homeland, no palm trees, no crocodile, no iguana. He described his London as made up of frenzied motion and large stone buildings and incessant noise. He spoke of thick fog and even thicker coal smoke. Yet, despite all this, Daniel insisted that he wanted to return. And he wanted her to return with him.

To leave the jungle.

Although Vanessa had long dreamed of flying away, of seeking out people more like her—people able to express their passions—she was not fully convinced that leaving Eldra'to was the path the Mother had chosen for her. It disturbed her to think of traveling across an ocean to a new land, foreign and strange. It disturbed her very much. But those concerns were almost nothing compared to how she knew she would feel in a few days' time, when she watched Daniel sail away from her forever.

A welcome breeze brushed over her shoulders as Vanessa stretched her arms overhead. While she still had much to think about, she was, at least, refreshed following a hot meal and a bath. She felt alive again, invigorated.

Alive? Vanessa frowned, her arms falling back to her sides as her thoughts clung to that word. She did feel alive, and it had naught to do, she realized, with a meal or a bath. This feeling was due to Daniel. It was he who made her feel vital, more vital than she'd ever felt before.

Simply being with him stimulated her thoughts, her emotions . . . her body.

What was it in Daniel that made her feel so? Was it only because he was a man that she responded to him like no other person she'd known? Or was there some other reason for his effect upon her, a reason she did not understand?

Once or twice these past days, she'd caught him watching her in a way that made her breasts tingle and her stomach grow taut. Even now the memory of his eyes upon her caused her skin to itch and pull.

She shivered, wrapping her arms about herself, as she stepped from the pond. Perhaps she should ask Daniel about it, she thought. He understood much that she did not. And he had been with many women. . . .

Vanessa picked up her pelt and shook it a handful of times before heading back to their encampment.

Daniel was sitting some distance from the fire, staring broodingly into the flames, his brown eyes flecked with the reflection of red, orange and bronze sparks. He glanced up as she emerged from the trees. She saw his throat work, and then he averted his gaze.

"Enjoy your bath?" he asked gruffly, threading his fingers through hair still glossy and wet from his own bath earlier.

"Yes," Vanessa answered. "It was lovely."

His eyes skittered toward her, then away

again. "What are you doing with your—ahem—dress?"

With one last shake, Vanessa draped the pelt over a dead limb. "It needs to be brushed."

As she turned to fetch her comb from the pack, she noticed that Daniel was staring at her again. Staring at her in the same way that made her insides curl and her lungs feel tight.

"Wh-why are you looking at me like that?" she asked breathlessly.

"Like what?"

"Like—"

Vanessa splayed her hands across her chest in an instinctively protective gesture. One she'd not used before.

"Do you not want me to look at you, Vanessa?" he asked in a quiet, careful voice.

"I—I don't know." She peered down at her body, washed gold in the firelight. "Is it . . . wrong for you to see me unclothed?"

He did not answer, but continued to study her as if he were searching for something. An answer.

With a crook of his finger, he beckoned her forward. "Come here, Vanessa."

She debated a moment, uncomfortable, uncertain. Yet, at her core, she knew she wanted to be close to Daniel—so why deny her instincts?

Inching over, he made room for her on the mat as she circled the fire ringed by stones. As she seated herself at Daniel's side, she gave a subtle tilt to her head, sending her hair forward over her shoulder to partially obscure her breasts.

From beneath her lashes, she watched Daniel very slowly reach out and take a lock of her hair between his fingers, rubbing the strands back and forth.

"Vanessa."

For some reason her voice failed her, and she managed but a murmur.

"Do you know," Daniel asked, "the meaning of desire?"

She had to swallow over the dryness in her throat. "It means want, longing."

"Yes. Very good," he whispered, smiling his approval. He twisted his wrist, so that the ends of her hair wrapped around his fist. "Would you understand then, Vanessa, if I were to tell you that I desire you?"

"Perhaps."

He arched a brow in question, his gaze still intent on the strands of her hair stretched across his knuckles.

"Perhaps?"

"I-I might understand," she stammered, as her hands fluttered aimlessly in her lap. "If desire is wh-what I am feeling, then I might understand."

"Oh?" His gaze, curious and bright, lifted to hers. "And what are you feeling, Vanessa?"

She licked at her lips, noticing how Daniel's

shirt gaped open to reveal the soft crisp curls on his chest.

"I am feeling as if a fire creeps through my veins."

"Hmm?" He smiled at that, then pushed her hair aside, exposing her, baring her nakedness to the night.

"Does it feel," he asked, "as if this fire must be stoked—"

She gasped when his fingernail scraped across the tip of one breast.

"—to soothe your hot, dark places?"

She nodded, her breath suddenly very fast. "Y-yes."

He nodded. "That is desire."

In the ensuing silence, a macaw chattered, and the breeze dipped and swayed.

Taking her chin into his palm, Daniel directed her gaze to his. Her heart leaped.

"I want you, Vanessa," he said in a low, harsh whisper. "I long to touch you and to taste you and to sink myself into you. To know you as a man knows a woman."

"But . . . I am not yet a woman."

Daniel circled her nipple with his finger. She shuddered, closing her eyes.

"Would you like to be?"

She shifted forward, seeking his touch, sensing a wildness stir within her. "Yes," she whispered. "Yes."

He smiled again, and Vanessa recognized how rare a sight it was. Yet none of Daniel's smiles had ever been like this. Full of fierce promise.

He leaned toward her, a lock of chestnut hair falling across his brow. His lips hovered just above hers.

"Are you going to possess me with your mouth again?" she asked.

"I am," he murmured, then did.

As before, when his mouth settled over hers, Vanessa felt the caress in each and every inch of her body. It was as if his lips and teeth and tongue were reaching to every part of her. To her toes and neck. Her breasts and belly.

Daniel wove his fingers through hers, gently pushing her onto her back.

"This is so nice."

He laughed softly. "It's supposed to be."

She lay beneath him as he taught her love games with his mouth—a playful nibble at the base of the throat, the seductive pull of lips on the fleshy lobe of her ear.

The way Daniel touched her made Vanessa feel as if she were being devoured, as she longed to devour him. To taste and savor and drink of him, to assuage her unquenchable thirst and hunger.

"More," she whispered.

"More?" Daniel responded, letting his deep voice slide like honey into her ear as his tongue did the same.

Breathless, Vanessa struggled to murmur

even a series of single syllables. "More . . . of . . . me."

"You want me to taste more of your body?" Daniel punctuated the last word with a slow, warm lick from the hollow of her throat up over her chin and onto her bottom lip, which he then began to suckle.

"No."

"No, Vanessa?"

"Not more . . . of me."

"Tell me, Vanessa."

"All . . . of me."

Daniel's face, which had these last moments been hidden from Vanessa as he nuzzled against the flesh of her lips and ears and throat, now lifted above her. She could see his eyebrows raise and a smile tease at the corners of his mouth.

"Good. Because I have been hungry so long."

Vanessa did not think she could stand the wait as he slowly lowered his lips to her left nipple, where he tugged and tickled her alternately, making her grow hot, as if she'd tumbled into the fire.

Daniel held the rest of his body like a bridge, so that their only point of contact was lips to nipple. And yet Vanessa felt as if his mouth was everywhere. Her whole body wet and warm and raw-feeling.

But now, even that did not seem enough.

"More . . . all . . ."

"Yes, Vanessa. Like this?" And his lips and

tongue threaded a trail down her belly, until his face met her special place. The womanly spot where Vanessa had been taught that all life emerged. She now began to learn what she had never been taught. That this was where life would begin.

With her eyes clenched shut, her fists grasping the grass and earth on either side of her body, Vanessa saw herself, in her mind's eye, at the brink of the precipice. At the special place where she had always gone. When she was hopeful, and when she was afraid. Always, she had longed to let go, to fly off and away. Always duty and fear had kept her earthbound. Not this time.

Daniel's tongue, light and quick as the wings of a hummingbird, urged her to the edge. Her toes curled. Her fists clenched. *No. I cannot go.* His tongue told her yes.

"No, no, no, no."

Daniel stopped to answer aloud, softly, "Yes." And he blew between her legs, giving wind to her wings. With one more kiss, he blew her over the edge, and she fell, until her falling turned to flight.

Vanessa's lips formed his name, though no sound came out. Daniel no longer touched her, but laying there with her eyes closed, Vanessa's body continued to tingle. Slowly, the tingling turned to a general, gentle warmth, and she opened her eyes.

Daniel lay next to her, his manhood a shaft of heat against her outer thigh.

"May I go with you?"

In answer, she reached for him, and he rolled her over on top of him, unerringly bringing her down upon him, quickly piercing through the shield of her virginity. She cried out and he cradled her hips in his hands, gently stroking until her muscles relaxed.

Then, again, he rolled over, taking her with him.

"Come here, my cat," he whispered. He pulled away from her, drawing her onto her hands and knees, kneeling behind her as he reached forward and cupped her breasts. He pushed into her again, gently rocking her forward and back as she arched and cried and ultimately soared over the precipice again. She was still calling his name when she felt his body jerk at her hips and he ground against her, a low guttural sound coming from his throat.

Finally full and sated, they dropped to the blanket and slept.

Chapter Eleven

Daniel awoke in the early hours of morning with a foul curse upon his lips. A foul curse and the sweet, sweet taste of Vanessa.

She lay half atop him, her arm sprawled across his chest, a knee hooked over his leg, the hemp blanket draped over the both of them. Her head was pillowed on his shoulder and, as he gazed at her profile in the fresh light of dawn, Daniel thought how surprisingly young she looked. Young and . . . innocent.

With a huff of disgust, he closed his eyes, suddenly overcome with guilt. If Vanessa had been an innocent before—and she had been—he'd sure as hell taken care of that last night, hadn't he? Taken care of it not once but twice, blast his lustful soul.

Stifling a groan, he peered up at the canopy of green, asking himself what he had done.

Damn it all, he hadn't planned to make love to her. In fact, during the last few days he'd tried not to think of Vanessa as a woman at all, which was hardly easy. Tempted every minute of the day by the gentle sway of her hips, the erotic flash of her gold-green eyes, he had tried to view her only as a guide, a helpmate. Not once during these last days had he allowed himself to wonder what it would be like to introduce Vanessa—sensual, sensitive Vanessa—to the ultimate experience shared between a man and a woman.

But last night, God help him, all that had changed. Drunk with relief and the realization that he'd cheated death at the hands of the Ama'zon, he had felt invincible. Powerful. Capable of reaching out and taking what he wanted with godlike impunity. And, yes, he had wanted Vanessa. When she had emerged from her bath, a vision of raw, untouched beauty—

Daniel grit his teeth until his jaw began to ache, wishing himself to perdition and back. He, who was so proud of his ability to keep his passions on a tight leash, had simply lost control. He'd let his desire run away with him. Or . . . was that merely an excuse?

No, no excuse, he told himself with angry desperation. He had made love to Vanessa because, after months of forced celibacy, he'd been presented with a siren in the flesh and he'd responded exactly as any other redblooded man would have done under the circumstances. He had made love to her because, at the back of his mind, he'd been fantasizing of nothing else these last grueling weeks. Because she intrigued him as no other woman had ever done. What he had *not* done—he couldn't have—was make love to Vanessa in an attempt to lure her to England.

His conscience was not so easily convinced. After all, he had successfully resisted his attraction to her until yesterday. Until yesterday, when she had shocked him by not leaping at his invitation to travel home with him on the *Angela.* Her reluctance to accompany him to England had been unsettling. Very unsettling. Daniel had not anticipated that she might actually refuse. What about his plans? He'd begun to doubt, to question.

Had he, by chance, acted on those doubts? Could he honestly claim he'd harbored no ulterior motives in taking her virginity?

Or had he secretly hoped to bind her to him? To seduce her so thoroughly that she would agree to forsake the only home she'd ever known in exchange for . . . what? Physical release?

Against his side, Vanessa snuggled closer, whimpering like a child troubled by bad dreams. That small, seemingly insignificant act was like salt in a wound, intensifying Daniel's guilt. Already the changes had begun. Vanessa was seeking comfort from *him*. Vanessa, the Ama'zon, who, only a few days earlier had stared down a pair of snarling ocelots as fearlessly as one might chastise naughty housecats.

Good God, what had he done?

No one was to blame but himself. He had hoped to present Vanessa to his colleagues as "Eve"; woman in her natural state, unsullied by modern man. But it was he who had sullied her, tainting his findings as surely as if he'd painted dots onto the wings of a newly discovered species of butterfly.

But perhaps . . . perhaps the damage was not so significant, Daniel argued with himself. Although he could not deny that he had erred in bedding her, Vanessa would not have been expected to remain pure forever. According to the Ama'zon's barbaric practices, she had already been "slated" to be deflowered. And by him, no less. He had only sped up events, changed the venue.

It was small consolation, but Daniel clung to it. His career as a naturalist depended upon it. His view of himself, as well.

But now what? If he hoped to introduce Vanessa as a scientifically acceptable model of an Ama'zon, she needed to remain an Ama'zon in the most absolute sense. Which meant that under no circumstances should he repeat his trespass of the night before. In fact, inasmuch as it was possible, he should strive to limit her contact with all men, all people. Everything that

Vanessa learned from this point forward about the world outside the jungle would only corrupt her experience and make her less of an Ama'zon.

Against his chest, Vanessa's fingers twitched as her eyelids began to flutter open. Carefully, Daniel slipped out from under her, prepared to alter the unfortunate course he'd begun.

"Good morning," he offered as he pulled on his trousers, then walked a few steps away from their cozy pallet.

"It is good, isn't it?" she answered, her voice a sleepy, husky purr.

"Hmm. I was thinking that we probably should get started before good morning turns to good noon."

Vanessa shifted up onto her side, leaning on her elbow. She tilted her head toward Daniel, her expression quizzical, alert. "There is still much time before noon."

"But there is no reason why we shouldn't set off now, is there?" he asked brusquely.

"Well, no." Vanessa plucked at the edge of the blanket. "No reason."

Turning his back to her, Daniel quickly pulled on his shirt, his fingers clumsy as he fumbled at the neck's closing. He was reminded of his first time with a woman, when he'd been but a callow youth, inexperienced and self-conscious.

"I believe there is still some fruit from last night. If you are hungry," he said.

"Yes, I am hungry."

He turned around and she smiled hopefully, pushing herself up onto her knees, fully baring her rounded shoulders, bosom and long, slim torso. "You must be also?"

"No, not really," Daniel lied, his voice low and scratchy. Another pang of guilt shot through him as he saw the pain of rejection dawning in her gold-green eyes.

"Well." Daniel spun away from the guileless confusion on Vanessa's face. "I'll wash up while you get ready to go."

Before she could answer, Daniel was tucking in his shirt and briskly stepping down toward the water.

Kneeling in front of the cool, dark spring, Daniel plunged his hands into the water, splashing his face and neck. He looked down at his glistening hands and remembered the look of their dark roughness against the smooth, golden skin of Vanessa's hips. She had been unsophisticated, yet so willing to learn, to experiment. He had never been with a woman who had offered both innocence and raw passion.

"Daniel."

He started, her husky voice sending a shiver of remembrance through his limbs.

"Yes?" He stood, adopting a rigid, unapproachable posture, very much like the one he'd seen his father use time and time again.

"I am ready," she said, although the statement sounded like a question. She appeared to be searching, inviting an explanation for his sudden reserve.

"Nothing to eat?" he asked.

"I am not hungry now."

Daniel met her eyes, reminding himself that what he did was for the best.

"Then let us move on." He took the pack of supplies from Vanessa and slung them over his shoulder. Since they would now be following the course of the river, he would assume the lead position.

Daniel made himself concentrate on each step, careful to keep his mind focused on the surrounding jungle and its hidden dangers. He watched the ground they trod, the walls of foliage on all sides, the river's slippery bank on their left. It was a helpful exercise in keeping his thoughts from straying to the events of last night.

For hours, they moved purposely through the dense forest in just this way, saying nothing to each other, except when Daniel offered "Water?" and Vanessa answered "Yes." Even then, he disciplined his eyes to avoid her direct gaze, tempered his voice to bland courtesy.

Daniel half expected, half feared that if they spoke beyond these simple politenesses, Vanessa would ask him the question he could not answer: *What is wrong?* Yet, to his relief, she said nothing. He wondered if she was too confused by what must seem his emotional betrayal of her, or if she merely understood that last night was last night, and this was a new day.

After they had been walking for several hours in this manner, Daniel in the lead, Vanessa's sure, light footsteps just behind him, keeping pace, seeming not to challenge his leadership in this leg of their journey, Daniel began to doubt his own sense of direction. Tiny insects ringed his head in a thick, moving screen, while unfamiliar sounds popped and whistled all around him. The river branched and forked and twisted into hundreds of streams and outlets, any of which might lead to his ship.

He had been so confident when he'd left the *Angela*, confident in his survival skills and his knowledge of the jungle. But now he recognized that he was less capable than Vanessa, less knowledgeable. She was a denizen of these wilds; he was merely a visitor.

What if I've made a mistake? What if the ship is farther upriver than I remembered?

But he could not reveal his doubts. He could not turn and ask, "Is this right?" He had been trained by his father to never reveal weakness, to never abandon the role of command.

"Daniel. Listen!"

Vanessa reached forward and gripped his upper arm.

He paused, amazed to feel himself respond to her touch even after hours of awkward silence. Even though she might have been warning him of impending danger.

He heard nothing but the constant low buzz of gnats and mosquitoes.

Vanessa's lips nearly touched his ear.

"I hear English."

I do not understand, Vanessa had been silently, rhythmically chanting to herself during their long, uncomfortable hike through the jungle.

The Daniel she had awoke to this morning was so very different from the Daniel she had known last night. He had changed, when last night it had been he who had changed *her.*

Channeling all of his strength and power and passion into subtle and delicate touches and gestures, he had transformed her. He had awakened the woman inside, the woman who had been desperate to feel all that she'd known Daniel was capable of making her feel. It was as if he'd opened tiny pinpricks all over her body, through which new and wondrous sensations had entered.

"The cistern contains; the fountain o'erflows," Daniel had whispered. And they had overflowed together. But like the river, once its waters overflow, then they must eventually retreat. As Daniel was retreating from her.

Though she did not understand him, she recognized his behavior. It was like that of an animal threatened, unpredictable and thoughtless. She remembered many seasons ago, a young Ama'zon had inadvertently cornered an enormous bull caiman while out gathering herbs. The error had cost the girl her life. Not because the animal was hungry and desired food, but simply because the girl had come too close. She had threatened the animal with her nearness.

Somehow Vanessa suspected that the same was true of Daniel. Perhaps she had come too close last night? Perhaps she should do as the young Ama'zon ought to have done—wait until the threat passed, then proceed cautiously?

Yes, Vanessa decided, that would be the wisest path for her to take. She would be patient while trying to gain a greater understanding of Daniel. And then once she understood him, she could make him understand her. Understand the reason for her feelings of hurt and confusion.

Lost in thought, Vanessa did not initially recognize the strange noises in the distance. She strained to hear, but the unfamiliar sounds were obscured by Daniel's footsteps ahead of her. *Again.*

"Daniel. Listen!" She leaned closer, her lips brushing just below his left ear. "I hear English."

"What? Where?"

"Follow the water with your eyes, as far as they will travel. Now let your ears follow. Do you not hear the voices?"

After a moment of weighty silence, Daniel's face erupted into a smile, sweat pooling into the craggy dimples on either side of his mouth.

"Mac!" he yelled. "Mac!"

Then he plunged forward into the brush.

No! Vanessa's heart thudded in the cage of her ribs as she started after him, her gaze slashing anxiously from right to left. In his excitement, Daniel had forgotten the principal rule of survival in the jungle: Never take your environment for granted and never drop your guard.

From straight ahead, a terrible cry sounded, only a few short paces in front of Daniel. Vanessa grabbed for him, trying to pull Daniel to safety, but he was just a hair too far out of her reach.

"Aaaghh!" the cry came again.

Alarmed, Vanessa watched as a large red creature emerged from the thicket—

"Mac!" Daniel shouted.

A man? The large red-faced creature was, in fact, a severely sunburned man, dressed from head to toe in bleached and tattered rags.

"Ah, Cap'n, I canna believe it!"

Daniel hurried forward and slapped the man on the shoulder. "Believe it, Mac, believe it. I made it back."

"Faith, I was worried when we hadn't heard from ye, that's fer sure. But I damn well wasn't goin' to pull anchor 'til I knew fer certain what had come of ye."

Daniel mopped his forehead with the back of his sleeve. "How's the *Angela*?" he asked. "The crew holding up?"

"Well, we've lost a few, Cap'n. One to fever, and three more just up and run off together one night. Like to've gone crazy just waitin' here, I s'pose. I did send a party to look for 'em, but then decided 'twas best to let 'em go. There's a small village of a few dozen savages down the river a mile or more. They mighta made it that far."

The man named Mac glanced past Daniel, evidently unable to detect Vanessa standing so quietly in the tall brush. "And what of the men who went with ye?"

Vanessa saw the sudden stiffness in Daniel's bearing. "Native ambush," he said, his words revealingly spare. "All dead. But for me."

The naked emotion in his voice caused Vanessa to instinctively reach out to him. Her small movement drew the attention of Mac.

His faded blue eyes rounded and he staggered back a step.

Daniel turned around, his expression surprised, as if he had completely forgotten of her existence. "Oh, Mac, allow me to introduce Vanessa. She, er . . . helped save my life, you could say. Vanessa belongs to a very interesting culture that I stumbled across. Very interesting. At any rate, she will be accompanying us back to England." He hesitated, then, for the first time in many hours, gazed directly into her eyes. "Or at least I hope she will be joining us."

The question lay between them.

"Yes," she said, "I will be."

Mac made an odd sound at the back of his throat. "Uh, Cap'n. A word if I may . . ."

Mac and Daniel drew their heads together and proceeded to engage in a heated exchange of whispers. Every few seconds, Mac shot a fretful glance in Vanessa's direction while she waited, weary and tired, the tension of the last few days finally catching up with her. Finally, the discussion concluded, Vanessa was wrapped up in the hemp blanket—at Mac's suggestion—and escorted onto the smelly, creaking structure Daniel called *Angela*.

Although tired, Vanessa was curious to examine the ship, for she'd only seen one or two from a distance before. But Mac quickly hustled her across the deck, past a cluster of gawking crewmen. Vanessa smiled a cautious greeting, amazed by the differences in the group. Her entire life, she had known only three men: Harold, Daniel and Reeves. Now here were dozens of them in so many varied sizes, shapes and colors.

"Come on, lass," Mac urged. "This way."

She followed him to a small, dark room: the captain's cabin. Daniel's cabin.

"Now, the cap'n says ye should rest, lass," Mac said. "He says the two of ye have had a rough time of it."

Vanessa gave a vague nod, positively fascinated by all the unfamiliar items surrounding her. Round things. Shiny things. Things with arrows and numbers.

"There's a flask of water over there"—Mac pointed to the table—"and over there ye'll find the, ahem, chamberpot. Ye need anythin' else, just holler."

Vanessa dragged herself away from the study of a silvery mirror. "Thank you. Thank you very much."

As Mac shut the door, Vanessa collapsed on the bunk, exhausted and pleased to find the mattress so comfortable. So comfortable, in fact, that when she again stirred, it was to the aroma of food cooking and to the odd sensation of being rocked. She had fallen asleep. And to judge from the sunshine filtering into the cabin, she had slept away most of the afternoon.

Scrambling from the bed, she stood in the middle of the cabin, her feet spread far apart to steady herself. Though she longed to look carefully at Daniel's things, the smell of meat roasting proved a more powerful lure, particularly since she'd gone all day without eating.

Vanessa opened the door of the cabin and glanced around. The smell of seawater was everywhere. She headed down the narrow passage, turned the corner and walked straight into a man. A tall, thin man with red, peeling skin, he stood directly in front of her, blocking the way.

"Well, hallo there," he said, his breath damp and sour and too close. "Harris is the name, miss. I was hopin' to 'ave a chance to meet ye."

"Hello," she offered tentatively. "I am Vanessa."

His watery gaze took in her animal pelt wrap. "Gor, and what's this ye're wearin'? Or not wearin', I should say?"

He chuckled heartily, revealing teeth uneven and discolored. In his hand he held a dented metal cup that sloshed liquid onto Vanessa's toes as he wobbled on his feet.

"This is what my people wear—"

Midsentence, she abruptly realized that this man was not truly interested in her answer. Her nerves signaled an alert as his gaze slid over her body. She'd never experienced a similar reaction, but she felt herself feeling immediate distaste for the man. "If you will excuse me, I need—"

Harris stepped closer, dropping his full cup onto the ground.

"Wot is it you need?" He ran two scalelike palms down the length of her arms, squeezing each few inches. "P'raps ole Harris here can fill yer need, eh? I know wot I need and I'm thinkin' ye can help me out."

"Remove your hands," Vanessa said, straightening to her full height. She attempted to step back but ran into the narrow hall's wall just behind her. "I do not want to hurt you."

He laughed and tightened his grip. His bony knee attempted to push between her legs.

"Ah, don't worry, missy. I don't want to hurt ye, either."

In the next moment, a hard mouth was on hers, and his grasping hands had dropped to her hips, dragging them roughly against him. The taste of him was foul, the smell of him worse yet.

Taken by surprise, Vanessa did not think to struggle or to pull away. Her instincts drove her to action before she fully recognized what she was doing. With little effort, she sent her fist into the side of the man's temple. Down he fell with a faint grunt.

Frowning, she regarded the figure crumpled at her feet, her fingers sliding curiously across the contours of her mouth. What a world of difference there had been between the effect of this man's lips on hers and the kisses she'd enjoyed with Daniel. She wondered at the difference, wondered what it meant.

Eager to seek out Daniel, Vanessa moved through the short, shadowy hallway and up several steps into fresh air and what seemed the companionable noise of a celebration. Several of the men were playing music on instruments she'd not seen before, while others sat cross-legged on the deck eating from metal platters, talking and laughing.

The music and laughter stopped, however, as Vanessa emerged into the warm light of dusk.

"Bloody—"

"Have you ever seen the like?"

"I wouldn't mind a piece of that. . . ."

Awkwardly, Vanessa stood her ground, unsettled by the attention she was receiving from the crewmen, many of whom were staring openly, mouths ajar.

"Vanessa!"

She pivoted around to see Daniel rushing toward her, a thunderous scowl marking his brow. He snatched a shirt that had been left to dry in the sun from the side of an oak barrel.

"Put this on, for God's sake," he muttered, moving to block her from the men's view. She pulled the shirt on over her head.

"Whatcha got there, Captain?" she heard one of the men call out.

"Yeah, aren't ye goin' to introduce us?"

The tension in Daniel radiated from his every pore.

"Vanessa is an expert in South American flora and fauna who is returning to England to help me in my research. She will be staying in my cabin—"

"Captain's privileges, I suppose," another man shouted out.

"—while I'll put up with MacDougal in the first mate's cabin," Daniel continued, ignoring the comment. "Our guest is *not* to be disturbed, is that clear? She'll be working and won't have time for idle conversation."

There was a threat hidden in Daniel's words, Vanessa noticed. A threat and a fair degree of anger. When he turned around and grabbed her by the elbow, she realized that his anger was directed toward her.

"Back below deck," he murmured tightly. "Now."

"But I am hungry and I smelled the—"

"I'll have Mac bring you something to eat."

Virtually dragging her across the deck, Daniel hurried her down the stairs into the lower passageway, where he came close to tripping over the man Harris, who was just beginning to regain consciousness.

"Harris, what the devil!"

The man was sitting up, rubbing at the side of his head. His gaze swerved away quickly when he saw Vanessa standing behind Daniel.

Evidently Daniel had noticed the man's guilty behavior, for he slowly turned to Vanessa and asked, "Do you know what happened here?"

"I-I struck him."

Daniel's eyes froze. "Why?"

Before Vanessa could answer, Mac came running from the direction of the stairs, boots pounding. He halted directly behind Vanessa, his breath rapid.

"Why?" Daniel repeated.

Harris tried to stand up, but Daniel placed his boot on the man's ankle. With considerable force.

"H-he attacked me. With his lips and hands. I reacted without thinking and struck him. I did not mean to hit him so hard, but . . ."

A vein in Daniel's neck throbbed, heavy with blood. "He touched you?"

"Yes," she answered uncertainly. "As I said, I

did not mean to hurt him, but I—I did not enjoy it."

On the floor, Harris was attempting to scoot backward, when he was brought up short by Daniel's warning. "Move another inch, Harris, and this ankle I'm using as a footrest will be of no further use to you."

"Cap'n, I'll take care of this," Mac suddenly offered, edging around Vanessa. "Looks like the lad got hold of more than his share of ale and needs to sleep it off. A night in irons'll teach him a lesson, and I doubt he'll soon forget what the little lady has shown him today."

Mac reached out as if to pull Harris to his feet, but Daniel clamped his fingers around the first mate's beefy wrist.

"No, MacDougal, *I* will take care of this. Go above and assemble the crew."

"Cap'n—"

"Do it."

"Wot are ye goin' to do to me?" Harris blurted out.

Daniel did not even deign to look at him. "I'm putting you ashore."

"Wot?"

"And should I hear your voice again, Harris, you'll be put ashore . . . without provisions."

The man's face blanched, but he held his tongue. As did Mac and Vanessa.

Less than a half-hour later, Harris was standing alone on the banks of the Amazon as the *Angela* continued its journey toward the wide

Atlantic. From the sober expressions of the crewmen on board, Vanessa soon realized that Daniel's purpose had been broader than the punishment of one errant sailor; he had meant to issue a warning to them all. And, since not one man had so much as glanced at her these last minutes, she deduced that the warning had been effective.

She was taboo, off-limits. Just as Daniel had been kept isolated from the other Ama'zons in Eldra'to, she was to be kept isolated from the other men on the ship.

"Come," Daniel said, drawing her away from the railing. "If I hope to still have a crew to get us home, you are going to have to keep to your quarters. You are going to have to remain completely out of sight. I cannot have another incident like this, do you understand?

She nodded and turned to gaze at the slowly fading image of Harris alone at the river's edge.

"Yes," she said. "I understand."

"Good." He tugged at her elbow to lead her below, but she resisted.

"What do you think will become of him?"

Daniel huffed derisively under his breath. "Hell, for all I know, Harris may father the next generation of Ama'zons."

Chapter Twelve

Vanessa's first two weeks on board the *Angela* were a time of discovery. Not so much a discovery of knowledge, but rather a discovery of the role she was expected to play on the long voyage home. She was, as she'd thought before, almost a prisoner in Daniel's cabin, confined to the tiny quarters every minute of every hour. In the first few days, she had wondered if it was possible that Daniel was exacting some manner of vengeance to compensate for his time in Eldra'to. Though she'd not believed him so petty, neither did she think that a short stroll on deck once or twice a day should be forbidden her.

"I do not see what harm I could cause," she had argued.

"Dammit, Vanessa, did you learn nothing from Harris's fate?"

"I learned it is not acceptable in your culture for a man to use his mouth and hands on a woman without first asking her permission."

"Yes, yes, but that's only part of it. It's not just your safety I am trying to preserve here, but the safety of my crew as well. If you go parading around, looking as you do—" Daniel had groaned and threaded a hand through the thick hair at his nape.

"Look, Vanessa, you probably cannot appreciate this, but in my world when a man goes many months without the benefit of a woman's company, he becomes . . . edgy, irritable."

"Why are you irritable and edgy then?" she'd asked, frowning. "You have had my company. And you could have more of it, if you so choose."

He hadn't appeared pleased by her offer. "Dammit, we're not talking about me! I'm irritable all the bloody time, all right?"

"All right."

Nonetheless, she did think Daniel seemed especially irritable and edgy since they'd arrived on the ship, and she longed to know what prevented him from recapturing the closeness they'd shared their last night in the jungle. How could he *not* want to experience again that rapture? The way they had fit together so perfectly, moving in rhythm and harmony, arching and writhing and shouting and weeping with joy?

Yet, if anything, it was as if Daniel had forgotten that night—or wished to. If she mentioned it, he hastily changed the subject. If she attempted to touch him as she'd done during their lovemaking, he slipped away, evading her.

She wanted to ask him: *Why can't we experience those feelings again?*

But she did not know how to ask, nor how to answer the question herself. She felt that she needed to understand Daniel in order to understand the answer. Or perhaps . . . she would first have to answer the question in order to understand Daniel.

With a weary sigh, Vanessa tugged unhappily at the waist of the trousers she was now required to wear, clothing borrowed from Daniel and other sailors on board. The shirt she did not object to so much, but the trousers felt strange, chafing her inner thighs and rubbing against her woman's place.

Mac had said that Daniel might purchase her a real lady's gown when they reached Belem, where the *Angela* had stocked up with supplies before beginning the long trek across the ocean. But they had left port yesterday and Daniel had not brought her a gown. Instead, earlier that evening he had brought to her cabin a pen and paper and had begun quizzing her about Ama'zonian practices.

Pleased with her responses, he'd finally relented, agreeing to escort her twice a day around the deck. As repayment, he'd said, adding something under his breath about the men having blown off enough steam in port.

But now, lying on her bunk, Vanessa could not feel happy about the promise of daily strolls abovedeck. She could not feel happy about much at all when Daniel continued to treat her with such painful reserve. As if he was a stranger to her, and she to him.

Rolling onto her stomach, Vanessa buried her head under the blanket, trying to quiet both her melancholy and her body's stirrings. Stirrings that simply being with Daniel had provoked in her this evening. She lay like that for many minutes, when a hand abruptly patted her back in an awkward cadence.

"There, there, lass. It can't be as bad as all that, now can it?"

Vanessa shifted onto her side. "Hullo, Mac," she said, her voice muffled.

"Are ye sad to be leavin' yer family? Is that what's got ye so low-spirited?" Framed in the lantern's light, his wispy red hair looked like a cloud at sunset.

"No, it's not that. It's Daniel."

"The cap'n, eh?" The Scotsman glanced nervously toward the cabin door.

"I swear, Mac, I do not understand him. His lips will say one thing, yet I can tell he's feeling something else. It's as if he hides the truth from me, his words and his emotions not in . . . agreement."

"Ach, no, lass. His lordship—er—the cap'n

wouldna lie to ye. He's an honorable man, he is. A hard one, a fierce one. But an honorable man."

"I do not mean to say that Daniel lies to me with purpose. Only that he is acting a lie."

Mac's thick red brows raised, creating a wave of wrinkles on his forehead. "Well, I dinna know about *acting* a lie, lass—"

"I express myself poorly, I fear. You see, Mac, at home I have always been someone who understood others, understood how they felt without their putting it into words."

"That musta made you a right important person, then, eh, lass?"

Vanessa laughed, thinking nothing could be further from the truth. "Well, no. But it is something in myself I value, this ability to identify emotions in others."

Mac smiled broadly. "Well, I confess I do fair 'nough with the lads, but I've never understood ye lassies at all."

Answering Mac's smile, Vanessa wondered if it was common for men and women not to understand each other in this world.

"Mac," she asked, now curious, "what is meant by 'the cistern contains; the fountain o'erflows'?"

Mac's brow folded into deeper wrinkles. "I beg yer pardon?"

"A cistern," she said. "What is it?"

"Well, I dinna rightly know, to tell ye the truth." He glanced around the cabin. "But the cap'n might have a dictionary somewhere abouts."

"A dictionary?"

"Aye, a book that explains what words mean."

"English words? Oh, that could be very useful, Mac. Especially since my English is not always correct."

"Ach, there it is." Mac ambled his round figure over to a shelf and removed a thick book, like the Bible Vanessa remembered Harold carrying.

"Cistern, cistern . . . can't find it under *s*," Mac mumbled, thumbing through the pages. "Ah-hah! 'Cistern, a tank or re-re—ahem—receptacle for holding water or other liquid.' " He looked up proudly from the book. "Like a jar, I imagine."

Vanessa's wistful gaze fell to the dictionary. A long time ago, Harold had introduced her to the English word through his Bible. If only she could remember what he had shared with her. . . .

"Mac?"

"Hmm?" he answered, returning the book to its place on the shelf.

"Would you teach me to read?"

"Me?" His florid face flushed a deeper shade of red. "Faith, lass, I'm not so good at it meself."

Vanessa shuffled forward on her knees. "But you will teach me what you know?" she asked hopefully.

"Ah, why not? Though ye canna complain if

I teach ye to read with a good Scots accent now, agreed?"

Smiling, Vanessa jumped up and, stooping over, hugged the first mate, whose stiff shoulders implied he was just a bit unsure whether this was proper.

"Can we begin tomorrow?" Vanessa asked, as Mac headed for the door.

"Sure, lass. I dinna see why not."

He left and Vanessa turned to stare wide-eyed at the many shelves of books lining the far wall. By the Mother, she could not wait to unlock their secrets and, through them, perhaps learn more of Daniel. And if not Daniel, then certainly England, which he had been loath to describe or prepare her for. Whenever she had asked Daniel about his homeland, he had evaded her queries, saying, "England is not nearly as interesting as your culture, Vanessa. Let us focus on the Ama'zon." And then he'd turn back to his paper and pen and his note-taking.

Running her fingertips along the spines of the heavy, worn leather covers, she found one with numerous slips of paper protruding. She pulled it from the shelf and set it on the small captain's table. The book fell open to a particular page, as if it had been opened to that page many times before. Three-quarters of the page was covered with what Vanessa knew to be English print: neat, tidy, all of one size. In the white margins ringing the print were scrawlings of a decidedly less tidy appearance, in circles around the tidy print.

In the middle of the page was a small drawing of what looked to be an animal one part monkey, one part human. Though its posture, muscles and body hair reminded Vanessa of the many families of apes that lived in the jungle surrounding her home, its expression was quite disturbing. Its face hairless, its eyes intelligent, its mouth smiling in a kind, familiar way. Vanessa looked up from the book to the mirror hanging over the table.

I am nothing like this. She could see that her own flesh was much smoother, the structure of her cheeks and jaw more delicate. But there was something in the creature's expression that oddly enough reminded her of herself. Something sad.

She placed her hands against her cheeks, reassured by the texture of her skin. From there, her fingers smoothed over her neck and collarbone. In the mirror, her complexion grew rosy. Rosy with the memory of the sensations she had known when Daniel had touched her neck, her face. Is this how she had looked to him? Beneath the jungle moon, had her skin glowed as it did now under the soft lamplight?

Curious, Vanessa pushed down the shoulder of her oversized shirt, revealing one breast to herself in the mirror. She tilted her head to the side, remembering how Daniel had touched her. Lightly. Like this.

With the flat of her palm, she brushed the pink tip, watching it strain and pucker as it had done for Daniel. It was not the same, her touch, but its effect, coupled with her memory of Daniel's caress, rekindled something of the strange, achy pressure she had felt that night. She repeated the caress and felt a tightening at the pit of her belly.

What else had Daniel done? How else had he touched her? Could she make herself feel as he had made her feel?

His mouth had kissed her there, yes. Tentatively, she put her finger to her lips and wet it, then rubbed the tip of her breast, pretending it was Daniel's lips and tongue.

She stared at the reflection of her hand on her pale skin, her eyes misty, her lips parted. She shivered and cupped her breast, the soft flesh filling her hand, as she captured her nipple between finger and thumb, gently twisting, sending sparks shooting into her woman's place. *Oh, this is dangerous.* These sensations only made her yearn for more. Yearn for Daniel more.

Touching herself alone, she felt alert and alive, but also cold. The sensations pleased her, but they were not enough, reminding her of the full spectrum of pleasure she had known with Daniel. A sadness stilled her hand.

The emotional chill that had stopped her now turned into a physical chill as Vanessa noticed in the mirror's reflection that the cabin door had blown open a fraction. A draft was moving through the room.

With a frustrated sigh, she pulled up her shirt and crossed the room. The door shut with a desolate *click.*

Daniel stood transfixed in the shadow of the doorway to his cabin, feeling like a man on fire.

He had come to gather the items he would need for morning, having forgotten them in the rush to get out of the cabin a few hours earlier. Even though Vanessa had been discussing Ama'zon medical practices, talking about poultices and infections and the like, Daniel had been so very aroused by her that he'd found himself incapable of concentrating.

Somehow the warmth of the amber light, the way her hair had shone like velvet, the sound of her voice describing the natural, uncontrived manner in which her society treated the body—all of this had made Daniel keenly aware of her. Too aware.

I cannot endanger this project, he had told himself. Too much was at stake. After meeting with the Naturalists Society, he planned to present to the Linnean Society and the British Association for the Advancement of Science. His treatise proving the existence of an independent female society would stagger the scientific world. If . . . he did not sabotage it first.

And so Daniel had ruthlessly driven his passion underground. He had cut short the interview, trying his damnedest to conceal the evidence of the desire bulging so prominently in his trousers. He did not believe that Vanessa had noticed—she'd not said anything—yet he could not be certain. During these last two weeks, Daniel had been aware that her silences had become more meaningful. It was not confusion that held her silent but observation.

Truly, in many respects, Vanessa reminded him of a child. She possessed that instinctive wisdom, the ability to see through pretense, undistracted by superficiality. He feared that she was beginning to see through him. To see through to aspects of his personality that even he did not—or would not—recognize.

Unfortunately, his body refused to consider her a child. Not by a long shot. And particularly not now.

Now she stood before the mirror like a vision, like his fantasy come to life. Vanessa, the most strangely exotic, sensual woman a man could imagine, touching herself, exploring herself, for pleasure.

As her long, delicate fingers lightly traced the tip of her nipple, her lips drew together in the shape of a kiss, her eyes closing with delight. Daniel had to bite into his cheek to hold back the moan that rumbled up from his loins. God, how he wanted her. Wanted her with every bit of himself. Every aching bit.

When she licked her finger and massaged the rosy bud until it glistened damp and swollen, he was forced to move away from the doorway, afraid his labored breath would reveal his presence. Reveal him to be the voyeur he was.

Leaning against the wall, Daniel struggled to regain control of himself. *Control.* That word held more significance for him than any other he could think of. *Be in control. Take control. Never lose control.* It was the philosophy his father had drilled into him from the day he'd been born. The philosophy Daniel had lived by.

Until now.

Until Vanessa.

Blast the woman, she did not realize it, but she put everything in jeopardy. His self-control. His career ambitions. His personal ambitions.

How the old man would laugh to see me now, Daniel mocked himself. Risking all he had worked for merely to be with a cat-eyed jungle woman. *No, dammit!* He would not give his father the satisfaction of seeing him succumb to temptation, of seeing him fall short of his goals yet again.

Furiously, Daniel shoved away from the wall and walked back to the small cabin he shared with Mac. Through the darkness, he fumbled his way to his narrow berth to lie down fully clothed. Closing his eyes, he concentrated on putting Vanessa from his mind. But his dreams that night were not restful ones, not restful at all.

The following morning, after breakfast, Daniel decided it was safe to return to the captain's cabin to fetch the notes he'd wanted. He knocked at the door and, when Vanessa called out, entered to a surprising tableau. Mac and Vanessa were sitting side by side at the small table, a book in front of them. Mac's gnarled finger held the place on the page.

"What the devil is this?"

"Poetry," Vanessa answered brightly. "Blake."

Mac jumped up from his chair, his aspect sheepish, a singular expression to be found on the face of a fifty-year-old seasoned sailor.

"Hullo, Cap'n."

"Just what are you doing, MacDougal?"

"He is teaching me to read," Vanessa explained, looping a lock of hair behind her ear, her eyes shining. "Is it not kind of him?"

"Well, there's not much to teach," Mac hurried to say. "The lass remembers much more than she gives herself credit for. She's a sharp one, all right. Sharp as a tack."

Daniel crossed his arms over his chest, a sense of frustration welling inside him. "You read?" he asked Vanessa in a tone of reproach.

She lifted a shoulder modestly. "Harold had taught me some English words from his Bible, but I thought I'd forgotten them all. Evidently"—her smile broadened—"I recall quite a lot of your written language."

Hell. His "Eve" was growing less primitive with each passing day.

"You do not object to Mac helping me, do you?" Vanessa asked.

"It is a long voyage, Cap'n," Mac pointed out hesitantly. "And if the lass is to spend so much time holed up in her cabin, it would surely help her pass the time, don't you reckon?"

Daniel felt himself trapped. Yet he could hardly forbid Vanessa from learning to read without appearing to be some sort of ogre.

"You are worried?" Vanessa asked, evidently reading his expression as well as she was reading Blake.

"Damn right, I'm worried."

"Why? What danger is there in my learning more of your world?"

The danger is that you will cease to be my perfect example of an Ama'zon. But he could scarcely confess that outright, now could he?

"There is the danger of you misinterpreting what you read, since you don't have the proper context in which to place this knowledge."

"Very well, then," she agreed, with a lively tilt of her head. "I promise that if I feel in danger of misinterpreting, I will come to you straightaway for a proper interpretation."

God, how could he resist that teasing glint in her eye? He couldn't, dammit. He'd never seen her like this. Like a young girl experimenting with her feminine powers, testing her flirtatious mannerisms on a brother or a favorite uncle. Not that she was flirting with him, exactly. Or flirting with Mac. But she was growing up.

"All right," he conceded. "But Mac, I want to

approve all reading materials in advance, understood?"

"Aye, Cap'n. Understood."

"Aye, Cap'n," Vanessa echoed playfully. "Understood."

Chapter Thirteen

Vanessa jerked awake, alarmed by the sense that something had changed. Something momentous.

Though the pre-dawn gloom offered few clues, Vanessa listened closely, noting how the slap of water against the ship's side had taken on a different rhythm, how the air wafting through the cabin smelled less salty than before. Then her instincts told her. They had arrived. At long last, they had arrived in England.

With a soft sound of wonder, Vanessa blinked into the darkness, her heart going pitter-pat beneath her ribs. She had looked forward to this moment for weeks, thinking that their arrival in England would herald a new stage in her relationship with Daniel.

She hoped that once his feet were planted on solid ground again, and once he was relieved of the responsibilities of captaining the ship, he would be less remote with her, more like the Daniel from the jungle. During the long, tedious voyage, the irritable, unpredictable commander of the *Angela* had been like a stranger to her. A stranger at a time when she had had only Mac as a friend. When she'd often felt very alone.

Yet now that she knew they had finally reached their destination, Vanessa did not feel the keen gladness she had anticipated. Her enthusiasm was shadowed by trepidation and self-doubt. Emotions utterly foreign to most Ama'zon.

While she sincerely looked forward to exploring this new world, Vanessa could not help but feel anxious. In the jungle she had had no cause to fear; she knew every animal, every plant, every danger. Her knowledge of the forest had kept her safe. But she knew nothing of England, nothing more than she'd learned from a few passages from books. Here she would have only her instincts to guide her; would she be able to trust them? More importantly, would she be able to trust Daniel?

Despite a childish desire to retreat under the covers of her narrow bunk, Vanessa gathered up her courage, wrapped her blanket around her and climbed out of the berth. Slowly, she made her way through the dank and oppressive passageways.

On deck, the chill hit her with surprise, a cold, white wetness that penetrated straight into her bones. The cold was followed by wind, the icy touch carrying a disagreeable blend of fish and smoke and sweat.

Shivering, her blanket pressed to her nose, Vanessa huddled against the wall, watching as the purposeful crew scurried back and forth through the dark gray morning, hauling ropes and tying down sails, shouting orders from one man to the next. The activity was dizzying, exhilarating, and Vanessa felt some of her anxiety ease as she became caught up in the crew's excitement.

As she watched, the sun's first weak rays began to lighten the sky, providing a glimpse of what lay beyond the *Angela*'s deck. The ship had settled up against a long, creaking wooden platform, which in turn edged up to several squat buildings. Other ships dotted the water, their masts craning through the fog like hungry long-necked birds.

To Vanessa, all looked awash in the color of ash—the fog, the buildings, the people scrambling up and down the docks. Even the sun's struggling rays lacked the golden warmth of home, and she found herself wondering where one found bright greens and cheery yellows in this place called London. Where too were the cries of animals, the moist smell of soil, the gentle hum of women at their business?

"Well, what do you think?"

Daniel's voice at her ear gave her a start. She'd not heard him approach, so fascinated had she been by the sights and scents around her.

Immediately she noticed that Daniel was attired differently today. He'd donned a heavy gray coat, long and pinched at the waist, and had enclosed his neck with some sort of white scarf. Instead of boots, shiny, black shoes that shone like a mirror covered his feet. He looked formal to her. Alien.

"It is not like the jungle," she conceded with a wan smile. "Is it always so cold in England?"

"No, not always, though the winters can be harsh." He glanced at the blanket she'd wrapped around herself, then at her bare toes. "I suspect you'll become accustomed to the weather soon enough."

Vanessa nodded, keeping her doubts to herself.

Daniel withdrew his pocket watch, his eyes narrowing as he checked the time. "The carriage has been summoned and should be arriving any minute," he told her, refusing to look up from the timepiece. "Why don't you go below and gather your things? We'll be disembarking soon."

His distant, unfeeling tone did little to allay her feelings of uncertainty. Would Daniel never again speak to her as he had that night in the forest?

"Where is Mac?" Vanessa asked, searching

the deck for a flash of red hair. "I would like to say good-bye before we go."

"Mac has already gone ashore to speak with the portmaster."

"Oh, but—"

"I will meet you back here in ten minutes," Daniel said, clicking his watch closed with a determined snap. A snap that shut her off as decisively as it had the timepiece.

As he stalked away, Vanessa had to remind herself that she was not a puppet to be strung along by Daniel's moods. She would greet this day with a smile, no matter how he behaved toward her.

Less than a half hour later, she sat across from Daniel in the strange, round structure that he had called a *carriage.* Clinging to the bouncing seat as best she could, she labored to control her shivers beneath the coat Daniel had thrown over her head and shoulders before they left the ship.

At first pleased by his thoughtfulness, she'd soon questioned whether he'd been more concerned with keeping her warm or with concealing her. When she'd tried to adjust the overcoat during the short trip from ship to carriage, he'd whisked her along, one strong hand holding the lapels together over her eyes so that she could scarcely see where she was going.

Once in the coach, he'd released her only to pull closed the curtains, enveloping them in gloom. Vanessa's curiosity, however, refused to be so easily restrained. She lifted aside a corner of the curtain to study the sights rolling by outside the small window.

London, she soon determined, was entirely made up of fog, stone and people. Literally hundreds and hundreds of people. Everywhere Vanessa looked men and women of varying shapes and sizes filled the streets, talking and laughing and shouting. The din was tremendous, made worse by the clatter of horse hooves and the metallic rattle of carriage wheels and the cries of street vendors from every corner.

Across the way, two men were shoving each other, wrestling over the contents of a burlap bag while an agitated dog barked furiously at their struggles. A one-armed boy juggled balls nearby, while a group of painted women applauded his efforts.

Farther down the road, Vanessa watched as a woman no bigger than a child was nearly run over by a bearded man on a large brown horse. The woman screamed and fell to the ground, yet none of the passersby seemed to pay any attention to the incident, least of all the horse's rider, who sped past without a second glance.

Disconcerted by the mayhem, Vanessa looked across at Daniel who, with his eyes closed and his arms folded across his chest, appeared to be drowsing peacefully. Certain that no one could sleep through such chaos, Vanessa wondered whether he feigned sleep in order to avoid speaking with her.

Determinedly, she set her jaw and turned back to the window. She would not beg for his conversation. She had her pride, after all. She was an Ama'zon.

As they continued to wend their way through London, the streets gradually became quieter, cleaner and less crowded. Though more pleasing to the eye and nose, the landscape still appeared very cold to Vanessa. Gray and barren. The few trees that managed to poke through the mist were wanting for leaves, their naked limbs brown and frail. Here and there, a stray shrub could be found fronting a brick building, but even that bit of greenery looked dull and ashen to her eye.

Vanessa, curious whether all of England was so colorless, peered at Daniel again. His eyes remained closed but, from the unnatural stiffness of his shoulders and the way the muscles in his upper arms flexed, she knew that he did not sleep. Yet he chose to pretend. Why?

If only I understood him, she thought in frustration, *understood his odd behavior.* But men were an enigma to her, as they were to all her kind. They were beings of whom the Ama'zon knew little more than what had been passed down to them through history and legend.

Frowning, Vanessa sat straighter upon her seat. Could this be the mysterious mission of which the Seer had spoken on her deathbed? Was this Vanessa's purpose—the reason she'd been led to leave the jungle? *Perhaps the Great*

Mother wants me to learn of men, to understand them, and then to take that knowledge back to my people.

Although the idea had not occurred to her before, she thought it reasonable. Over the centuries, the Ama'zons' contact with men had been limited to a few short months once every ten years. Perhaps the time had come for her people to learn more. . . . Perhaps there was important information they were meant to learn to preserve their society. . . .

Vanessa pondered the notion, until she was abruptly yanked from her thoughts by the carriage's sudden halt.

Before she could peek around the curtain, Daniel was jostling past her.

"Wait here," he instructed.

The footman pulled open the door and Daniel descended in front of a tall, narrow house, sober and uninviting. He walked a few steps to the open doorway where waited the oddest-looking man Vanessa had ever seen. Dressed all in red and black, he reminded her of a bird, with his beaklike nose and bright plumage. Daniel spoke to the man, who then disappeared back into the house. Daniel pivoted and gestured for her with a peremptory wave.

She glanced uncertainly at the footman waiting below. He encouraged her with a small nod of his head. She climbed down, clutching the coat around her, as Daniel waited on the porch, his expression strained with polite impatience.

Swallowing, she squared her shoulders, taking comfort from the same words that had first set her on this journey around the world: *Follow your heart.* And, for Vanessa, no matter what else she might feel, following her heart meant following Daniel. Wherever he might lead.

Professional and efficient, Daniel's town house staff was accustomed to their master's eccentricities, especially those relating to his varied scientific pursuits. Guided by the Italian-born butler Rollo, the servants had been trained and trained well. One did not interrupt his lordship when he was deep in his books. One did not touch the piles of dust-coated papers scattered across the study floor. One did not dispose of any insect, alive or dead, that might be found littering his lordship's desktop. A well-disciplined group, they had learned to accept without question if they hoped to remain in Lord Heywood's employ.

Nonetheless, Daniel knew a moment of uneasiness as he ushered Vanessa into the foyer.

"Welcome home, m'lord," the staff murmured as one, standing side by side in a neat little row of crisp white aprons and scarlet livery.

"Thank you. It's good to be back." Daniel inclined his head, drawing Vanessa forward by her elbow. "As you can see, I have brought home a guest."

All eyes obediently converged on Vanessa,

first on the wildly tangled hair tumbling over the collar of the woolen greatcoat, then on her feet, bare and blue-tinged, against the creamy white marble floor.

Despite himself, Daniel allowed his gaze to linger, a disconcerted frown working between his brows. After so many weeks, he had nearly forgotten what a powerful impression Vanessa made at first meeting. With but a single glance, there could be no mistaking that she was . . . different.

Her extraordinary height and the unusual color of her yellow-green eyes clearly distinguished her from the typical English society lady. But there was even more to it than that, Daniel decided. There was a wildness to Vanessa, a watchful, wide-eyed alertness that set her apart from the average woman one passed on the street. Her tense stance and wary expression gave the impression of an animal cornered. An animal frightened.

With a light, reassuring squeeze to her elbow, Daniel cleared his throat and continued addressing the servants. "Vanessa is a native of the South American jungle and will be staying with us for a while, assisting in my research."

One of the younger maids may have tittered with nerves.

"Due to the sensitive nature of my research, it is imperative that no one outside this house know of Vanessa's presence. I will be inviting other naturalists here to consult with me. All other callers are to be denied admittance. You are not to discuss Vanessa with your families or your friends. You are to disclaim all knowledge of her if asked. Any violation of this edict will result in immediate termination without references."

The ensuing silence was strained and Daniel questioned whether his zeal had made his pronouncement sound overly harsh.

"I ask that you all treat her with the same courtesy you would extend to any houseguest, bearing in mind, of course, that she is unfamiliar with many of our modern practices."

"Will Miss, um . . ." Rollo hesitated, apparently not knowing how to address their unusual visitor.

"Vanessa will do," Daniel told him.

"Ah." The butler's heavy nose wrinkled, signifying that he didn't approve of such familiarity. "Will Miss Vanessa be staying with us long, m'lord?"

Daniel's brows gathered. He hadn't thought ahead to the particular hows and whens and whatfors of Vanessa's eventual departure. His primary concern had been getting her to England for his presentation, and, frankly, that was all he could be bothered to think of at the moment.

"If you anticipate a lengthy visit, m'lord, Miss Vanessa might prefer the more commodious west suite," Rollo suggested. "It would take but a minute to make the room ready."

Fingers twitching with annoyance, Daniel released his hold on Vanessa's elbow. When one considered the rugged conditions the two of them had lived with these last few months, he didn't think it much mattered which bloody bedchamber she occupied.

"Very well," he answered curtly, finding himself more than ready to end this interview with his staff. For whatever reason, he was growing increasingly aggravated by the curious, surreptitious glances being slid in Vanessa's direction.

Eager to begin preparation for his lecture, he started to take a step toward his study when Rollo's next question arrested him in midstride.

"Pardon me, m'lord, but will Miss Vanessa be requiring a bath?"

Daniel's impatience unfurled. "For the love of God, Rollo, I—"

"Yes, thank you. I would very much like a bath."

A hushed gasp rose from the line of servants as Vanessa stepped forward, her softly spoken words hovering in the cool air of the foyer.

"She speaks English!" someone whispered.

"Like a toff," another added sotto voce.

Daniel's jaw clenched. His staff knew better than to conduct themselves in such a manner.

"Rollo—" he warned.

With a terse word, the butler dismissed his charges, who quickly scurried from the hall like so many ants fleeing a flattened ant hill.

"My apologies, m'lord. I assure you, I'll attend to the problem."

"See that you do," Daniel muttered, sending an uneasy glance over his shoulder to gauge Vanessa's reaction.

She stood in the center of the foyer, her fingers tightly clutching the lapels of the oversized coat, the muted light of early morning touching her bare head. With her eyes huge and uncertain and her teeth worrying at her lower lip, she seemed deceptively small and almost fragile in the marble cavern of the town house's front hall. Her face, so brown from the tropical sun, did not look as if it belonged in pale, wintry London; she looked exotic and out of place. . . .

Because, Daniel abruptly reminded himself, she *was*. Vanessa was a being from another world, another culture. Naturally she would look peculiar in this setting. It was only to be expected.

Yet that truth did not prevent a pang of emotion from tweaking Daniel's conscience—a pang he did not care to investigate, for it too closely resembled guilt.

"See that she's taken care of," he told Rollo in a low voice. "Then come to me in the library. We've much to do before this evening."

Rollo bowed, and Daniel marched down the hall toward his study without sparing Vanessa even a backward glance.

Chapter Fourteen

"Miss? Uh, Miss Vanessa, are ye in here?"

A freckled female face peeked tentatively into the bedroom, the accompanying white cap and splash of orange-red hair just visible from around the painted door. With anxious eyes, the young maid scanned the room's perimeter, apparently unable to see Vanessa where she was standing in front of the billowing green window hangings.

The redhead had already begun to slip back out the door when Vanessa answered, "Yes?"

The maid jumped as if startled, her heels clicking sharply as they landed on the polished wood floor. Initially bewildered by her behavior, Vanessa suddenly realized that the woman was afraid. The little maid was afraid of her.

"Lord Heywood asked that I bring ye this," the girl said, her voice aquiver as she inched through the doorway, extending her arm. Vanessa's pelt hung between two stubby fingers. "His lordship asked that ye put this on and join him downstairs as soon as ye can."

Vanessa glanced at the animal skin with a confused frown. She'd not worn it since she'd left the jungle over two months before. As Daniel himself had requested.

"Did he say . . . why?"

Lifting the hem of her borrowed robe—a robe she guessed belonged to Daniel—Vanessa crossed the room, her toes sinking into the soft carpet. The chill at the room's center brought goosebumps to her flesh.

"No, miss, he didn't." The maid stretched out her arm as far as she could, flinching as Vanessa took the pelt from her. "Will ye be needin' anything else?"

Vanessa smelled the fear in the young woman and wondered at it. Wondered what on earth had inspired it. "No. Thank you."

"Then I can inform his lordship ye'll be down shortly?"

"Yes. Please do."

The maid needed to hear no more. Within a heartbeat, she and her freckles were gone, and Vanessa was left staring curiously at the panels on the closed door.

Fear was not an emotion she'd witnessed frequently, and the young maid's obvious discomfort had surprised her. Were Englishwomen easily alarmed by strangers? Or only English servants? Or rather, could it be that there was something in particular about Vanessa herself that had elicited the girl's reaction?

Slowly she turned away from the door, thinking back to the pair of maids who had prepared her bath earlier that morning. Speaking less than three or four words between them, the two servants had gone about their business with a speedy efficiency, their expressions closed, their movements economical. At the time, Vanessa had been preoccupied with exploring her chambers and had not given much thought to the women's demeanor. Now, however, she wondered if they too had been fearful of her. But why?

Atop the mantel, the clock showed that the hour was approaching two. Vanessa's stomach let out a hungry, low-pitched growl. She'd not yet eaten today; in fact, she'd done nothing since arriving at Daniel's home but bathe. Bathe and huddle beside the fire, and pace back and forth from this room to the connecting one next door. She had expected that Daniel would send for her much earlier. But the hours had passed until eventually morning was gone, and still no word had come.

At least he had sent for her now. She gave a small shrug and tossed the pelt over the back of a chair. Difficult as it was, Vanessa knew she would have to accept that life would be different for her here in England. She would have to learn to adapt.

Within five minutes, Vanessa had doffed the silk robe and donned the jaguar skin. To her surprise, the animal pelt felt heavy and coarse to her skin, now that it had grown accustomed to the soft, weathered cottons she'd worn onboard the *Angela.* She straightened the pelt on her shoulder, fought another shiver and headed for the door.

As she walked past the oval pier glass, she happened to glance at her reflection. She stopped dead center in front of the mirror. Something was not right.

Her forehead creased as she studied her reflection, studied her waist-length hair and the familiar brown-and-black pelt skirting along her thighs. She looked the same—did she not? So why did something now appear amiss?

Her gaze strayed from her own image to the lavishly appointed chamber at her back, at the room's silk-covered walls and coordinated furnishings, its gilded picture frames and plush tasseled pillows. The fringed bed hangings were shimmering, as the light from the chandelier picked out the gold flecks in the swirling leafy pattern. It was all so very elaborate, so very complicated. . . .

Vanessa rubbed at her arms as another chill wafted over her. Although she sensed it intuitively, she could not seem to explain this feeling of "wrongness." Nor, she realized with another glance to the clock, had she the time to examine it. Daniel was waiting for her downstairs. With a conscious effort, she smoothed the worry from her brow, ran her hands one last time over the front of her pelt and started for the hall.

She'd only just shut the door behind her when Rollo, the parrotlike man, appeared from around the corner, his black eyes as sharp as those of any bird.

"If you'll come this way, miss," he bid her.

Vanessa hesitated for a fraction of a second before nodding and following the manservant down the corridor. Despite his strange aspect, she felt comfortable with this man. His face suggested kindness behind that overlarge nose and, unlike the maids, he did not behave as if she frightened him.

They descended a secondary staircase at the end of the corridor, an icy, drafty staircase that had Vanessa gritting her teeth before they were halfway down. Never in her life, not even during the jungle's worst storms, had she known a cold such as this, the way it reached deep into her bones and chilled her very blood. She was beginning to understand the reason the English wore so many layers of clothing, and the reason they'd built these towering houses of thick stone.

At the bottom of the steps, they turned down a hallway and were greeted by the low drone of many voices from the front of the house. Vanessa did not recognize the voices—all of them male—and her pulse quickened.

"You *are* taking me to Daniel?" she asked, feeling somewhat foolish in need of reassurance.

"Yes, miss," the butler answered, and a hint of—could it have been compassion?—glinted in his dark eyes.

"Daniel is not alone?" she persisted.

"No, miss," and this time Rollo did not meet her gaze. "His lordship has invited a few guests."

Guests.

Vanessa flicked a strand of hair from her face, licking at lips chapped and dry with nerves. Her stomach felt unsettled and she wanted to blame it on lack of food but sensed that more than hunger lay at the heart of her discomfort. As she had upstairs, she knew a sense of foreboding, a vague, pervasive apprehension.

She sent a series of rapid glances from one wall to the next, fixing on objects as if they were markers leading her down a path. Sconces shaped like trumpets of gold. Paintings of landscapes foreign and distant. An almost imperceptible tear in the silk wall covering. She swallowed as Rollo led her toward a pair of doors. Her stomach twisted painfully. She wondered if she was going to be ill.

"Glad you could make it, Wilson. I apologize for the short notice, but it couldn't be helped."

Daniel, barely managing to contain his enthusiasm, ushered the last of his guests into the library with an eager, if somewhat forceful, pat on the back. The fourteen men already assembled were all members of the Naturalists Society; all, like Daniel, with a special interest in the development of theories for biological evolution. Among them this afternoon was Daniel's mentor and friend, whose five-year expedition on board the *Beagle* had inspired Daniel to make his own fateful voyage to the Americas.

"I must say," Charles Darwin announced, his gently rounded face pleasant yet serious, "we never expected you to return so soon, Heywood. Figured you'd be gone a good two years or better."

Daniel gave a faint smile. "You weren't alone in anticipating a lengthy expedition. But, as you'll soon see, I stumbled across something so important I felt I needed to return home with it immediately."

"Hmm, well, I look forward to sharing this discovery of yours; though, if I were to judge by your appearance alone, I'd have to believe you located the legendary Fountain of Youth, my friend. The South American climes evidently suited you far better than they did me." Darwin turned his head and coughed delicately into a handkerchief. Plagued by fevers he'd contracted during his voyage, the man had never fully recovered his health here at home.

Daniel shrugged and glanced down at his

hands, noticing in the back of his mind how dark they appeared when compared to the pasty complexions of his colleagues. Darwin had a right to be envious, he supposed. Most scientists returned from their South American expeditions weakened by disease and hardship, yet Daniel had returned to England stronger and more fit than ever before. It would seem he had Vanessa to thank for his good health.

"Lovely specimen, Heywood," Sir Frederick broke in, indicating a butterfly displayed on one of the many easels Daniel had placed about the library. "Mimics the *Danaus plexippus,* does it?"

"Yes."

"And this here?" Archibald Wright broke in, pointing toward another easel. "I'd like to hear the details on where you found it, Heywood. Orchidae are a keen interest of mine, you know."

"Of course," Daniel answered politely, although he was far less interested in his minor findings now that he had Vanessa to present to the assemblage. These assorted insects and bits of cuttings would pale in significance once his fellow naturalists understood the magnitude, the far-reaching consequences, of his discovery of the Ama'zon.

The fifteen scientists continued to mill about the library, sipping their tea as they examined and discussed the different drawings and specimens. Daniel answered the occasional query while keeping one eye fixed on the ormulu clock. *What in the blazes is keeping Vanessa?*

The maid had said she'd agreed to come right down. . . .

A soft knock at the double doors acted like a kick to Daniel's gut. This was it. This was the moment he'd been waiting for.

"Gentlemen," he said loudly, addressing the room with more bravado than he genuinely felt, "may I have your attention please?"

"Ah-hah," Sir Frederick said knowingly. "I knew he had something more up his sleeve. Are you finally going to sate our curiosity, Heywood, old boy?"

"Yes," Mr. Lancing-Smythe said, adjusting his spectacles with a shaky hand, "what is it you have brought back for us?"

Daniel inclined his head in Lancing-Smythe's direction. "Proof, gentlemen. I have brought back proof."

"Good God, save your cryptic evasions for the ladies," Wright teased. "Proof of what?"

"Proof of what our colleague here"—he lifted his hand toward the bemused Darwin—"has set forth. Proof of natural selection in its most startling form. And, even more importantly, proof that a society, a race of people heretofore believed to be nothing more than myth, exists. Exists in the darkest recesses of the South American jungle."

"What?"

"Does he claim to have discovered a new race?"

Daniel watched Darwin's expression, knowing that should his friend sanction the veracity of this discovery, the rest of his colleagues—indeed, the world—would accept Daniel Heywood's claim to fame.

"Charles, if I may—" Daniel bowed to the openly curious Darwin. "I would like to present to you, woman in her natural state. I submit for your approval . . . an Ama'zon."

His heart beating fiercely, Daniel threw open the double doors with an uncharacteristically dramatic flourish. The silence was instant and complete.

One by one, Daniel registered his colleague's reactions with a sense of almost boyish glee. Wright's jaw had dropped open to reveal a row of sadly crooked teeth while, at his side, the seventy-year-old Reverend Grampling had frozen with a teacup at his lips. Lancing-Smythe was blinking furiously behind his spectacles, as if he did not trust what was revealed to him on the other side of the lenses, while Darwin . . . Well, Darwin's reaction was not precisely what Daniel had anticipated. The naturalist looked surprised, yes. Surprised, but also concerned.

Well satisfied by the initial response, Daniel turned toward Vanessa and felt his breath catch. By God, she was a sight to behold. Taller than most of the men in the room, she stood before them, her shoulders raised, her muscles flexed as if for flight, her head tilted down so that her catlike eyes were gazing up at them through a fringe of black lashes. Her hair, newly clean, shone like light on still, dark water, spilling over her right shoulder to fall in an enticing curve at the sharp peak of her hipbone.

"Upon my honor," Wright breathed in awe and, all at once, the room exploded.

"Heywood, explain this!"

"An Amazon, you say? But how on earth—"

"Is it a hoax?"

"No, no hoax," Daniel quickly assured them.

"But how—"

"Where—"

As the roomful of scientists peppered Daniel with shouted questions, they all slowly began to close in on Vanessa, eager for a better look.

Vanessa's eyes widened and, though she scarcely looked to move, her body shifted lower into a half-crouch.

"Easy, now," Daniel warned. "Back up a bit; you're making her skittish."

"But where did you find her?"

"What makes you believe she's an Amazon?"

Though pleased with his colleagues' reaction, Daniel felt vaguely bothered by the intensity of that same interest. "If you will but calm yourselves, you may ask her these questions yourselves."

"What do you mean 'ask her yourselves'?" the reverend demanded with outright skepticism.

"I mean," Daniel explained, "that, as a young girl, Vanessa learned English from a missionary who visited with her tribe."

"Come now," Wright interjected. "This is all

rather farfetched, ain't it, Heywood?"

"It would seem so, but I am here to tell you that it is true. Hidden in the South American jungle lies a self-contained society made up exclusively of women. Women like Vanessa. Unusually tall, unusually strong and completely untouched by the civilized world. Incredibly enough, throughout the last centuries, these people have managed to escape discovery. Until now."

"And how was it that you located them?" Darwin asked.

Daniel phrased his answer with care, uncertain how much he wished to reveal of the role the Ama'zons had planned for him. "I was taken to live within the walls of their fortress, where I remained for over a week. It was there that I met Vanessa and came to understand the astounding nature of her society."

"But why were you taken, Heywood?"

"Yes, why you?" other voices chimed in.

"Please," Darwin interrupted, raising his hands in a bid for quiet. "I would propose that we allow *her* to tell us the story."

The room immediately hushed.

"Vanessa?" Daniel invited.

Wary yellow-green eyes that had been moving swiftly over the crowd of scientists, shot upward to meet his gaze. He forced what was meant to be a reassuring smile.

"Tell them who you are," he said.

Vanessa wrapped her arms around herself,

clutching at her elbows. She started to speak, then hesitated. "I . . . I am Ama'zon."

"Hmmph. I could have taught her that much in the carriage ride 'cross town," Reverend Grampling protested.

"Perhaps, but where would you have come by those eyes?" Wright pointed out. "Have you ever seen a like color? Not on any human, I'll vow."

"I own they're uncommon," Grampling conceded with gruff reluctance, leaning forward into Vanessa's face.

Vanessa recoiled, and Daniel resisted the urge to push the good cleric to a safer distance.

"Uncommon?" Wright echoed. "They're the eyes of a cat! Have you identified the genus and species, Heywood?"

Daniel's brows knit. "I presume Homo sapiens. . . ."

"Can she say anything else?" Wilson asked.

Daniel waited for Vanessa to speak, but when she remained silent, he answered for her. "Indeed. She speaks English as fluently as you or I. Initially, her vocabulary was somewhat limited, but she is very quick to learn and even taught herself to read and write during the voyage home."

"You don't say," someone murmured.

"And how does she prove Darwin's theory of natural selection?" Wright asked, "as you suggested?"

Daniel folded his hands behind his back, shifting his weight onto his toes. "First, take a look at Vanessa's extraordinary height and muscular development. All the Ama'zon women exhibit these same physical characteristics, presumably to make them better fit to survive the duress of jungle life. Their conditioning is exceptional, at a level one generally finds in only the finest of athletes.

"Secondly, and even more convincingly"—Daniel paused for effect, slowly drawing out his pronouncement—"the Ama'zon, through the process of natural selection, have ceased to bear male progeny."

A score of eyebrows shot toward the coffered ceiling.

"Once having concluded that the male was a destructive and unnecessary force in their culture," Daniel explained, "the women, over the years, began to produce only females. Females such as you see here before you."

"Is such a thing possible?" a younger member of the group queried.

"Indeed," Daniel confirmed. "Through natural selection. You see, as I understand it, after the Ama'zon began to shift to a female-dominated structure, the women became stronger and the males weaker. Over time—many, many centuries, I would presume—the reproductive process naturally selected out the less desirable male in order for the fittest, the female, to survive."

"Remarkable," Darwin muttered. "Simply remarkable."

"But in the absence of males—Good Lord, never say they multiply through parthogenesis?" Wilson demanded, obviously shocked by the notion.

"Are you mad?" Wright questioned his fellow scientist. "Do you realize that you're talking about self-propagation?"

Before a heated discussion could erupt, Grampling reached out and took hold of Vanessa's arm, holding it as if it were a dusty artifact he wished to study.

"Look at this," the cleric said. "Just look at the length of her forearm, and the development of her musculature. I suppose any modern British woman might have a physique this developed if she ever did anything more strenuous than the occasional hoisting of her vinaigrette."

A young naturalist, Hyatt, snickered at the churchman's sarcasm.

Daniel pried Grampling's fingers from Vanessa's arm feeling a sudden need to apologize for the older man's conduct.

"How can you be certain she's Homo sapiens, Heywood? I should think a thorough examination would provide evidence to the contrary," Wilson suggested. "Especially when one considers the eye color—"

"Quite so," Wright added. "We might be looking at a link between man and his ancestors—"

"May I see the pads of her feet?" interrupted the Viscount Maxim. "I'd be very curious to study the formation of the tarsals as they relate to similar species."

Horrified, Daniel watched Maxim kneel down and proceed to take hold of Vanessa's bare foot.

"Believe me when I say that she is most assuredly Homo sapiens." Daniel proclaimed in a near growl as he forcibly hauled Maxim upright, then placed himself in front of Vanessa as a shield.

He frowned at the assembled group of scientists, thinking that the lot of them had spent far too much time in their laboratories. For heaven's sake, one only had to look at Vanessa to see that she was a woman. A *real* woman. A woman who could make a man crazy with wanting . . .

Daniel shook himself, realizing that he was growing uncomfortable with the manner in which Vanessa was being discussed by his colleagues. He hadn't anticipated this sort of reaction.

"I think we've seen enough for today," he announced, starting to wave back the group of gentlemen.

Then it happened. Vanessa released an alarming sound, closer to a hiss than a scream, as Daniel turned to find the cleric running his hand over Vanessa's hip with shocking and grotesque familiarity.

"Hmm," the cleric said. "Interesting—"

In the next instant, Vanessa shoved at the reverend with both hands, sending the old man sailing across the room as if he was nothing more than a child's rag doll.

In the chaos that ensued, Daniel reached for Vanessa, but she eluded his grasp. In the flash of an eye, she had fled the library. He ran after her, catching the barest glimpse of pelt as she flew out the front door into the streets of mid-day London.

Chapter Fifteen

Vanessa ran like the wind itself, wild and free and without direction. She ran with the cool kiss of the afternoon air on her face, her long hair lashing at her back, urging her to greater and greater speed. She knew not where she was headed; she did not care. She only knew that she had to get away from those men. Those men with their purse-lipped questions and prying eyes. Those men who touched her as if she were somehow less than human.

Less than human. Good heavens, no wonder the maids had been frightened of her; they did not know if she were man or beast. Was she so very different from them, then?

A vision flashed through her mind's eye, the picture of the apelike creature she'd seen in

Daniel's book, the picture that had continued to haunt her. Did those men honestly believe her to be some manner of beast, some sort of dangerous and exotic animal?

After long, breathless minutes of blind flight, Vanessa became aware of the blurred scenery around her, of the fact that what had been all gray and square was now brown and open. She'd entered a field where people were passing by on horseback and in open-topped carriages. She caught glimpses of shocked faces buried beneath hats, heard faint cries of surprise that were directed toward her. Panic invaded her, a kind of panic that she'd never experienced before: She was completely lost and alone in a world she did not understand. Without Daniel, she belonged to no one. To no place.

Lungs strained with fear, Vanessa stopped in the middle of the field and whirled around as horse-drawn carriages slowed and fingers pointed with shaming accuracy at her. At her. The Ama'zon.

She glanced up and found the unfeeling gray sky frowning down upon her. She did not feel at all well. The cold was stabbing at her flesh like hundreds of tiny knives. Her lungs, filled with the stench of coal smoke, ached for fresh air. She felt light-headed, unsteady.

"Vanessa!"

Across the field came Daniel, his chestnut hair fluttering, his neckcloth loose and flapping in the wind. Vanessa blinked and rubbed her arms, a part of her gladdened that he'd followed her, but another part equally saddened that she would now have to go back to that house where those men waited.

"Vanessa," Daniel called again, shrugging from his coat as he ran up to her side. His chest heaved and his breath made soft puffs of white in the air. "Good God, are you all right?"

Vanessa shook her head, unable to lie. "I feel unwell."

Concern flashed in his brown eyes and he proceeded to help her into his coat, his head jerking left to right, taking notice of the many stares they were receiving.

His touch was firm as he drew her against his side, his fingers coming to rest intimately at her waist. Vanessa stared at her feet, at the dead grass poking between her toes, and realized that Daniel had not shown her such tenderness since the night they had shared in the jungle. That night seemed many dreamlands away.

"Come," he said, his words brushing against her temple. "Let's get you home."

Vanessa bit at her lip, thinking of home. Her home. Although she sorely missed the forest's verdant beauty and the security she'd known in the jungle, her feelings were conflicted at the thought of returning to Eldra'to. Was she ready to leave Daniel? And what of the Great Mother's purpose for her? What of the mission the old Seer had spoken of? She did not want to fail. Yet she'd been in England not even one full day and already she was assailed with doubts, questioning whether she'd be able to survive in this strange, uninviting place.

As Daniel led her from the field toward a bordering street, Vanessa lowered her gaze, embarrassed by the blatant scrutiny from passersby. The street was busy, peopled with scores of shoppers, an apple-cart vendor, a troupe of musicians and a trio of young boys playing with sticks and a ball. Yet, despite Vanessa's best efforts to melt into Daniel's side, everyone seemed to take notice of her amid the din and hubbub.

"Keep your head down," Daniel quietly instructed.

Vanessa nodded, detecting the tension in his strong fingers upon her ribs. They were walking rapidly, their long strides matched in a hurried, anxious rhythm.

Suddenly, Daniel made a small sound, akin to a relieved sigh. "Bless the old idiot," he murmured. "Rollo sent John Coachman after us."

Vanessa glanced up to see Daniel lift his hand and wave, drawing the attention of his driver, who was battling his way through the congested thoroughfare. The carriage pulled up alongside them and Daniel swiftly pushed her inside.

To Vanessa's surprise, Daniel did not move away once they'd settled into the carriage, but continued to hold her in his arms, his hands moving up and down over the coat sleeves, as if to warm her.

The carriage moved off with a sharp jolt, the motion jarring Vanessa's queasy stomach. She was glad for the ensuing silence as she fought back the nausea roiling in her middle.

After a minute or two, Daniel shifted slightly on the seat. "Vanessa, I, uh . . ."

She waited, her eyes downcast.

"I owe you an apology," he said in an awkward rush.

She pursed her lips and said nothing, for some reason most reluctant to make easier his confession.

"I ought to have anticipated that this afternoon's presentation would result in . . . excitement. I failed to prepare my colleagues properly and their enthusiasm surged out of control. I am sorry. I have asked the gentlemen to leave and I promise you that I will not invite them until you tell me that you are willing to meet with the committee again. And," he added grimly, "until we agree on a few rules of conduct."

She hid behind the curtain of her hair. "You did not know they would treat me that way, did you?"

"Lord, no. Of course not."

"You merely wanted to introduce me to your colleagues?" she pressed, needing his reassurance.

"Naturally, I wanted to introduce you," he said. "You've an intriguing . . . background. My fellow naturalists would understandably be amazed."

Yet she sensed that Daniel was not wholly comfortable with his own response.

He cleared his throat, changing the subject, "Rollo also pointed out to me—albeit too late—that, while I was preoccupied with my guests' arrival, I forgot to have a meal sent up to you. I don't suppose you've eaten at all today, have you?"

Vanessa wagged her head.

"Hell," was Daniel's self-disparaging response as his boot tapped out an irritated beat upon the coach floor.

"Apologies aside, Vanessa, I must insist that you never again leave the house unescorted. Never. Under *any* circumstances," he stressed. "You cannot begin to appreciate the danger you were in today."

"Danger?" She lifted her face to his. She'd not enjoyed the feeling of being lost, but neither had she felt threatened or in peril. "I did not sense any danger, Daniel."

His expression hardened, his sleek brows veering together. "Well, simply because you didn't *sense* it doesn't mean it wasn't there."

"I do not understand. Were there venomous snakes or spiders in the field?"

"No, but—"

"Surely no panther or jaguar could have been hidden in those bare-leafed trees?"

"Of course not, Vanessa, don't be foolish. I

told you there were no such animals in England."

"What, then? Crocodile—"

"Men, Vanessa, men!" Daniel shouted.

Startled by the heated outburst, Vanessa reared back, her hand at her throat.

"And, dammit, I am not referring to natives with poisoned darts, either! In the civilized world, men's weapons are far more dangerous and far more subtle. Too subtle for you to possibly recognize."

She sucked in her lower lip. "Should I not then be made aware of such dangers?"

"No." His answer came curt and quick. "It is unavoidable that you should eventually be exposed to the unpleasantries of my world, but I see no reason to accelerate your education."

"But . . ." Why would Daniel wish her to remain ignorant?

Ignoring the question she'd left hanging between them, Daniel sighed heavily and pulled his arms from her, withdrawing back into himself and away from her. The moment of closeness was gone. With a familiar and bittersweet feeling of resignation, Vanessa tucked her feet beneath her and huddled under Daniel's coat, savoring the heady male scent captured within the wool. The smell of him, at least, was a comfort to her.

Rollo was waiting for them as they pulled up in front of the town house, and Daniel wasted no time in delivering her into the butler's care. Before Vanessa could share another word with

Daniel, she'd been bundled in blankets and ushered back to her room, Rollo sending a maidservant to the kitchens to prepare another hot bath for their guest.

Vanessa stood in her bedroom as the tub was dragged in for the second time that day and pondered the afternoon. She knew that she needed to speak frankly with Daniel. To speak frankly about his plans for her future. His stated reluctance to "accelerate her education" concerned her greatly, for she knew that she could not rely upon Daniel alone to learn her way in this English world. She had to rely upon herself. She had to educate herself about her new environs, this new culture, especially if she was to take this knowledge back to her people.

Determined that her concerns not be brushed aside, Vanessa made her way down the hall to the servant's staircase she and Rollo had used earlier. She chose not to take the main stairs and thus be forced to walk through the foyer again, draped in blankets like the workhorses she'd seen on the street.

As she approached from the rear of the house, Vanessa heard a voice that was not Daniel's come from behind the partially open library doors. The voice belonged to one of those men, those scientists. The round-faced man named Darwin.

Disappointed to discover that Daniel was not alone, Vanessa started to turn back when the man's next words froze her in place.

"She must go back, Daniel. You must send her back to South America as soon as possible."

Vanessa's heart leaped into her throat. They were speaking of *her*. Quietly, she crept closer, her pulse so loud in her ears that she had to strain for Daniel's response.

"Dammit, Charles, why? Surely you of all people grasp the importance of this discovery. A civilization never before studied, a culture never before explored. And, my God, man, the evidence the Ama'zon offer for natural selection—with this evidence we can take your theories to an entirely new level."

"Hmm, yes, I agree that the possibilities are fascinating, and I would welcome the chance to explore them more closely. Also, Daniel, believe me, I do understand what these findings would mean for your career. It is a coup beyond compare, a chance to turn the scientific world on its ear. My God, Ama'zons . . ."

Vanessa imagined she could hear the man shaking his head in wonderment.

"But," Darwin continued, "I strongly suggest that you seek other avenues by which to substantiate your claim, my friend. Take a history from the girl, if you must, to supplement your drawings and the handful of artifacts you've brought home. Record your own experience while the memories are still fresh and alive in your mind. You need not abandon the hope of establishing proof of their society, Daniel. But you cannot do so by using this woman. It is wrong.

"As you know," Darwin said, "I have had personal experience with introducing natives into civilized societies. Sadly, the results have been nothing short of disastrous. Even should you plan to keep her here only a short time, Daniel, she will not be the same once returned to her native environment."

Papers rustled as if disturbed by agitated fingers.

"What if she chooses not to return?" Daniel asked. The question was posed cautiously.

"Impossible. You cannot allow it. From what you have told me of her background, it is inconceivable to think she could ever adapt to our modern existence. She is a primitive, Daniel, a being raised without any of the benefits of contemporary society. Yes, she may understand the fundamentals of our language and may speak well and have even taught herself to read—but it does not change her history, her very nature. . . . Only consider what happened in this very room an hour ago."

"Hmmph. How is Grampling?"

"By the grace of God he suffered only a sprained wrist."

"He deserved worse, the old fool."

"Perhaps," Darwin prevaricated. "However, you must understand that many of the gentlemen present did not view your Ama'zon as . . . as—"

"As one of us?" Daniel supplied, his words bitter. "As a human being?"

Darwin cleared his throat. "Which leads me rather awkwardly to my second point. . . . If you and I agree that she is a woman like any other, then you must realize that it is not altogether proper for her to remain unchaperoned in your home, Daniel. She's not merely an artifact to be kept upon a shelf, you know."

Daniel snorted. "I doubt Vanessa is concerned as to whether or not a few old hens are gossiping about her over tea."

"Well, if she is not concerned, you ought to be. Especially if you decide to keep her in London."

Daniel did not answer, and the silence stretched into long seconds. Vanessa held her breath.

"She belongs in the wild, Daniel. You must send her back."

A ragged sigh rasped through the room, sounding to Vanessa like acceptance. Or defeat.

"Dammit, Charles. I do not know if I can."

Chapter Sixteen

The scientific world was abuzz the following morning, as word of Daniel's claim filtered through the ranks of London's many naturalists, botanists, biologists and the like. By the time Daniel came downstairs for breakfast, he had already received a half dozen notes, begging an introduction to the "fascinating creature" he'd brought back from the South American jungle.

Daniel sat at the dining room table, flipping broodingly through the notes one by one. He'd scarcely slept a wink during the night, tormented by his conversation with Darwin the previous day.

He trusted Darwin and valued his friend's judgment. Often throughout the years, Daniel had turned to his colleague for guidance, especially as his estrangement from his family left him more and more isolated. Darwin was one of the very few men whose opinion held any sway with Daniel, one of the very few men whom Daniel respected and trusted.

So, why, then, was he resisting his friend's advice?

Daniel knew that Charles, unlike most of their colleagues, had accepted Daniel's claim of the Ama'zon's existence without prejudice or doubt. Not only did he accept it, but Darwin appreciated the profound impact such a discovery would have upon Daniel's future, upon Daniel's search for immortality in the annals of scientific exploration.

So when Charles suggested that Vanessa be sent home, Daniel knew that the man did so with her best interests at heart. Darwin had no ulterior motive, no secret desire to undermine Daniel's accomplishment.

Therefore why was he so quick to disregard his friend's counsel? Perhaps, his conscience argued, he should send Vanessa back to Eldra'to. Perhaps it was the only moral decision left to him.

Dammit, when he remembered how he'd felt yesterday . . . The guilt and relief that had twisted his gut when he'd finally caught up with her in Hyde Park. Vanessa had been so strong in the jungle, so competent. Yet yesterday afternoon, she'd looked like a frightened child, standing there in the middle of the bleak field, shivering and lost.

He was to blame. He should send her back.

He would.

Hot liquid splattered onto his fingers and wrist as Daniel realized that he'd unconsciously tightened his grip on his teacup.

"Hell," he muttered, returning the cup to its saucer and shaking his hand dry.

"Did you burn yourself?"

The soft question spun Daniel around in his chair.

"Vanessa, I didn't hear you come—Good Lord, what the devil are you wearing?"

Vanessa's smile wavered and she ran her palms down the sides of her faded yellow dress. A dress that looked as if it belonged on a washerwoman a stone heavier and a good foot shorter than Vanessa.

"Wherever did you come by that rag?"

Yellow-green eyes flickered with doubt. "One of the maids kindly lent it to me."

Daniel winced. He was no authority on women's fashions, but this particular garment had to be the most atrocious excuse for a gown he'd ever laid eyes on. Cheaply made and festooned with rows of limp lace, it hung on Vanessa like a tent, the skirt dangling a few inches longer at the back. And the color . . . Lord, the color made her golden skin appear sickly and green. Nightmarish.

"Why on earth would she lend you *that?*"

Vanessa released a shaky breath, her chest quivering. "Because I asked her to. Isn't this how an Englishwoman is expected to dress?"

"An English charwoman, perhaps," Daniel answered uncharitably.

Vanessa's face fell; then she seemed to recover herself, her jaw firming with conviction, her fists clenching in the folds of the gown. "Well, since I no longer wish to go about in animal skins or sailor's cast-offs, this was the best I could manage."

"Oh?" Daniel's brows inched upward, and he leaned back in his chair, crossing an ankle over one knee. "What is this about, Vanessa?"

"This is about me . . . fitting into your world." She took another deep, quavering breath. "I don't wish to stand out, Daniel, to be seen as some sort of aberration or oddity. I want to be like any other person. I want to be able to walk down the streets with the same freedom that you do, to go riding and exploring and to do as I please."

"Do as you please? Vanessa, you are a woman."

Her forehead creased. "What difference does that make?"

Daniel lifted a shoulder, privately thinking it a sound question. "Society has its rules. Separate rules for men and separate rules for women."

"Can you not teach me the rules for women?"

"No, I can't." He frowned and studied the fine

stitching on his Hoby boots. "And, to tell you the truth, I don't know that anyone *should* teach you. I have been thinking . . ." He flicked a stray thread from his trousers, half watching her from beneath shuttered eyes. "And I am beginning to wonder if I may have erred in bringing you to London."

Her posture grew rigid. "You no longer want me here? Am I not welcome in your home?"

"You are welcome," he said with an irritated bob of his foot. "It's not that. It is only that I must question whether it was right of me to encourage you to leave your own kind."

"I wanted to go with you."

"Yes, but perhaps you and I rushed that decision. Perhaps the wisest course would be for you to—"

"Daniel."

He raised his gaze to hers, and, in an instant, wished that he had not.

She stood before him, her back ramrod straight, her shoulders square and strong, her expression proud. Even garbed in the maid's sorry tatters, she looked to him like a queen. Like some pagan goddess of field and forest. Like woman in her purest form.

Desire coursed through him, then, hot and sweet and potent. Desire and admiration and envy. Envy for Vanessa's ability to feel emotion, to express it, yet not allow that emotion to make her weak.

Dropping his gaze to his boot again, Daniel

stamped down the desire surging through him.

"Perhaps, the wisest course," Vanessa said, with a hint of unfamiliar arrogance, "would be to allow me to make my *own* decisions."

Despite himself, Daniel almost felt himself smile.

"I want to learn, Daniel. I want to learn what it means to live in this world of yours."

With the tips of his fingers, Daniel traced the scalloped rim of the china saucer. The sharp aroma of tea lingered between them. Only moments ago he had resolved to send Vanessa back to South America. Yet already that resolve was crumbling.

And, really . . . why should he send her away? Admittedly, Darwin was well intentioned, but what of Daniel's own intentions? They were not immoral; he wished Vanessa no harm. Rather, he simply did not want her to leave. Was that surprising?

After all, she is an intriguing woman. A beautiful woman. A woman who held the key to a treasure trove of knowledge—knowledge that could ultimately determine Daniel's future. He needed Vanessa. He could not argue the existence of the Ama'zons without her.

Blast it, why should I torment myself over this decision?

Especially when there was still so much he did not know, so much he had yet to understand about the Ama'zons' history and tradition. So much he would need to research before he could hope to deliver his treatise to his fellow naturalists.

If I were to proceed with greater caution . . . No more presentations such as yesterday's— Of course, if he allowed Vanessa to stay, he would have to abandon all hope of "preserving" her in her natural form. He'd have to submit to her request. She would no longer be the same woman he'd met in the jungle; her Ama'zon state would be forever compromised.

But if the alternative was to send her away . . .

"If you cannot teach me," Vanessa continued to argue, "I ask that you find someone who can."

Daniel's conscience played tug-of-war with his ambition, as he examined a scar at his wrist. "Are you certain that this is what you want?"

Her answer was firm. "Absolutely."

That afternoon, Vanessa was curled up in a chair in the library, reading Defoe, when she heard Daniel return. He'd been gone the better part of the day, having left the house without a word to her, shortly after their discussion that morning.

Not knowing what to do with herself, Vanessa had passed the hours impatiently awaiting his return. She'd contemplated taking a walk, but Daniel's warning not to leave the house still lingered with her. Instead, she had relieved her boredom by running up and down the stairs and by gazing wistfully out the windows and, finally, by poring over Daniel's book collection.

She jumped from the chair at the sound of his voice.

"I am in your debt, Miss Perkins. This is really very decent of you."

"Truly, Lord Heywood, it is my pleasure. I am delighted to be of assistance."

Miss Perkins? Who was this Miss Perkins, with a voice as soft as the down of a newborn chick? Curious, Vanessa peered through the slit between door and jamb.

A woman, extremely small and extremely fair-haired, stood at Daniel's side, smiling up at him, her tiny gloved hand resting upon his coat sleeve. She was like nothing Vanessa had ever seen before—a hundred times more lovely and a hundred times more delicate than any woman she'd observed on the streets of London. In fact, Vanessa thought, she did not appear to be a woman at all. Swathed in a rose-colored mantle, her heart-shaped face framed by a white, lacy bonnet, she appeared to be a flower or a butterfly or some other such thing equally as fragile and fine.

"Let me have Rollo fetch Vanessa," Daniel suggested.

Vanessa scowled and glanced with anxious displeasure at her borrowed yellow gown. If Miss Perkins illustrated the way an English lady should attire herself, Vanessa could now well understand Daniel's reaction of that morning. In no way, shape or form did she resemble the blossomlike Miss Perkins.

"Rollo," Daniel called.

Vanessa bit into her lip, casting around for somewhere to hide. But, of course, she could not hide, she chided herself. She was being foolish.

With head high—and feet bare—Vanessa walked from the library into the front hall. As she met the other woman's gaze, she saw Miss Perkins's smile falter for but a moment before the woman quickly recaptured her expression of pleased expectation.

"Ah, Vanessa, there you are. Come here. I'd like you to meet Miss Perkins. Miss Perkins, this is Vanessa, of whom I have spoken."

Miss Perkins extended her hand and Vanessa came forward to clasp it. The woman's slim fingers all but disappeared in her palm, and Vanessa could not help but picture herself as a giant, dark elm towering over a dainty water lily.

"M'lord?" Rollo appeared from the direction of the dining room.

"Is there a fire in the parlor, Rollo?"

"Yes, m'lord."

"Good. We'll take our tea in there." Daniel accepted Miss Perkins's cloak and bonnet, then handed them to the butler. Beneath her mantle, Miss Perkins wore a matching rose-and-mint gown cinched at the waist—an impossibly tiny waist—with a satin bow.

Vanessa tugged at her own gown as the three of them entered the seldom-used parlor. After taking a seat on the creamy brocade sofa, Miss Perkins turned with a bright smile to Vanessa, who had sat opposite her. Daniel walked to the fire, distancing himself from the discussion.

Eyes the color of a forest pond addressed Vanessa with kindness. "Lord Heywood tells me that you've only recently arrived in England."

Vanessa nodded, inexplicably tongue-tied.

"I do envy you," Miss Perkins said, "the amusement of discovering London's delights for the first time. I do so adore my rare visits into Town."

"You don't live in London?" Vanessa asked.

"Oh, we keep a house in Mayfair, but Father prefers the quiet of the country." She leaned forward, as if sharing a girlish confidence. "I confess that I too, after a few months of the social whirl, welcome the peace Devonshire affords."

Without turning from his study of the fire, Daniel explained in a flat, disinterested tone, "Devonshire is an area of eastern England."

"Oh. Yes." Miss Perkins seemed embarrassed, her cheeks flushing the exact color of her sash. "I am sorry; I hope I don't appear insensitive. I must remember that all of this is unfamiliar to you."

"Please, Miss Perkins." Vanessa gave a small, rueful smile. "I am the first to acknowledge that I still have much to learn."

Miss Perkins reached over and patted Vanessa's fingers with her own. Vanessa tried very hard not to compare her brown, sturdy digits to those encased in pink kidskin, or to notice how her exposed nails showed broken and uneven. She doubted that Miss Perkins's nails had ever appeared untended.

"Oh, would you do me the favor of calling me Samantha? I would like to think that we could be on familiar terms, Vanessa dear, especially since I have come to help you. To help you learn, just as you asked."

Vanessa shot a surprised look at Daniel's broad back. "You have?"

"Indeed. You see, Lord Heywood and I became acquainted last year through my cousin Charles, who is also a devoted student of the natural sciences. Since Lord Heywood knows of my interest in Charles's studies, it was altogether understandable that he would seek me out to ask for my assistance."

Samantha's blond brows arched. "However, I do not wish to presume, Vanessa dear. I would be honored if you'd allow me to help introduce you to the ways of society, but if you don't believe I will suit, I assure you that I shall not take offense."

Vanessa blinked and tried to form a response. She was having a difficult time following Samantha Perkins's dialogue; although she was listening to the other woman's words, Vanessa found herself not tending to their meaning. Rather, she was admiring the musical quality of Samantha's voice and finding her speech exquisite and refined.

Such delicacy, such daintiness. Vanessa tried to guess at Samantha's age, wondering if the lovely Miss Perkins had yet experienced the rites of womanhood. Somehow, to judge from all those tight-fitting buttons, Vanessa suspected the answer was no.

"Do you understand my offer of assistance?" Samantha asked with concern.

Again Vanessa glanced at Daniel. He was stabbing at the fire with a poker.

Vanessa chewed at her lower lip. "If I were to learn the proper etiquette for eating and dressing and talking, and whatever else I'm meant to learn, then would I be able to go about as you do? To musicales and museums and . . . ?" She could not think of what other entertainments she'd read of on the *Angela.*

"I do not see . . . why not," Samantha answered haltingly, a hint of a shadow passing through her blue eyes.

Vanessa studied Samantha, struggling to determine the source of that darkness. At last, she said, "Yes, I accept your offer, Miss Perkins. I accept it gratefully."

"Splendid." Samantha smiled, her small white teeth shining like a row of polished pearls. "Shall I help you pack your things?"

"Pack?" Daniel, poker in hand, spun around and glared at Samantha Perkins as if she'd lost her very wits.

"Why, y-yes," Samantha stammered, obviously unnerved by Daniel's brooding glower. "I see no reason why Vanessa should have to put up at a hotel when we've more than enough room at Cavendish Square."

"She is staying here."

"Ah. Is the countess coming down from Lincolnshire, then?"

"No."

Samantha's fine lashes fluttered before realization drew her eyes wide. Her lips compressed into a firm pink line. Her fingers threaded uncompromisingly in her lap.

"Vanessa, my dear, would you excuse Lord Heywood and me for a few minutes? We need to clarify the terms of your tutelage."

Vanessa's gaze flitted back and forth between Samantha and Daniel. Neither of the two looked very pleased.

With a small shrug of her shoulder, Vanessa rose and nearly bumped into Rollo, who was entering the parlor with the tea tray.

"Not now," Daniel growled.

Wordlessly, the butler spun on his heel and followed Vanessa from the room. She hoped to linger in the corridor, her curiosity strong, but the butler pointed her to the foyer with a tilt of his chin. Sighing, she did as she was bid and went to sit on the last riser of the staircase, her foot tapping impatiently.

As the cold reclaimed her, Vanessa huddled against the wall and tucked her feet beneath her skirt. She traced the wallpaper pattern with a lazy finger, reflecting on Samantha's invitation, not altogether sure that she welcomed the prospect of going to stay with the Perkins family. While admittedly kind, Samantha Perkins prompted strange and uncomfortable feelings in Vanessa. Feelings of rivalry and envy. Feelings that made Vanessa ashamed of herself.

Of course, Samantha was not at fault. Not at all. And Vanessa knew that if she were to go stay with the young woman, she would have to work diligently at overcoming such ignoble sentiments. They were beneath her, these petty jealousies, beneath an Ama'zon.

The light *tapping* of boots on the hardwood floor signaled Samantha's approach from the parlor. Vanessa stood, wondering if she ought to go upstairs and gather her meager belongings. As Rollo materialized with a cloak and a bonnet, Miss Perkins emerged from the short hallway, her features tense.

She saw Vanessa and tried to smile, but Vanessa could see through to her masked distress. Instantly, Vanessa felt contrite, for she truly did like Samantha Perkins and sensed that the young woman was more ally than rival.

"Heywood and I have agreed that I will commence with your instruction tomorrow morning," Samantha said in a tone too bright to be sincere. "If it pleases you, I will be here at eleven?"

Vanessa nodded her agreement, watching as Samantha slipped into her outer garments, yanking at the bonnet's ribbons and fumbling with her mantle's clasp. She turned to leave, then hesitated, gauging the distance between Rollo, who stood ready at the front door, and Vanessa at the foot of the staircase.

Samantha took a step toward Rollo, then paused again, evidently struggling with some kind of decision. At last, she whirled back to Vanessa, her gaze laced with anger and confusion and perhaps . . . pity?

"Be sure," she said in a defiant whisper, leaning far forward, "that you lock your door tonight, will you, dear?"

Then, not waiting for an answer, the petite Miss Perkins marched out the door.

Chapter Seventeen

"Would it not be easier for the guests to serve themselves?" Vanessa asked. "It would be less work for the servants and easier for those at table to choose what they wanted to eat."

"Dear, you must understand that often one may have as many as fifty or sixty people to dinner," Samantha Perkins pointed out. "It would never do to have so many ladies and gentlemen running around the dining room with overloaded plates dripping onto your carpets."

Daniel saw Vanessa give a thoughtful nod as she tugged at the bodice of her new gown, one that had been delivered that very morning. The color of a persimmon, the dress was evidently giving Vanessa some difficulty. She'd not stopped tugging and pulling at it since she'd entered the parlor five minutes earlier.

Ensconced in a quiet corner of the room, Daniel was pretending to thumb through the *Weekly Dispatch*. He'd been away at his solicitor's during the first two days of instruction but had asked Rollo to maintain a watchful eye on the women's activities. The butler's reports had been unsettling enough to keep Daniel at home today.

"Now." Samantha Perkins referred to her neatly penned list. "Let us move on to general appearance. You do look well in your gown, dear, but we need to refine some of the points of presentation. First, you must cease poking at yourself."

Caught in the act, Vanessa's hand stilled at her waist. "I am sorry. But my dress seems to be shifting around to my front."

"Hmm, yes." The diminutive blonde squinted her eyes assessingly. "I know it feels that way, but you look perfectly aligned to me. Come now, hands front and center, folded nicely."

Vanessa meekly linked her fingers together before her.

"Much better. Now, let us practice our walk, shall we?" Miss Perkins wiggled a commanding finger. "To the window and back."

Daniel peered over the top of his newspaper, watching as Vanessa strolled across the room and back. God, she was utterly magnificent—

"No, no," Miss Perkins murmured, flattening her fingers to her chin in obvious dismay.

Vanessa pivoted, sending a glorious cloud of hair floating around her shoulders. "Is it wrong?"

"Not wrong, precisely. However, I believe it might be improved with less movement. Less sway to the hips, perhaps?"

Daniel frowned and lowered his paper. "I like the way she walks."

"Oh!" Miss Perkins gave a little hop, her blond curls bouncing like springs. "Gracious, Lord Heywood, I did not see you there!" Her mouth pursed with disapproval. "You ought to have announced yourself."

Daniel's frown darkened to an outright scowl. "Vanessa is the one receiving lessons in etiquette, Miss Perkins. Not I."

Across the room, Vanessa stood quietly in a shaft of rare winter sunshine that lit her golden eyes, making them glow like amber. Daniel suspected that she had been aware of his presence all along.

He shook his paper irritably. "Proceed."

"Thank you," Miss Perkins answered, not without a touch of sarcasm. "Now, Vanessa, will you please try again? And this time, be conscious of keeping your spine erect and of allowing as little motion as possible in your shoulders and hips."

Vanessa did as she was asked. Over and over again until the tyrannical Miss Perkins declared herself satisfied. And until Daniel's jaw was throbbing, his facial muscles tight with frustration.

Dammit, what was the matter with the way Vanessa walked? It was natural, lovely, provocative. Must a woman mince about like a pigeon in order to be socially acceptable?

"Slowly," Miss Perkins advised. "A lady must not ever appear rushed. Stand up and try again."

Vanessa rose from the settee, then sat down again, folding herself cautiously onto the sofa.

"Very good. Very fluid and ladylike."

Vanessa beamed, her smile sending a bolt of heat racing through Daniel's chest.

"Now remember," Samantha cautioned, "I know that you are accustomed to a natural directness of regard, Vanessa, but if you were to look at a gentleman so openly, he would most likely think you bold."

Vanessa obediently shuttered her gaze behind a sweep of lashes.

The Perkins woman patted her hand approvingly. "It is such a pleasure to work with you, Vanessa. I find your eagerness to learn immensely gratifying. Mark my words, we'll have you presented at court yet."

Vanessa smiled, obviously pleased, while Daniel cursed beneath his breath. He'd sure as hell never agreed to a court presentation!

"I am going to ring for tea now so that we may practice pouring out." She shot Daniel an arch look. "Will you be joining us in a refreshment, Lord Heywood?"

"No." He rattled his paper.

Rollo answered the summons, returning soon thereafter with the tea service. Daniel tried his damnedest to keep silent during the lengthy process of teaching Vanessa how to pour from a teapot and how to hold a spoon and how to sip from a cup with the exact degree of delicacy required. But it wasn't easy. More than once, he quite literally was forced to bite his tongue to keep himself from spouting off about the ludicrous nature of it all.

Serviettes and sugar bowls? *Nonsense.*

And always at the back of his mind, as he watched Vanessa cling to every word Samantha Perkins uttered, he was tormented by the question: Is this right? Was it not almost immoral, profane even, to take a woman unaffected, spontaneous and genuine, and turn her into something artificial and practiced and unnatural?

How could he allow it? How could he participate in it? He remembered Darwin telling him of the three natives on board the *Beagle* whom the ship's captain had hoped to "civilize." After being instructed as Vanessa was in the practices of civilized peoples, the Indians were taken back to their homeland, where they immediately reverted to their primitive ways. Yet, in that case, the natives were being trained against their will, whereas Vanessa had insisted that she be taught English manners and customs in order to fit into society.

So was it wrong? To give her what she asked? Even though, each day, she became less of an Ama'zon and more of an aristocrat?

An inexplicable anger began to simmer within Daniel, an anger that was directed at himself. Blast it, he was no better than a child, a selfish, shortsighted child, who could not decide what it was he truly wanted. Though proud of Vanessa's progress, Daniel secretly resented it, wanting to hold fast to his Jaguar Eyes, his virgin of the jungle.

And he wanted her. Wanted her desperately, wanted to feel her bucking beneath him as she cried out his name, weeping and sobbing with pleasure. But did he take her? No. Again like a spoiled child, he could not accept the consequences of his actions. He just sat here, gnashing his teeth, tormenting himself with the memory of their shared passion.

"Now, now, you must not play with your hair," Samantha Perkins said, as Vanessa flicked a long strand from her face.

Daniel remembered that hair sliding across his naked chest, its sweet sandalwood fragrance . . .

The smaller woman wrinkled her nose contemplatively. "In fact, although I think you have simply lovely hair, a more fashionable cut—"

"That's it!" Daniel exploded from his chair, the newspaper flying from his lap in a papery jumble. "Teach her all you want about teapots and vinaigrettes, but I draw the line at allowing you to cut her hair!"

Both Vanessa and the Perkins woman turned toward him, their eyes round with surprise.

"Goodness," Miss Perkins gasped.

Recognizing that he had just made a royal ass of himself, Daniel glanced at his boots. But he could scarcely back down now.

Squaring his jaw, he repeated firmly, like a general issuing a military directive, "Do not cut her hair."

Then, with an almost imperceptible shake of his head, he stormed from the room.

"My, my, what was that all about?" Samantha asked breathlessly.

Vanessa set her teacup on the tray, her gaze trained thoughtfully on the parlor door. "I do not know. Daniel's moods have been unpredictable of late. I fear he's been testy, irritable."

"He has, has he?" A discerning note crept into Samantha's voice.

Vanessa turned toward her friend, curious. "Do you understand it?"

Fingers tapping against the edge of her saucer, Samantha's blue eyes narrowed. "Hmm," she murmured. "Let us just say I have my suspicions."

Chapter Eighteen

One painfully long week later, Daniel stood outside Vanessa's bedroom and listened to the darkness. The thick, satiny darkness that fell only after midnight and only after a man had downed his second bottle of port.

He knew he had no right to stand outside Vanessa's door and even less right to consider knocking. Yet he stood there nonetheless in the dark, drafty hallway, wishing Samantha Perkins to perdition.

Blast the infernal girl anyway, he muttered peevishly, forgetting altogether that it was he who had first requested Miss Perkins's interference. Outwardly a prim and genteel miss, the soft-spoken Miss Perkins had turned out to be a pint-sized dragon beneath all that pink and lace. She'd been tutoring Vanessa as agreed, abiding by the terms of their agreement. Each day she spent up to six hours locked away with Vanessa, instructing her in all that a proper Englishwoman needed to know. And each day Miss Perkins made it a point to express to him her extreme dissatisfaction with Vanessa's living arrangements.

Only this morning, the impertinent chit had gone so far as to take him aside to ask if his intentions toward Vanessa were honorable. *Honorable, by damn!* After he'd hemmed and hawed and scowled and finally told her that it was none of her blasted affair, the Perkins girl had merely pursed her lips and then gone on to convey—in no uncertain terms—her opinion of gentlemen who took advantage of young ladies placed under their protection.

Young lady? Jaguar Eyes isn't a young lady, Daniel tried to argue as he stared hungrily at the door latch. *But, by Jove, she wants to be one, doesn't she? My cat-eyed jungle queen wants to be an English gentlewoman.*

He scratched lazily at his temple, wondering why in blazes Vanessa had taken it into her head to don bustle and buttons. *Why?* He supposed if his thoughts were a bit less fuzzy, he'd be able to make sense of it. After all, Vanessa had come to England on a quest for new experiences, hadn't she? And exactly what did he think she could experience without venturing outside, without venturing into London itself?

Daniel leaned his forehead against the door, feeling his frown press into the wood. But did he want Vanessa to venture out? He rather thought not. Not now that he'd witnessed how men, educated and gently bred men—men he called colleagues—had reacted to Vanessa. She'd never be safe from scorn or scrutiny; she'd never be able to live up to society's ludicrously stringent standards of comportment and conduct. Yet what was to be done? He could scarcely keep her a prisoner in his home, as he himself had been imprisoned in Eldra'to.

Shaking his head, Daniel stifled a laugh that came upon him without warning. It came upon him as he realized what a first-rate fool he was. Why, if he'd had his wits about him, he ought to have jumped at the opportunity to send Vanessa off to the Perkins town house on Cavendish Square. Indeed, he should have. To flaunt temptation right under his nose was utter folly, a test of endurance and self-discipline a hundred times more rigorous than any to which his father had ever subjected him. Another laugh, this one slightly more bitter, swelled Daniel's chest as his thoughts turned to his father, the earl.

Daniel knew for a certainty that his father was not ignorant of his return to England. According to his own solicitor, during his absence subtle inquiries had been made into the state of his finances. His father had been keeping an eye on him even half a world away. Was it concern, Daniel wondered, or did the earl plot his financial ruin? Dammit, he'd show him, wouldn't he? He'd show Bretton he could be a success.

Or would he?

"It's all so damned confusing," he mouthed, his lips moving against the oak door, his wits wallowing in wine. A slight headache threatened at the base of his skull.

There were so many factors to consider. His future, Vanessa's future, his need to prove something to himself, to prove something to his father . . .

Most confusing of all was this inexplicable and unshakable need for Vanessa. Good God, how much longer would he be able to deny it, to pretend that his blood did not boil at the mere sight of her, the mere memory of her body sliding against his, the wild, grassy perfume of her skin that was hers and hers alone?

Agh. Those same memories had brought him to this point, had brought him to stand outside her door like a lovesick swain. Or, as Miss Perkins would surely claim, like an unprincipled libertine, an unscrupulous debaucher of naive Ama'zons, a—

He stumbled, almost toppling onto his face as the door to Vanessa's bedroom suddenly swung open.

"Daniel?" She clutched at his sleeve to keep him from falling. "Are you unwell?"

Clumsily, he reclaimed his feet. His mouth went dry. Miss Perkins had evidently located a nightdress for Vanessa—a lady's nightdress, no less, not some secondhand cast-off from a chambermaid. Of a pristine white, the gown cloaked Vanessa from chin to toe and was arguably the most erotic thing Daniel had ever had the pleasure to view. With a chaste ruffle circling the neck, it gave his Jaguar Eyes the appearance of a well-wrapped gift, one that tantalized, hinting of the pleasures concealed within.

A cool palm settled across his brow.

"You're warm. Have you a fever?"

"I do," he answered and grabbed hold of her wrist. He vaguely understood that he was far deeper in his cups than he'd planned to be.

"Shall I call for someone?"

He held on to her. "No."

The faint light in the hallway illuminated her concern. It also revealed a luscious shadowy outline beneath the floor-length linen of her gown.

"But Daniel—"

"It's not that kind of fever." He drew her hand down from his forehead, flattening her fingers against his chest. "Don't you ever simply feel the need to be touched, Vanessa? To know someone's touch other than your own?"

Her lips parted in a shocked, wordless confession.

Daniel smiled, blood flooding his loins as he

remembered that night on the *Angela* when he'd spied on her trying to pleasure herself.

"I—I didn't think you wanted to touch me or I to touch you. Not since that night . . . in the jungle."

His lips tightened with chagrin. There was no point in trying to explain the difference between what he wanted for his body and what he wanted for his career.

With his free hand, he reached out and took a heavy section of silky hair into his palm. It slid through his fingers in a nerve-tingling caress.

"We probably shouldn't," he whispered, wondering if he was talking to her or to himself. "But perhaps just this one night? Just one more night."

As he spoke, he was backing her up to the wall of her bedroom, his gaze roaming over her as if he could not decide where to begin, his fist still clenched in her hair.

"I—"

Her shoulder blades met the wall.

"May I kiss you?" he interrupted.

In the dim light, her eyes glowed like golden embers. Her hand was still pressed to his chest.

"If you like," she answered.

"Oh, yes. I would like."

Tentative he was not. He swooped down upon her like a bird of prey, claiming her mouth with an intensity that forced a gasp from her. But it was a contented gasp, he noticed with a man's secret satisfaction. A gasp that boded well for the rest of the evening.

Their tongues met and began a dance as old as time, a dance of thrust and parry, forward and retreat. Daniel pushed closer, fully pinning Vanessa to the wall. Her breasts were a soft, warm heat against him, a pleasure he could scarcely endure.

He kissed her, the delicate scent of soap floating up from the crisp folds of her linen ruffle, as he cupped her neck with his hand. On his tongue, the fresh scent seemed to mingle with the taste of port. The taste of Vanessa.

His mouth trailed from her lips to her ear, savoring the texture of her satin-smooth cheek.

"Vanessa, you make me wild. You make me wild and hard and so crazed with need that nothing else matters but this." He defined *this* by grinding his manhood against her hips until he was certain she'd felt every inch of his desire.

"I too feel wild," Vanessa murmured.

Daniel smiled and bit into the lobe of her ear, his hand seeking the fullness of her breast. She sighed when he found her and he rewarded her with a gentle squeeze, kneading her, sensitive to the way she pushed into his hand. His lips returned to hers. She welcomed his kiss, whispering his name over and over again.

All around them, the shadows bore witness to their stolen embraces, their labored breath singing harsh and fast in the room's deep quiet.

He brushed her nipple with his thumb, and

the pure woman sound she made shot straight to his heart. Not his loins, he recognized from a distance, but to his heart. He let the realization go, however, when his fingers became entangled at the neck of her night rail. A small tearing sound all but floated away into the darkness. He'd torn her gown. Daniel knew a moment's surprise at this sign of his urgency; then the small tearing sound was followed by a louder one. The front of Vanessa's gown gaped open.

So many months of wanting and not having—

Daniel lowered his head and dipped his tongue in the vee between her breasts. Vanessa did not shy away, but instead cradled his head in her hands, her fingernails raking through his hair. His body had begun to shake. He could not remember ever before shaking with need for a woman.

"Vanessa, Vanessa, what am I going to do?" he groaned in a low, hoarse voice, his cheek nuzzling the side of her breast. What was he going to do the next night and the next and the next, knowing that he could not—should not—have her?

Vanessa misunderstood his meaning. "You are going to touch me, Daniel," she whispered. "And I am going to touch you."

His mouth opened and pressed a wet kiss where her breast curved up from her ribs. "Yes."

He flicked his tongue over her nipple and felt her stomach muscles clench.

"Yes," he repeated. With his knee, he nudged her legs apart so that his hand could snake under her gown. Her thigh was cool and sleek as water as he traveled up its length. When his fingers found her, she gasped and he suckled her harder. She gasped again.

"Daniel, I—"

His thumbnail flicked across her most sensitive flesh and her knees started to buckle. He held her upright with one hand and continued to play her with the other. With every twist of his fingers, he drew on her nipple with his teeth and lips, setting a rhythm that matched his raging pulse.

Vanessa was vibrating like a fine instrument under his ministrations. His hand grew damp with her juices, and the smell of her sex drifting onto his tongue proved a thousand times more intoxicating than the port had been.

She trembled violently. He knew she would not be able to stand should he let her go. He held on to her more firmly, a joy invading his lungs as he sensed her approaching climax. Her fingers tugged at his hair. Fast, tiny pants came faster and faster as she neared her peak. Daniel feared he too was about to erupt.

Then a long, shuddering gasp pushed Vanessa flat against the wall as, around his fingers, her woman's muscles contracted in an explosion of spasms. They clenched over and over with a power he'd never felt in a woman, while she cried out his name on a quiet sob.

He held her for a long moment, not moving his hand, afraid to let her go. Her skin was moist and sweet-smelling. Her muscles were now lax with relief. He was about to lead her to the bed when a noise from the corridor turned his gaze to the open doorway.

Blast. Why didn't I think to close the door? The last thing he desired was for a curious maid to come investigating.

What had been an indistinct noise became footsteps and, with a fleeting kiss, Daniel left Vanessa panting and limp against the wall as he raced toward the threshold.

He'd planned to shut the door, but instinct forced him to look down the hall. His gaze collided with that of a startled Rollo.

Under normal circumstances Daniel wouldn't have given a damn whether or not his butler knew of his nocturnal exploits. In fact, over the years, Daniel had even called on Rollo once or twice to help whisk away a lady friend intent on overstaying her welcome. But tonight . . . Tonight, haunted by Samantha Perkins's accusations and Charles Darwin's warnings, Daniel felt an acidlike guilt wash over him. A guilt that burned.

Rollo dropped his gaze quickly, but not before Daniel heard himself blurt out, "A nightmare."

"She's had a nightmare," Daniel repeated, disgusted to realize that he was explaining himself to a servant. "But she's all right now."

Rollo gave an abbreviated, respectful bow. "Very good, m'lord."

Calmly, Daniel reached for the latch, then pulled closed the bedroom door. Without another word to Rollo, he turned and headed for his own room. Already his mouth felt dry and cottony, his headache more severe. As he strolled down the hall, intent on walking a straight line, he had the feeling that, come morning, he might just owe Vanessa an apology.

"You're doing splendidly, Vanessa," Samantha whispered. "Very well indeed." Samantha's blond head barely reached the top of Vanessa's shoulder as she leaned forward, talking from the side of her mouth. "All your hard work is paying off, my dear, don't you see?"

"You do not think people are staring?" Beneath the sheltering brim of her bonnet, Vanessa anxiously scanned the crowded bookshop.

"Heavens, my dear, any attention you are receiving is complimentary, I assure you. That burgandy velvet is a wonderful color for you, and your new coiffure most flattering. Don't fret, dear. No one is staring."

Vanessa gave a small nod, although she knew that Samantha's senses were not as keen as her own, and thus her friend could not have heard the smattering of whispers as they'd entered, or noticed the heads spinning around every few seconds for a quick peek. A quick peek at Vanessa, the curiosity.

She wasn't supposed to be aware of it, but Vanessa knew full well she'd been the subject of gossip this past week. Evidently, one or two of Daniel's colleagues had spread word of "the jungle woman" brought back from the South American wilds. The stories had spread, embellished with each telling, until Vanessa was reported to stand over ten feet tall, sport claws like a tigress and eat raw meat at every sitting.

Eventually, as the tales grew more outlandish, Samantha had decided to nip the rumors in the bud by suggesting an outing. A very safe and easy outing to the bookshop.

Adjusting the lace at her cuffs, Vanessa lifted her head, acting as if she were perusing the titles. She took a calming breath, careful not to breathe too deeply lest her corset bind and pinch. Oh, she'd learned her lesson about corsets, she had. About corsets and petticoats and drawers. About ointments that bleached the complexion and salves that softened the hands. About sleeves so tight one dared not raise an arm above the waist and shoes so confining that one's toes were squeezed into sharp and painful points.

And while these lessons had proved trying, they were nothing compared to the instruction Vanessa was receiving on etiquette. The "dos" and "don'ts" seemed endless, especially as they pertained to a lady's conduct. Often Vanessa felt compelled to fall back on her Ama'zonian training in order to maintain the necessary self-control. A lady must not raise her voice. A lady must not appear hurried or rushed. A lady must not shake hands with a gentleman, or make casual eye contact lest she be thought forward. A lady must not . . .

Yes indeed, Vanessa had learned that being a woman in 1840 London was not for the faint of heart.

Nonetheless, she could not help but think her training was making her more attractive to Daniel, for, last night, he had finally come to her. At last. After so many months of yearning, he had come to her room and she'd known the pleasure of being with him. It had not been the same as what they'd shared in the jungle—he had not taken his own pleasure—but it had still been very meaningful. She had still floated to the stars in his arms. Of course, she had been disappointed when he'd left again, but she was encouraged that he'd come to her at all. Perhaps as she continued to improve her manners and appearance, as she continued to become more like the typical English lady, he would come to her more frequently.

She would have to work very hard.

"Heavens," Samantha suddenly announced, "I fear I've lost my brooch." She patted futilely at the now empty hollow of her collar. "Oh, dear me, where can it be? It belonged to my grandmother and has great—Ah, there it is!"

Vanessa followed her friend's gaze and spied a spot of glittering gold near the entrance to the bookshop.

"I'll be right back," Samantha said before swinging toward the door.

Not wishing to be left alone, Vanessa was going to start after her when she was addressed from her right, from the direction of a tall wooden rack.

"Good afternoon."

Vanessa, remembering Samantha's warning about speaking to strangers, would most likely have refused to turn around, except for the distinctive timbre in the gentleman's voice. It was strangely familiar to her.

She pivoted slowly—she'd learned to do everything slowly in her restrictive attire—and was struck with the impression that she had somehow leaped into the future. The well-dressed man standing before her was Daniel thirty years from now. He was a sterner, stiffer version of Daniel, more intimidating, a touch more portly, but the resemblance was unmistakable. He had to be a relation of some sort.

"I am not usually in the habit of approaching young women in public venues," the gentleman said. "But I have been curious to meet you."

His curiosity, Vanessa noticed, did not seem to be a friendly one. There was about the man a vague hostility that made her believe he thought ill of her. Or, if he did not yet, he planned to.

"We have not been introduced," she answered, straightening until she stood every inch of her nearly six feet.

"No. I am Lord Bretton. The Earl Bretton," he said, as if the title held significance.

She glanced aside, pretending disinterest, when in reality she sought Samantha. Her friend stood near the door, brooch in hand, engaged in an animated conversation with two young gentlemen.

"I am Daniel's father."

Oh.

Careful to keep the surprise from her features, Vanessa returned her attention to the earl. Although Daniel never spoke of his father, she had overheard bits and pieces of discussions—enough to conclude that the father-son relationship was a strained one.

"How do you do?" she asked.

"Town gossip has it that you're residing in my son's home."

Vanessa's lips pursed and she glanced at the tips of her gloves.

While Samantha had been the essence of kindness and discretion, Vanessa had just recently begun to suspect that her living situation was not acceptable by society's standards. After all, according to Samantha, a lady was not even supposed to call upon an unmarried gentleman; how, then, could it be seemly for her to share a house with one?

The earl snorted beneath his breath, then

tapped the floor with his walking stick.

"You should know that though I cannot keep the title from him, he's not going to get a penny of my money, if that's where your interests lie. I'll not see my coin squandered on those half-baked ideas of his, those pathetic dreams of scientific glory. The boy has to accept his fate like a man. Like a *real* man.

"And as for this ludicrous pretense of yours—" Bretton's eyes washed over her as cold as morning fog. "I don't know whether you are playing Daniel for a fool or not. I'm not certain that I even care. I only hope that, for the sake of his mother, he is not a party to this shameful deception that all and sundry are talking about. Not that it would matter to that spineless offspring of mine, but the Heywood name still means something, you know. Quite a lot."

This tirade left the earl flushed, and Vanessa suddenly understood where Daniel came by his passionate nature.

"Spineless?" she echoed.

Lord Bretton puffed out his chest in a show of belligerence. "He's got to stop running. He can't run from the truth forever."

"I've not known Daniel to run from anything."

"Hah. Then you don't know him."

Don't know him? Vanessa weighed the words, perceiving that they were false. She did know Daniel. She did. She might not always understand him, might often be confused by his manner—particularly his manner with her—but she knew him. She'd known Daniel from the very beginning, had recognized something of herself in the half-dead stranger thrashing feverishly upon the grass mattress, cursing the jungle. Cursing this man.

Vanessa pushed back her shoulders and leveled a calm eye upon the earl. "I do know Daniel," she corrected, "and he is not a coward."

The earl tapped his ebony-tipped cane upon the floor once more. At the back of her mind, Vanessa recognized that the man had no genuine need of the walking aid.

"You think not, do you?" He tilted forward at the waist, using his greater height in an attempt to intimidate.

Vanessa recognized the ploy for its worth and held her ground. "I do," she told him, then leaned forward herself until their noses were nearly touching.

Interest glimmered in Bretton's brown gaze. He eased back. "You're no coward either, are you, girl?"

"I was raised to be strong." Then, she added, "Just as Daniel was."

"He's spoken to you of his . . . education?" The earl's thin smile revealed skepticism.

Vanessa did not answer. Despite this man's belligerence, she felt as if she recognized the Earl Bretton. He was like any number of Ama'zon warriors she'd trained with in her youth and, because of this, she could not help but feel a measure of respect for the man. She'd been taught her whole life to admire strength.

"Well, I'll wager he's not told you what led him to South America, has he, girl?"

Shrugging, Vanessa glanced at Samantha, who was still in conversation. "He came to find me."

"Hah! The boy was searching for his manhood," Bretton scoffed.

Vanessa whirled around and spoke directly from her heart. "Yes. And he found it through me."

And with that, she achieved something. The proof was written in the earl's expression, in the telltale softening of the lines around his mouth. His eyes shifted toward the door, and Vanessa saw that Samantha was hurrying toward them as fast as her tiny booted feet would allow.

"Here." The earl thrust a square piece of paper into her hand. "My card. Contact me if you are ever in need of assistance."

Speechless with surprise, Vanessa studied the sharp letters inked in black. When she glanced up again, the earl was gone.

Chapter Nineteen

Daniel despised this sort of thing, despised it passionately. The crowded rooms, the insufferable heat, the clamor of hundreds of voices vying to be heard on the wearisome subjects of fashion and horses and politics. God, how he hated it. He'd sell his very soul to the devil to be at home this night, working on the first draft of his treatise, instead of trading banalities with perfume-soaked biddies while sipping weak punch. But Samantha Perkins had insisted. She'd insisted on hosting this little soiree, claiming that it was an important and necessary step in Vanessa's education.

Education, Daniel silently mocked, his eyes narrowing as he studied the pale yellow liquid filling his glass. For nearly two weeks now, Miss

Perkins had been working to transform the primitive into a princess. She'd brought in dressmakers and dance instructors and coiffure designers who had taught Vanessa the proper way to walk, to talk, to sit, to arrange her hair. Samantha had instructed Vanessa in subjects ranging from English history to table settings to cross-stitching, while not foregoing the gentle arts of menu planning and flower arranging. In short, they had done all they could to take the jungle out of his jungle woman.

And they'd succeeded.

As he glanced around, Daniel had to recognize, not without a sense of irony, that this society was every bit the brutal environment for Vanessa that the Amazon had seemed to him. In acquiring the so-called "gentle arts," Vanessa was simply learning survival techniques for a *new* jungle. This one known as London society.

His bored gaze landed on the Mayfair Trio, the much-beloved Misses Dalton. The heart of Samantha Perkins's social set, Alexandra, Julia and Susanna stood together, surrounded by a bevy of young bucks. The ladies simpered, giggled and blushed, to the general admiration of everyone around them, their fair skin a testimony to a life spent indoors, as if they were being raised as a commodity, as soft white meat to be purchased by the highest bidder. The highest bidder being in possession of the most lofty title or the most ample bank account.

Daniel felt disgust at the utter uselessness of

these women, all white and pink and weak. *This isn't what Vanessa is to become, is it?*

Dear God, he hoped not.

With brooding eyes, Daniel sought her from his hiding place behind a large potted urn. There she was, whirling past on the arm of Samantha's father, Sir Rodney. He had to admit that she did look lovely in an evening dress of blue-green silk, her hair pulled back in a cluster of glossy, flower-trimmed curls. In truth, if one did not look too closely, Vanessa might have appeared to be like any other English lady in attendance. Like any other corset-pinched, pale-cheeked, vinaigrette-sniffing miss he'd met a thousand times over in his lifetime.

With a muttered curse, Daniel drained his glass, questioning his sour mood. He had no reason to resent Vanessa's triumph. On the contrary, he was rather proud of her, proud of her for having proven Darwin wrong. Daniel knew that she'd had to work very hard for this evening; that she'd stayed up late each and every night poring over books on etiquette and social protocol. He knew this, of course, since he'd been spying on her. Or if not spying, watching the light spill under her bedroom door as a man dying from thirst watches water spill from a carafe.

Yes, by God, he was a man at death's door. A man about to expire from lust. Foolishly, he'd hoped that the brief interlude they'd shared—when he'd pinned Vanessa to her wall and brought her to a shuddering climax—would have helped assuage the need that had been burning him alive since their night in the jungle. But nothing could have proven further from the truth. That sweet taste of her had only whetted his desire until, last night, he'd gone so far as to visit one of the more discriminative bawdy houses tucked away discreetly on St. James's Street. He'd been determined to find a cure for his affliction, a remedy to the desire that was eating him alive.

Alas, female after female had been brought forward for his review without one managing even to stir his passions. Desperate and disgusted, he'd finally decided on a tall girl, certain that if he closed his eyes he could pretend it was Vanessa whose soft secrets he was plumbing. But the girl's smell was artificial and perfumed, not green and fresh and he'd not been able to see the deed done.

He'd realized then that only Vanessa could sate his desire. Only his Jaguar Eyes.

The dance concluded, and Daniel watched as Vanessa was claimed by her next partner, a short young pup whose nose seemed only to reach dead-center of Vanessa's bosom. Grumbling to himself, Daniel did grudgingly appreciate that Samantha Perkins had chosen her party guests with care. Although the Perkinses moved in society's best circles, it was clear that the evening's invitees were a select crowd—close family friends and associates who could be trusted not to gossip or to treat Vanessa with anything less than complete courtesy.

Which was more than he could say for himself. Daniel kicked at the heel of his shoe, painfully aware of the fact that he'd been behaving like a perfect ass these last weeks. More of an ass than he normally was. He'd been avoiding Vanessa for fear he'd lose control of himself and ravish her in the middle of the foyer with all the servants looking on. He'd been curt and severe with Miss Perkins, who had only done precisely as he had asked her to, and befriended Vanessa in the process. And to Darwin he'd been nothing short of rude, ignoring his friend's messages, too ashamed to confess that he'd not had the courage to send Vanessa home.

Good God, what is happening to me? He felt as if he could no longer recognize himself, recognize the Daniel Heywood who had sailed off to South America nearly ten months ago. The Daniel he remembered had been fixed on his goals, had been self-controlled and focused. He had known what he wanted and he'd gone after it with a vengeance, with single-minded ferocity, in keeping with the Heywood name. He'd sought recognition. Fame. Redemption of the most personal kind.

And all of this he'd found with the Ama'zons.

Yet how much had he written of his treatise? A half-dozen pages, perhaps? Why was he not pursuing his paper with greater fervor? Was he so addled with lust that he couldn't concentrate on his purpose?

Daniel cursed, loudly enough that an elderly lady standing a few feet away turned and glowered at him. He was of such a mood that he glowered back.

He couldn't go on like this. He had to either return Vanessa to Eldra'to or . . . find a way to keep her forever.

Scanning the dance floor, he found her spinning toward him in the arms of the fuzzy-faced young man, her chin held high, her face almost ashen. A flicker of unease shot through him. Instinctively, he edged toward the dance floor as couples twirled past like flocks of brightly colored butterflies. He saw Vanessa stumble, then regain her footing. Her dancing partner asked her a question and she started to nod. Her nod became a wobble—

In the next instant, Daniel was lunging forward, catching Vanessa before she could tumble to the floor. Her eyes were closed, her head limp, as he hauled her into his embrace. Around him, he heard voices rise in startlement, accompanied by a flurry of gasps.

"It must be the heat," he explained to the young man who'd been partnering her.

The lad swallowed, looking as if he might swoon himself.

"Heywood, oh, dear!" Samantha Perkins emerged from the crowd, the peach feathers in her cap fluttering frantically. "Whatever has happened?"

"The heat," Daniel suggested, although he knew for a fact that Vanessa was accustomed to temperatures significantly more severe than that of the crowded ballroom.

"Come this way."

Daniel swung Vanessa up into his arms and carried her through the gawking throng. He resisted the urge to bury his face in her hair, though the scent of her was triggering a deep response in him. He followed as Samantha Perkins led him from the ballroom, down the hall to a small, private parlor.

Dashing ahead to place a pillow upon the gold-fringed divan, Samantha stepped aside so that Daniel could lay Vanessa down. He did, then smoothed a stray silken curl from her cheek.

"Tell me exactly what happened," Samantha demanded, waving Daniel aside as she took Vanessa's gloved hand and knelt on the carpet beside her.

Frowning, Daniel edged around to the head of the divan, not pleased by the low color in Vanessa's complexion. "I was watching her dance when I saw her grow faint."

"You noticed nothing else? Did she appear agitated, perturbed?"

"No—See here, don't you think we should call for a doctor?" he demanded, his tone a shade too harsh even for his liking.

Samantha Perkins tilted her face up and studied him for a long, long moment. "Yes," she said slowly, "that's what we should do. Would you be so good as to ask Father to send for someone?"

Disinclined to leave Vanessa, Daniel knew he could hardly refuse.

"Of course," he said, casting another concerned look at Vanessa's pallor. "Do you think you ought to loosen her stays?"

Miss Perkins's eyes rounded.

"Ah." He'd forgotten he was not supposed to speak of such things. "I'll find your father immediately."

And Daniel flew from the room as if an entire contingent of Amazon warriors were hard on his heels.

Vanessa regained consciousness, wondering why the sky looked more white than blue and why the trees were not arching above her in giant sprays of green. She also wondered if she were about to lose the contents of her stomach.

"Vanessa?"

She rolled her head toward the woman's voice, her memory returning in a rush. The party, the dancing, Daniel brooding in the corner. . . . "Samantha, I—What has happened?"

Samantha patted Vanessa's hand, her smile gentle and ever so comforting. "You fainted, my dearest. Have you not been feeling well?"

"I don't know. I have been nauseated."

Samantha stopped her patting, growing suddenly rather still. Sensing her friend's concern, Vanessa felt the need to explain.

"I assumed I've not felt well due to the change in diet. The food in London is very rich compared to what I am used to."

"Of course. But, um, have you been experiencing this nausea for some time?"

"A few weeks. But generally only in the morning."

"The morning—" Samantha's smile grew strained. Her nose gave a tiny twitch. "Tell me, dear, have you noticed that you've been particularly fatigued?"

Vanessa sighed. "Well, I have been reading until very late."

"Hmm-hmm." Samantha lowered her gaze, her fingers touching the buttons on Vanessa's glove one by one, as if counting them off. "I hate to be impertinent, and I do apologize for asking you such a personal question, Vanessa dear, but I like to think of us as friends and I know you've no one else to talk to. . . ."

Vanessa lifted herself into a half-sitting position, noticing with surprise the blush staining the curve of Samantha's cheekbones.

"On the day we met, I suggested to you that you keep your bedroom door locked. Do you remember?"

Vanessa bobbed her chin.

"Did you understand, dear, why I made that suggestion to you?"

Vanessa gave a self-conscious shrug. She had learned so much over these past weeks, she hated that she could still appear ignorant to her more learned friend. "No. And I am sorry, Samantha, but I forgot to do as you asked. Was it important?"

Samantha huffed out her breath, the feathers on her head dancing in response. "It may have been very important," she said quietly, lifting her gaze from her study of the pearl buttons. "I am going to ask you to think carefully now, Vanessa. . . . Have you noticed a change in your—pardon my bluntness—your woman's cycle?"

"Oh." Vanessa did not understand the correlation, but answered, "It has stopped."

Samantha squeezed shut her eyes before reopening them. "How long has it been stopped?"

"Since we left the jungle, I believe."

"And, before you left the jungle, was Lord Heywood . . . intimate with you?"

"Intimate?"

Samantha blushed an even brighter hue of red. "Did he take liberties with your"—she waved a hand across Vanessa's torso—"person? Kiss you, touch you? More?"

"Oh." Vanessa suspected that Samantha was not going to approve of her answer. "Yes."

"Dear me." Samantha closed and opened her eyes once more, taking a moment to compose herself. "Do you comprehend what this means, Vanessa?"

"I do not think I do."

Wrapping both her hands around Vanessa's, Samantha said in a sober whisper, "It means that you are with child."

With child? Vanessa's lips curved in a smile of surprised wonder. "I am?"

"Oh, my goodness, Vanessa, I fear you cannot appreciate the gravity of the situation. Someone will have to speak with Heywood."

"Why?"

"Because he must be told that he is to be a father!"

"But Daniel cannot be the father."

A choked sound came from Samantha's throat. Her fingers clenched harder on Vanessa's. "Have there been others?"

At Vanessa's blank stare, Samantha persisted in a ragged voice, "Have you been intimate with any man other than Lord Heywood, Vanessa?"

"Oh, no!" She sat up straight on the divan, turning to face Samantha. "Daniel is the only one who has touched me. Another man tried, but I did not let him do so."

"Praise God." Samantha truly did look as if she wanted to weep now. She swallowed hard, her eyes shimmering in the gaslight. "But what then makes you assert that Heywood is not the father?"

"Daniel told me that he was incapable of fathering children."

Indignation flashed through Samantha's blue gaze. "He *told* you that?"

"Y-yes."

"Oh, the black-hearted scoundrel . . ."

"You are angry?"

"Dash it all, Vanessa, I am more than angry!

I am outraged. Lord Heywood is supposed to be a gentleman, if not by action, at least by birth. For him to compromise you in this manner is simply reprehensible."

"By *compromise,* do you mean get me with child?"

"That is precisely what I mean," Samantha said with breathless vehemence, her eyes shooting sapphire sparks. "I am shocked. Shocked and disappointed."

"But I don't think Daniel intended for me to become pregnant."

"Heavens, my child, they never do!"

Confused by Samantha's ire, Vanessa began to deduce that her pregnancy was not the cause for celebration that it would have been had she been home in Eldra'to.

"Will my being with child reflect poorly on Daniel?"

Samantha made a disparaging snort. "If he does not do the honorable thing, it will go very badly for him, I daresay. After all, he is heir to an earldom, you know."

"And what would be the honorable thing for him to do?"

"Why, marry you, of course!"

Vanessa sank back into the cushions, overwhelmed, a multitude of emotions rioting through her. She knew of the English practice of marriage but had never considered that she might be party to it.

"Will Daniel want to marry me?" she asked doubtfully.

Samantha's gaze shifted. "What he wants to do is irrelevant."

"So what you are saying is that, whether he wants to or not, Daniel may feel that he is duty-bound to marry me?"

"I, um—" Samantha flicked a blond curl from her shoulder. "I do not know that Heywood has ever been greatly influenced by public opinion or the threat of scandal, but I should hope he would demonstrate a degree of decency in this instance."

"I see."

And Vanessa was beginning to see. She was beginning to see that her pregnancy had placed her in a terrible predicament.

Would Daniel even believe that she carried his child? As she recalled, he had been firmly convinced of his infertility. Convinced and disillusioned and bitter. Yet might he not be glad to learn of a child? Glad enough to wed her? Or would he too be placed in a terrible predicament? Compelled to marry her even though he was at heart reluctant to join himself to a woman his friends considered something less than human?

Vanessa laid her hand upon her abdomen and came to a decision.

"Samantha, I must ask a favor of you."

"Anything, dear."

"I must ask you not to speak of this. To tell no one of my condition."

"Why, Vanessa, darling, I'd sooner cut out my own tongue than spread tales about you; you know that."

"I do and I am grateful. I am more grateful than I can say to have found your friendship." Solemnly, she added, "However, when I ask that you tell no one, I do mean *no one.*"

Blond brows spiked upward. "Good heavens, not even Heywood? But he has to be told, for your sake, if nothing else."

Vanessa pressed her fingers to her temples, fighting another onslaught of dizziness. "But I do not wish him to be told right away. I must first decide what is best for my child before I can consider discussing marriage or any other feasible alternative with Daniel."

"Vanessa, there is no other feasible alternative," Samantha said in a voice that sounded almost frightened. "You cannot bear a child outside of wedlock and still hope to be received by good society."

Vanessa's smile felt stiff and bittersweet. "I doubt whether good society will receive me in any case, dear Samantha."

Tears pooled at the back of her friend's eyes before they were brushed away by a hastily retrieved handkerchief. "Very well, then. I promise I will say nothing to Lord Heywood on one condition: You must come live with me. I do not want you spending even one more night under the same roof as that odious man. I never should have let him bully me so with that beastly scowl of his. I ought to have insisted that you stay with me right from the start."

Vanessa hesitated, realizing how difficult it would be for her to be parted from Daniel. She had relied on him. She had relied on him emotionally—even during the days when he'd blatantly avoided her—by believing that Daniel was a constant in her ever-changing world, a landmark in the perplexing landscape of her life. He might have ignored her, shunned her, rejected her; but he had been there. At least, in her own mind, he had been there for her.

Nonetheless, Vanessa was not blind to the fact that she'd approached a crucial point in her relationship with Daniel. One that required much prayer, contemplation and time. And all of those, she thought, would be better found in the calm of the Perkins house, away from Daniel's unsettling influence.

"Perhaps it would be for the best."

"Most definitely," Samantha agreed. "I will go find him now and explain your decision." As she stood to go, Vanessa reached out and grabbed hold of her hand.

"Please say nothing."

Samantha's lips tightened, but she nodded her acquiescence. "As you wish, Vanessa, though he will have to be told eventually, you know. A man has the right to know he's going to be a father."

Chapter Twenty

The next morning, Daniel was still in a fury. A red-hot, teeth-grinding, fist-clenching fury. He didn't like being manipulated. It reminded him far too strongly of his dealings with his father. But manipulated he'd been, all right, by that conniving Perkins woman. Under the guise of the soiree, she had managed to maneuver Vanessa into her home and out of his.

"Damn," he muttered, as the carriage pulled up in front of the Perkins house. "Damn, damn, damn."

Samantha Perkins had used Vanessa's illness as an excuse, arguing that Vanessa required the care of a woman as she recovered from her "unexplained ailment." When Daniel had gruffly pointed out that he employed any number of housemaids, Miss Perkins had fluttered her dainty fingers and dismissed him out of hand. No, she'd said, Vanessa needed a friend, not a servant. Then the impertinent woman had ordered him to send for Vanessa's things.

Only after he'd done so had Daniel realized that the doctor had never been sent for. Pressed, Miss Perkins had confessed that Vanessa's malady appeared not to be as serious as first believed. At that point, however, his Jaguar Eyes was already firmly ensconced in a first-floor bedroom of Perkins House, Cavendish Square. And unless he wished to storm upstairs and carry her off, he'd had little choice but to return home, where he'd roamed the halls of his town house until dawn like some poor, crazed, senseless animal.

But enough was enough. Vanessa was coming home with him today.

The coachman yanked open the carriage door and waited patiently for Daniel to descend. He started to when a small voice inside urged him to return home and make himself presentable, as he'd not even bothered to shave that morning and was still wearing the same evening clothes from the night before.

Frowning, he ran the back of his hand across his beard. *The hell with it,* he thought. He was a scientist, not a dandy. And a perverse part of him rather enjoyed the forsaking of gentlemanly trappings, remembering the man who'd fought his way, shoeless, through the overgrown rain forest, subsisting on fruit and roots and pond water.

With a sharp yank to his silk top hat, Daniel clambered from the carriage, his jaw set at a belligerent angle. If the Perkinses didn't care for his less-than-immaculate appearance, that was unfortunate for them.

As it turned out, Daniel didn't have to worry about offending the Perkinses; the butler who admitted him related that the family was still abed. Then the cheeky servant displayed his pocket watch, confirming that the hour was not yet ten. No civilized gentleman went calling before noon.

"Doesn't matter," Daniel told him, "for I've come to see Miss Vanessa, not any of the family."

"M'lord, perhaps if you'd like to leave your card—"

Daniel silenced the man with a pointed look. "Send word to Vanessa that I will wait for her."

The butler knew when he'd lost. He bowed so deeply his forehead practically smacked his knees, then led Daniel to the front parlor, an expansive room, decorated *a la Grecque,* and nearly twice the size of his own drawing room at home.

As Daniel waited, he circumnavigated the parlor no less than four times, scrutinizing the Argand chandelier and bobbin-turned chairs as if he was planning to draft an article on drawing room furnishings. He didn't rightly know what it was he proposed to say to Vanessa, but he figured he would know once he saw her. Yes, once he saw her, he'd be able to put into words what had been eating away at him all night.

She had to come back. One way or the other, Daniel knew he had to convince Vanessa to return home with him. Although he'd yet to dissect it, he had finally accepted that he needed her. He had always needed her. He'd needed her in Eldra'to when he'd had no other ally but her. He'd needed her in the jungle when his very survival was in her hands. He'd needed her last week when his body had craved the feel and smell of her with a potency that bordered on insanity.

He needed her now.

The door to the parlor swung open and Daniel felt something twist in his chest. Vanessa appeared on the threshold, looking frail and unhappy, a sadder, paler version of her previously vibrant self. Dressed in a walking gown of striped fuchsia, she reminded him of an exotic orchid that had been plucked from its shaded stem and left to wilt in the tropic's hot sun. Something beautiful and rare savagely removed from its natural element and left to perish.

"That Perkins chit led me to believe that your illness was insignificant," he began in an accusing tone.

Vanessa lowered her gaze to the ribbon dangling from the bonnet she held. "Good morning to you, too, Daniel."

His eyes narrowed. Damn her, only she could rebuke him with such gentleness. "I only meant—"

"I know," she interrupted. "And Samantha did not speak falsely, for I am feeling much better. I truly am."

Her appearance belied her words. "What ailed you, then? Did you not eat enough at supper? Or did that overheated ballroom make you ill?"

"I cannot be sure." He noticed that she avoided his gaze. "I believe both probably contributed to my not feeling well. But really, Daniel, there is no need to be concerned."

Need. There was that word again, brazenly staring Daniel in the face.

"Vanessa, I want to talk with you."

She tilted her head to the side in silent invitation.

"Not here. Will you join me for a ride?"

She bit indecisively at her lower lip, a shallow sigh lifting the lace on her collar. A jolt of surprise shot through Daniel then, as he realized that she was actually considering refusing his invitation. Vanessa. His discovery. His goddess of the jungle. Refusing him.

"Please," he managed. The word sounded rusty dragged from his throat.

She smoothed a slow hand across the side of her neatly pinned bun. "Very well. Let me fetch my mantle."

Daniel had a few anxious moments as he

waited for Vanessa to return. What if Samantha Perkins intercepted her in the hall and convinced Vanessa not to go riding with him? As childish as it seemed, Daniel was beginning to feel as if he was in competition with the Perkins girl. Though he'd always been on good terms with Darwin's cousin, since tutoring Vanessa, Samantha Perkins had acted as if she'd taken a dislike of him. No doubt, he assumed, because she had learned the truth. She had most likely learned that he'd been unable to resist Vanessa's charms. How, in fact, he'd succumbed to his desire for her not once, but twice now.

Guilt reared its ugly head again, striking out at Daniel where he was most vulnerable. He loathed feeling guilty or ashamed, and it made him uncomfortable to have to question himself, question his motives.

Yet where Vanessa was concerned, Daniel could not hope to avoid those uncomfortable feelings. He knew he ought not to have taken his pleasure with her—it had been an act of blind selfishness—but his desire for her had been too strong for him to deny. Indeed, Daniel could not think of another time in his life when he had wanted anything with the same pure energy with which he had wanted Vanessa. Not even the fame and recognition he had been striving for all these years meant as much as—

"Daniel?"

He snapped back to the present. "Ah, are you ready?"

As they settled into the closed carriage, Daniel was glad he'd not ordered the gig brought around. Although the weather had finally changed, allowing the sun to shine down upon foggy London, he remembered that Vanessa was sensitive to winter's cold. Even with her heavy cloak, she'd not have been warm enough in the open-topped vehicle.

"Are you sure you're well?" he asked, struck again by her unnatural pallor.

"Quite sure, thank you." But when he glanced out the carriage window, he saw her give a surreptitious pinch to her cheeks.

"You enjoyed yourself last evening?" he asked. "Before you fell ill, that is?"

"Yes, I did." She fidgeted with the bow of her bonnet. "Everyone was most kind. I did feel conspicuous, but I doubt that can be helped. I will always be noticeably taller than the average Englishwoman, won't I?"

Daniel frowned. "I like your height."

"Thank you," she said, although there was a touch of melancholy in her words.

"Are you homesick?" he suddenly asked, wondering whether her apparent sadness might be due to a longing for her homeland.

"Homesick?" Her gaze clouded, as if her inner eye sought to re-create a picture of the jungle. "No," she said slowly. "Not really. Although I do miss the . . . sounds, the music. The way the monkeys would chatter loudest at dusk, and the birds take turns, singing one after the other from tree to tree to tree. . . ."

Her voice trailed off, carrying Daniel back with her to that place of green, lush memories. That place so far from the crowded streets of wintry Mayfair.

They both fell silent, an unspoken tension rising between them—the same tension that had been born of a passion-filled night shared under the Amazonian stars. Nothing had been the same since that night. Nothing.

Tapping his fingers upon the window ledge, Daniel wished he might find a way to diffuse that tension. . . .

"I've an idea. What would you say to a visit to London Zoo?"

A quizzical frown curved Vanessa's brow.

"I've not been for many years, but I understand the Zoological Society has made many worthy improvements. You'd enjoy it, I believe."

"I-I am not sure. Samantha might be concerned if I'm gone too long."

"She knows you are with me."

Daniel rapped at the roof and when the coachman slid open the communicating door, Daniel instructed him to drive to Regent's Park.

Upon their arrival, it became evident that the favorable weather had lured many of London's residents to the zoo that morning. Daniel kept a watchful eye on Vanessa, concerned that she would become nervous in the crowd. But as they strolled toward the first attraction, Vanessa did not appear to be uneasy, yet neither did she look to be particularly interested in her surroundings.

"You seem preoccupied," he said as they approached the Camel House, with its quaint, and much-admired, Gothic clock tower.

"Do I?" she asked listlessly, then did not elaborate, instead turning her attention to the hump-backed beasts resting in the tower's shade, lazily chewing upon their grassy cud.

"I've never seen such an animal," she said. "Where is its home?"

"Camels are desert natives. These were probably brought here from Northern Africa."

For the first time that day, Vanessa gave him a genuine smile. Genuine, and somehow wistful. "How splendid it must be to know so much, Daniel."

He made a wry face and tipped his hat, unaffected by the many curious glances from strangers questioning his rumpled evening attire and unshaven state.

"Now let me see," he said. "To our left is the aviary. The Society has collected a vast assortment of birds, many of which you ought to recognize."

Cupping Vanessa's elbow, he steered her down the path toward the symphonic potpourri of twitters, whistles and trills. The crowds were heavier here, as people loitered in front of the tall enclosure. Young boys stood nearby, attempting to mimic the different bird calls, their youthful mouths puckered into comical shapes. On the other side of the path, a fountain spilled prettily into a man-made pond.

Vanessa spent almost a quarter of an hour standing before the enclosure, searching for birds familiar to her. Once or twice she asked Daniel for the name of a particular species, reminding him of the fact that English was not her mother tongue. She'd become so fluent these last weeks, he'd nearly forgotten that she spoke another language. He made a mental note to begin working on a dictionary of the Amazonian language as soon as he returned home.

From the aviary, they proceeded to the bear pit.

"What are those men doing?" Vanessa asked.

Around the gate's perimeter stood a group of society bucks taunting the bears below by waving food above their heads and out of the bears's reach.

"One of the attractions here is the opportunity to feed the animals," Daniel explained.

"But they are not feeding the bears," Vanessa pointed out unhappily. "They are mocking them."

"I doubt the beasts understand that they are being mocked, Vanessa."

"Whether the bears understand or not, it is not right for the men to taunt the animals, is it? Or is that the purpose of this zoo of yours?"

"Come now, it isn't as if—" He stopped in midsentence. Vanessa was truly upset. Visibly upset.

"Would you like me to speak with them?"

"Yes, Daniel, I would."

Vanessa watched Daniel walk around the pit toward the quartet of nattily dressed young men. Even in his unkempt state, he exuded an air of authority and power. Her heart swelled with pride.

"I say," a voice behind her murmured, "isn't that Heywood over there?"

Vanessa was about to respond when another voice answered and she realized that the gentleman in question was not speaking to her.

"So it is. Egads, I haven't seen old Heywood in ages. Looks as if he's had himself a helluva night. What's he been about?"

"You've not heard?"

"Haven't had a chance to catch up on the latest since I got back from the expedition."

Expedition? Were the two men scientists like Daniel? Instinctively, Vanessa hunched over in an effort to minimize her height.

"By Jove, it's been all the talk. Don't know how you've not heard. Apparently, Heywood is claiming to have discovered the original Amazons."

"Amazons? Women warriors? Never say it!"

"I do. Word is, he's going to set the British Association for the Advancement of Science on its ear. He's said to be working on a paper to prove his claim, and it's even rumored he's got one of the ghastly creatures living at his house for him to study."

"Good God, I don't believe it. Must be some kind of sham. I never would have thought it of Lord Heywood, you know, but then again, he always has been desperate to make a name for himself. Never saw a man so hungry for fame. He'd do anything to leave his mark on the world of science." The man snorted. "As if wealth and an earldom weren't enough for the lucky sod."

Vanessa swallowed a lump of shocked tears, watching across the way as Daniel concluded his short conversation with the now sheepish-looking youths.

"Eh, now, here he comes. Should we say our hallos?"

"Faith, no. I still owe the old fellow a hundred quid from a bet we made at White's."

"All right, then. Let's slip off before he sees us."

Holding her breath, Vanessa gripped the iron railing before her, praying she would not swoon as she'd done last night.

Ghastly creature . . . keeping one to study . . . He'd do anything . . . desperate to make a name for himself . . .

Great Mother, was that why he'd brought her to England? To study her as he studied other animals?

Daniel smiled indulgently as he approached. "Satisfied?"

By some miracle, she managed to bob her head up and down.

"Onward to the Monkey House?"

In a daze, Vanessa allowed him to steer her toward an elaborate domed cage where dozens of monkeys leaped about on trees and ropes, shrieking furiously at the people on the other side of the bars. An unpleasant odor issued from the cage, a scent Vanessa decided had to be that of captivity.

She tried to calm herself as she stood there, but the angry cries of the monkeys scraped across her nerves like nettles, and suddenly, the mob of people seemed to be talking too loudly, all at once, in strident voices that matched the monkeys'.

Ghastly creature.

He'd do anything.

"Fascinating animal, the monkey," Daniel said, as if delivering a lecture to a classroom. "Darwin and I have often discussed the significance of the opposable thumb. . . ."

Her stomach was churning like the waters of a rain-swollen river.

"Why, heavens, would you look at that woman, Amanda?" a thin voice hissed. "Have you ever seen anyone of such a size? Do you think she could be the one Mrs. Hook was talking about yesterday?"

Vanessa swung around to find two elderly

women staring at her as if she was some sort of carnival attraction. Daniel, still expounding on the importance of thumbs, evidently had not heard their comments above the din the monkeys were making and his own monologue.

She spun away from the women, a panic coming over her, the sort of panic that left her mouth dry and her limbs quivering and weak. Mother help her, she had to know. Did Daniel see her as these women did? An oddity? A freak?

She had to know the truth. She had to know because . . . she had fallen in love with Daniel. She loved him when, only a few months earlier, she had not even known the meaning of the word. She loved him completely, painfully. Despite his shortcomings. Despite his faults. Throughout their relationship, Daniel had shown her both kindness and indifference, his behavior unpredictable from one day to the next. Yet it had mattered not to her heart. Her heart belonged to him. Belonged to this intelligent, enigmatic man of fierce pride and private fears.

And what was she to him? She had to find out. For in her womb, she carried their child, a child she already cherished with all of her being.

The world around her blurred into a watery landscape of indefinite colors and shapes, the ambient noise receding to a low, distant buzz. Vanessa breathed deeply, digging her nails into her palms, searching for the strength she needed to ask what she must. Inside the ornate enclosure, a small brown monkey watched her with compassionate, white-ringed eyes, looking as if he understood the reasons behind her distress.

"Daniel." She was surprised to hear her voice sound so composed, so quiet. "Is *this* why you brought me to England? To study me as you study these monkeys?"

At her side, she felt him go rigid, like a man turned to stone. No heated denials. No surprise other than that of discovery. Bravely, Vanessa forced herself to look into Daniel's face, only to find the awful confession written in the tight lines of his expression.

Pain shot through her then, twisting her gut, closing her throat.

"This is what I am to you? A creature to be studied? The subject of a treatise? A means by which to gain recognition among your naturalist peers?"

He opened his mouth. No words came forth.

Vanessa felt the panic inside her surge to suffocating proportions. All around her, she could feel people staring, whispering. It was unbearable.

She turned and vanished into the crowd in a matter of seconds.

Chapter Twenty-one

"You must know where she is."

"I do not. She refused to tell me where she was going, although I begged her to. I asked her if she might reconsider, if there was anything that I might do to help, but she insisted that she had to get away. She said only that she could not stay at Perkins House because you would most certainly come looking for her here."

In that moment, Daniel would have loved nothing more than to wring Samantha Perkins's pretty little neck. "Good God, woman, how could you let Vanessa leave without knowing where she was bound? Have you no sense at all?"

He raked both hands through his hair until the ends stood up like porcupine quills, privately wondering what right he had to question Miss Perkins's sanity when his own hung precariously in the balance. In the three hours since Vanessa had disappeared from his side, Daniel had felt as if he were slowly sliding toward the abyss of madness. One minute Vanessa had been standing there, her beautiful golden eyes awash with misery and hurt and, in the next minute, she was gone.

He'd searched the zoo for well over an hour, never imagining that she would be able to find her way out of Regent's Park, never believing that she could have disappeared as quickly as she did. But she had.

According to Samantha Perkins, Vanessa had arrived back at Cavendish Square almost two hours earlier, departing again within twenty or thirty minutes.

"Did she take all her things, her clothes and such?"

"She took two small traveling bags, and I insisted she accept my pin money."

"Pin money?" Daniel wanted either to laugh or to scream his lungs hoarse. "This is London, for God's sake, woman! Vanessa cannot survive out there with *pin money.*" He thrust his fists onto his hips with enough force to bruise them, his gaze sweeping through the Perkinses' parlor as if he hoped to find Vanessa hiding beneath an occasional table.

"Dammit," he burst out, "I cannot believe that you let her get away!"

Samantha regarded him coolly, her blond brows arching with disdain. "I cannot believe that you did, either."

That brought him up short. And cooled his temper a degree or two. After all, he was the one responsible for Vanessa's disappearance, not Samantha Perkins.

In a tone significantly more restrained and polite, he asked, "Did she give you any clues at all to where she was going?"

"No, not really. She asked me not to worry, saying that she knew of someone who would help her." Samantha shrugged in evident puzzlement. "But I do not know whom she could be speaking of, since she's scarcely met anyone since arriving in London."

"Unless she befriended someone at the party last evening." Daniel's eyes tapered into thoughtful slits. "As I recall, she was dancing with that redheaded chap when she fainted. Perhaps he said something to her, issued an improper proposal. . . ."

"Sir Stuart? Gracious, I should think not. Very respectable, very upstanding young gentleman. He's entering the clergy, you know."

"Is he?" Daniel asked, thinking that some of the most corrupt men he'd met in his lifetime had been men of the cloth. "Nonetheless, Sir Stuart is as good a place to start as any."

"What do you plan to do?"

"I plan to find Vanessa. And if that means hunting down every single person with whom she has come into contact since stepping foot on English soil, then so be it."

"Oh, my. Well, there cannot be *that* many people," Samantha said, striving toward optimism. "Except for last night."

"I'll need the invitation list."

"Yes, of course. I have it right here." Walking to a painted secretaire, Samantha shuffled through a pile of letters, emerging with a sheaf of paper. "Here."

She handed Daniel the list, then looped her hands together, twisting them anxiously back and forth. "I fear, however, it may take days, perhaps even weeks, to reach all of those people. Is there not a faster way to try to locate Vanessa?"

"I suppose I could engage a private investigator."

Although Daniel did not relish the idea of hiring a man to track Vanessa down, he relished far less the thought of her wandering unprotected through the dangerous streets of London.

"If only I could have prevented her from leaving." Samantha lowered her gaze to her knotted fingers, a slight quiver audible in her voice. "Beneath that gentle nature lies a strong and decisive character, Lord Heywood, and from what I could see, Vanessa was determined to leave. Nothing I said would sway her." Samantha shook her head sadly. "She seemed rather upset."

Another shot of guilt rushed into Daniel's gut. "Do not blame yourself, Miss Perkins. I am the one at fault, not you. I . . . apologize for my earlier ungraciousness."

Angry with himself—and rightfully so, he thought—Daniel shoved his hat onto his head, anxious to resume his search. Every minute was precious now. Every minute.

As he headed toward the door, Daniel caught a glimpse of himself in one of the silvered mirrors flanking the fireplace. He looked like hell. He'd have to clean himself up before he went knocking at doors if he hoped to be received anywhere.

"Ah, Miss Perkins, one more thing—" Daniel paused on the threshold and turned around, mangling the list in his left hand. "I know I've not done much to give you a good opinion of me, yet I would ask a favor of you nonetheless. If you do hear from Vanessa, would you send me a message right away? No matter the time of day?"

"Naturally, I will let you know if I have word of her." Her eyes clouded over to a dark blue-gray. "Unless, that is, Vanessa expressly forbids it."

Daniel's jaw clenched. He wanted to shout at the silly girl to do as she was asked, blast it all. Instead he nodded courteously and walked from the room, determined to turn London upside down if he had to. He had to find Vanessa.

* * *

"This is an unexpected pleasure."

The Earl Bretton rose and walked around his ivory inlaid desk to take hold of Vanessa's hand. His fingers pressed hers firmly, his touch impersonal, as his dark cocoa eyes, so exactly like Daniel's, bored into her with unsettling intensity.

"Please sit down."

He released her hand and waited until Vanessa seated herself in a stiff-backed caned chair before he took the seat opposite. Like Daniel, he was a large man by English standards, wide in the shoulders with heavy, well-developed arms and a broad chest. More particular in dress than his son, he wore a fashionably tailored coat, his simple neckcloth neatly tied and unadorned.

The earl said nothing, merely steepled his fingers before him in an expectant pose. And waited.

Vanessa swallowed and glanced at the earl's card, clutched in her fingers. "I need to leave London."

"Ah." His fingertips tapped together. "Where do you wish to go?"

"I think that I must return home. To Eldra'to."

A silvery brow lifted. "Eldra'to? I presume we speak of South America?"

Vanessa licked at her lips, wishing she'd stopped long enough at the Perkins house to eat. The scent of tobacco in the room was not sitting well on her empty stomach. "Yes. I need your assistance in arranging transport back to South America."

"Hmm." The earl's head tipped to the side, as if he were weighing her statement with care. "Is there a reason why Daniel does not simply book you passage on the next ship leaving London?"

Vanessa fought the rush of embarrassed color to her cheeks. "Daniel does not know of my plans."

She noted the interest that flared in the earl's light smile. "He does not know that you've come to me?"

She wagged her head, sending a silent prayer to the Mother that she had not erred in seeking out Lord Bretton. He was a hard man—she could see that. Everything about him was severe, from his uncompromisingly stiff posture to the austere cut of his jacket.

"I take it, then, that you and Daniel have quarreled?"

"No. Not exactly."

Those eagle eyes honed in on her. "What is it, then? Exactly?"

Brushing a lock of hair from her neck, Vanessa reminded herself that this man had no tolerance for weakness. She could not be weak.

"It is complicated." She filled her lungs, then emptied them, the lingering scent of tobacco clinging in her nostrils. "Daniel views me as a vehicle by which he can advance his career," she said, choosing her words with painstaking care. "I happen to see myself as more than that."

"Indeed? And just how do you see yourself?" Lord Bretton asked sharply.

Vanessa refused to be cowed. "I do *not* see myself as a savage, untamed creature plucked from the wilds. And I do *not* see myself as an oddity to be evaluated or studied by a team of gawking scientists."

The earl's mouth thinned. "So you persist in the pretense of this story?"

"Believe what you will, but I speak the truth. I am an Ama'zon."

Flicking his wrist in a cynical motion, he dismissed her claim summarily. "Not that it matters."

Vanessa rose from her chair, her fists clenched. "It matters to me, Lord Bretton. I do not tell falsehoods."

Their gazes locked and held. The earl appraised her through narrowed eyes.

"Sit down, girl," he finally ordered. "No need to get your back up."

She reclaimed her seat, as he continued to stare at her for another long minute.

"There is more to this tale, isn't there?"

Vanessa felt the cords of her neck tighten. "What do you mean?"

The earl leaned forward in his chair, light from the window glinting off the silver streaks at his temples. "There is something that you are not telling me."

Indecision held Vanessa's tongue silent.

Could she trust him? She knew she would have to trust someone soon, for she'd not be able to keep her condition a secret much longer.

"See here, I'll not help you," the earl warned, "if you are not completely honest with me. Withholding the truth is as good as lying, you know."

She squared her jaw, then took a deep breath. "I carry Daniel's child."

Lord Bretton's reaction was not what she'd anticipated. She had expected him to distrust her, to question her again just as he'd questioned her ancestry. Instead she watched, surprised, as the blood drained from his face, stealing a good dozen years from his youthful appearance.

"Impossible," he murmured, sinking into his chair. "Yet I had always wondered—Are you certain?"

Heat filtered into Vanessa's cheeks. "Of my condition? Or of the father?"

He nodded, asking for an answer to each.

"I am utterly certain of both."

The earl passed a shaky hand over his eyes, while Vanessa felt the tension in her shoulders ease. She felt so very relieved to realize that the earl had accepted her word. That he had not doubted her.

"You've not told Daniel, have you?" Lord Bretton said in a low, raspy voice.

"No."

"Of course not," the earl muttered. "He'd

never have let you out of his sight had he known. Are you aware that Daniel believes himself to be incapable of fathering children?"

"Yes, he told me."

"Do you plan to tell him of this child?"

"I . . . I do not know."

Lord Bretton scratched at his chin, the harshness of his features softened as he lost himself in private deliberation.

Observing him, Vanessa thought she might at last understand the reason for the apparent friction between Daniel and his father. Strong and stubborn, both men possessed wills of iron; both needed to be dominant and in command.

"You cannot travel," the earl abruptly announced.

"I beg your pardon?"

"It's not healthy for the babe."

Instinctively, Vanessa splayed a protective palm over her abdomen.

The earl's gaze followed her movement. "Just how far along are you?"

"Over three months."

"Hmm, good. Rarely will—"

He was interrupted by a quick rap at the door, which was immediately followed by a woman rushing into the room in a flurry of violet skirts. Gray-haired, with pale, nervous eyes that constantly shifted back and forth, she was small yet elegant, attired in the very height of fashion. Jewels glittered at her ears, neck and wrists.

"Bretton, I must speak with you."

"We have company." His expression cold with displeasure, the earl remained in his chair, not rising as courtesy demanded.

"Oh." The woman, who could only have been Lady Bretton, gave an anxious little start as her gaze fell upon Vanessa. *"O-oh,"* she repeated.

"Constance, this is—"

"I know what she is," Lady Bretton said, her nose tilting haughtily toward the coffered ceiling, a shudder of distaste shaking her frail shoulders.

Lord Bretton regarded his wife with scorn. "Vanessa will be accompanying us back to Bretton Hall tomorrow."

"Wh-what?" Lady Bretton blinked once, twice, then started to puff up like an irritated pigeon. "Bretton, have you not heard the gossip surrounding this—"

"Constance."

Even Vanessa, who had rarely known fear, felt a tremor pass through her at the threat implicit in the earl's voice.

"Go see to the arrangements," her husband directed. "Now."

Lady Bretton's hand rose shakily to her throat, her gold bracelets tinkling. Eyes wide, she glanced at Vanessa once more, then hurried from the room.

An awkward hush fell.

"I-I do not understand," Vanessa stammered.

"You wish to leave London, do you not?"

"Y-yes . . ."

"And since you cannot risk the safety of the babe on a long ocean voyage, you will stay with us in Lincolnshire until my heir is born."

"But, I—" *But I cannot bear to remain in England.* What if Daniel were to visit his parents and find her at Bretton Hall? Could her already broken heart suffer the pain of seeing him again?

"Don't be foolish, girl," the earl said. "I will stand for no arguments. You must consider what is best for the child now."

Vanessa nodded, her teeth worrying at her lower lip. Yes, she had to do what was best for Daniel's child.

"And after the baby is born, you will help me return to my home?" she persisted.

The earl peered at his fingernails, his fingers spread open on the arm of the chair. "If you still want to return to South America after my grandson is born, then . . . yes, I will help you."

Grandson? Vanessa was about to explain that Ama'zon did not bear male offspring, when she caught her tongue between her teeth. Could she be certain she carried a daughter? After all, Daniel had believed himself to be infertile, yet his babe was growing in her womb. Was it not possible that she, who had always been different than other Ama'zon, might give birth to a boy?

She had no way to be sure and, since the earl was obviously set on a male child, she did not want to disappoint him with her suspicions.

"You will not tell Daniel, will you?"

"No." The earl smiled cryptically. "The question is: will you?"

Vanessa turned away to glance out the window. She did not have an answer to that question.

Chapter Twenty-two

Spring had come to the city, laying her cloak of greenery across the land in the form of velvet tree buds and satiny sprays of flowering color. As Londoners emerged from their homes after the long, cold winter, they hit the city's streets in good cheer, pleased with England's political and economic climate, as guided by their happy queen, a newly wedded bride.

It was a time of peace in the city, a time when Daniel ought to have enjoyed walking the quiet paths of Hyde Park, listening to the birds celebrate the dramatic change of season. But Daniel Heywood could take no joy in this day or any other, for he was living a hell—and one of his own making.

Three long months he had searched, and

searched in vain. It was, as Samantha Perkins claimed, as if Vanessa had simply vanished into thin air. Although Daniel had employed six separate investigators during this time, none had been able to turn up even the smallest clue as to Vanessa's whereabouts. They'd interviewed hansom cab drivers and railway workers and hotel proprietors. They'd explored hospitals and whorehouses and prisons. Dozens and dozens of leads had been followed week after week, all eventually leading to the same discouraging place: nowhere.

Daniel had even traveled to Devonport in search of MacDougal, in the hope that Vanessa had sought out her shipboard confidant. But Mac had left on a surveying expedition for the Admiralty a full fortnight before Daniel's arrival. And, after talking to people in town, Daniel had quit Devonport convinced there had been no woman accompanying the friendly Scotsman on his journey to the west.

Rolling his neck on his shoulders, Daniel tried to ease the cramp at his nape. He was tired. He'd not been sleeping well these last weeks, tormented by visions of Vanessa as he'd seen her last, wounded and bewildered, her lovely cat eyes shining with unshed tears.

"Hell," he muttered, and savagely kicked out at a stone on the path, the toe of his boot digging through the dun-colored dust.

He was haunted by that day at the zoo, particularly by those few crucial seconds when he'd been shocked silent by Vanessa's painful questions. That silence had cost him, by Jove. It had cost him dearly. If only he'd not been so taken aback; if only he'd answered her immediately, instead of finding his tongue tied up in knots.

But she'd caught him off guard. Not only the nature of her questions, but the manner in which she had phrased them had left him stunned and speechless. And overwhelmed with guilt.

A creature to be studied? Like the monkeys in their cages? Lord, what had she thought? Did she believe he planned to bottle her in alcohol and place her on a shelf? Pin her to a cardboard square? Yet if she had not hit so closely to the truth, he would have been able to answer her. He wouldn't have stood there like an idiot incapable of coherent speech.

The truth, blast it, was that he *had* been studying her and that he *had* been using her. He'd been using her to advance his consequence in his circle of colleagues, to advance his career. Of course, Vanessa had known of his interest in her culture. She was well aware of the focus of his research.

Yet he had not been truly honest with her, had he? Never had he discussed with Vanessa his plans for the treatise, never had he revealed to her the scope of his aspirations. Because in the darkest, most secret corner of his soul, he'd been ashamed. Ashamed of himself for exploiting this woman in every way possible. Exploiting her mind, her heritage, her emotions . . . her body.

God help him, he had inadvertently treated Vanessa with the same lack of compassion with which he had been raised. Forced to become the man his father had envisioned, rather than allowed to grow as he needed to grow, he had rebelled. Yet had he not done the same to Vanessa? Objectified her, forced her to fulfill the vision of what he desired her to be?

The breeze ruffled through his hair in a soft caress, a bitter mimicry of Vanessa's gentle touch. How he ached for her. After so much time, he would have expected his need for her to have abated, but nothing could have been further from the truth. She occupied his every waking thought—and his sleeping ones, as well—to the exclusion of all else. Nothing mattered but that he should find her again. If for no other reason than that his conscience might finally be put at ease as to her well-being.

A squirrel scampered across the path ahead of him, drawing his gaze forward to the grove of newly leafed trees. The sun, sitting low on the horizon, shone bright in his eyes. It was time for him to make a decision. He had to decide whether or not to return to the Amazon. There was, after all, a very slim chance that Vanessa had been able to borrow money from this mystery friend of hers and book passage back to South America. God knows they'd not been able to find a trace of her here in London.

But an ocean voyage would take many long months. What if Vanessa was suddenly to resurface, looking for him? What if she was in danger and needed him?

Daniel shoved his fists under his arms, sighing with angry frustration, as he circled back in the direction of his town house. The hour was still early, the park virtually empty. Empty, he suddenly noticed, but for the lone figure jogging toward him. Lifting a hand to his brow, Daniel shielded his eyes from the sun, squinting east. The man was running in livery. *His* livery.

A spurt of heat rushed into Daniel's stomach as he too broke into a half-run.

"M'lord," the footman called, breathing heavily, as he neared. "Mister Rollo sent me to look for you, m'lord. A message has come."

"Go on. Fetch it."

The spaniel tilted his head to the side, his liquid brown eyes gazing adoringly at Vanessa, his tongue lolling wet and pink from the side of his mouth. He paid no attention to the slobber-soaked stick she'd just tossed to the other side of the lawn.

"Had enough, have you?" Vanessa squatted low, her distended stomach making the movement more difficult than it had been even a few weeks earlier.

She scratched behind the dog's floppy ears, the hem of her skirts growing heavy with dew. A pair of jays pecked through the grass nearby, hunting for their breakfast. The spaniel spied them and gave chase, his excited bark loud in the hush of early morning.

Vanessa pushed to her feet and smiled softly. This had become her favorite time of day, these untroubled hours following dawn. It was the only time that was truly hers, when she did not have to worry about encountering Lady Bretton's disapproving frown or Lord Bretton's proprietary scrutiny. It was the only time of day when she felt truly relaxed and free.

Since arriving in Lincolnshire, Vanessa had learned a great deal about the environment in which Daniel had been raised. To her dismay, she had discovered that it had not been so very different from her own. Like Eldra'to, there was an absence of emotion at Bretton Hall, a scarcity of feeling. *At least, feelings of warmth,* she thought to herself.

It had not taken her long to realize that the earl and countess disliked each other with a painful and unwavering intensity. Lord Bretton thought his wife silly and shallow and made no efforts to pretend otherwise; and Lady Bretton, while both fearing and resenting her husband, persisted in provoking the earl, rather like those young men at the zoo had enjoyed provoking the caged bear.

It was not a happy home, Bretton Hall. And Vanessa had felt very lonely within its walls.

Although the earl watched over her as if she were a priceless and fragile treasure, never allowing her to leave the grounds or to travel into town, Vanessa understood that his concern was not for her, but for the child she carried. He treated her politely—as politely as he was able—yet took no real interest in her aside from monitoring her health, and the food she ate, and the hours she slept. It was as if she were being kept in a cage. A beautiful, spacious cage called Bretton Hall.

Therefore, Vanessa had been glad to hear the earl announce last week that he needed to make a short trip to London. Not only would she enjoy seven days free of his constant supervision, but she'd seen the trip as the perfect opportunity to get a message to Samantha Perkins.

Lord Bretton had discouraged Vanessa from writing to Samantha these last months. He'd warned her that Daniel would learn of her whereabouts and come after her and the baby. But Vanessa had been unable to bear the thought of her friend worrying. Especially after all that Samantha had done for her. So she'd paid the coachman a pound from Samantha's pin money and asked him to secretly deliver the message once they'd arrived in London.

Vanessa had felt almost cheery yesterday afternoon as she'd waved off the earl's carriage. As cheery as she could remember being in quite some time.

A high-pitched barking pulled Vanessa from her thoughts as she watched the red-and-white spaniel scamper excitedly across the grass toward the manor house. To her surprise, Vanessa saw that it was Lady Bretton who had caught the dog's attention. Picking her way gingerly across the still damp lawn, the countess was fighting to keep the spaniel at bay with the tip of her parasol.

Vanessa frowned, wondering what had persuaded Lady Bretton to rise so early when it was her habit to linger in her rooms until well past noon.

"There you are," Lady Bretton grumbled, stating the obvious, as she took one more swat at the poor dog scampering around her skirts. "Come on, girl," she said, and waved with her parasol in the direction of the house. "We haven't much time."

Vanessa pressed a hand to her lower back. "Time for what?"

The countess's rouged mouth pursed with annoyance. "For you to catch your ride."

"Am I going somewhere?"

"You want to go home, do you not?" the lady snapped. "Home to your"—her upper lip curled—"jungle?"

"Y-yes."

"Well, then, let us be quick about it. If you miss the ship, I do not know when I'll be able to get you on another."

Vanessa rubbed at her back, feeling the baby give her a light kick near the ribs. "I do not understand. Lord Bretton has said it was unsafe for the baby for me to hazard an ocean voyage."

"Nonsense! He merely spouted that rubbish to prevent you from going home, stupid girl. Women in your condition have to travel overseas all the time—don't you know anything?"

Vanessa's brow furrowed.

"Listen to me." The countess's pale green eyes glittered with impatience, shifting back and forth in a now familiar nervous manner. "Do you honestly believe that Bretton will allow you to leave once you birth his heir? Hah! Not likely. He'd sooner sacrifice a limb than see the future Earl Bretton carried away from Bretton Hall."

Her gaze dropped to Vanessa's rounded middle, her revulsion manifest. "Though I daresay he may someday let *you* go if you agree to leave the baby behind."

"Leave the baby?" Outraged, Vanessa shielded her stomach with both hands. "I would never!"

The countess nodded knowingly. "Then you best be prepared to live the rest of your days as a prisoner in this house," she threatened. "For I assure you that, whatever Bretton promised, he'll never let you return to the jungle with that child."

Vanessa swallowed and glanced at the palatial hall that stood like a fortress against the Lincolnshire landscape. Of late, she had been feeling conflicted, listening to the earl argue the many reasons that her child should be raised in England. He'd spoken of education and opportunity; of the earldom and its attached privilege and wealth. He'd made her question whether she was acting selfishly in choosing to return to Eldra'to.

Yet, if what Lady Bretton said was accurate, what price would her child be required to pay for this supposed privilege and wealth?

"And what of the scandal?" the countess continued relentlessly. "Do you want your son or daughter to be the subject of gossip as you have been? It is bad enough that the baby will be labeled a bastard, but to be viewed by society as some sort of savage freak . . ."

Vanessa masked a wince.

The countess leaned forward, her breath hot in Vanessa's face. "Is that what you want?"

"I-I—no, of course not. . . . But what should I do about Daniel?"

Suddenly, Vanessa felt overwhelmed with indecision. She had planned to tell Daniel about the baby eventually, only choosing to wait until her broken heart had mended somewhat. Yet, whenever she had contemplated writing to him, the old pain had resurfaced and she'd not been able to face the prospect of seeing him again. Not that she was convinced the earl would have permitted her to contact him, in any case.

"What about Daniel?" Lady Bretton countered angrily. "You said yourself he does not even consider you a real woman. And how *could* he—a primitive raised in the wilds? If you mean nothing to him, I should think he'd care even less about the child you carry."

That blow hit hard, driving the breath from Vanessa's body. Could it be so?

"For heaven's sake, we haven't time for your dawdling. It's not been easy arranging all this without Bretton's knowledge, you know."

Vanessa hesitated. Did Lady Bretton hope merely to thwart her husband by sending Vanessa away? Or was there truth in what the countess was saying?

Of course there was truth in it, Vanessa knew. She herself had worried for her baby's future if she remained in England, as the earl wanted. At all costs, she did not want her child to grow up feeling like an outsider, an oddity. *By the Mother, no.*

Whereas, if she returned to Eldra'to, she would need have no fears that the baby would be accepted, for the Ama'zon revered children. Unless, of course, the child had inherited Vanessa's emotional weakness. Or, worse yet, the child was born male.

Vanessa groaned and pressed her fingers to her temples. What to do?

Underlying her confusion was the almost forgotten issue of the mission foretold by the Seer. At one point, Vanessa had convinced herself that her mission was to learn of men and to share that knowledge with her people. Yet what had she learned? Only that a man could make your heart bleed if you were foolish enough to let him steal it from you.

"The child belongs with its own kind," the

countess hissed. "That is how it is meant to be."

Vanessa's head jerked toward Lady Bretton. "What did you say?"

"I said that the child is meant to be with its own kind."

Vanessa's fingers slowly traced the outline of her stomach, an idea taking hold. Could it be that this babe in her womb fulfilled the Seer's prophecy? That it was her child who was destined to be the Ama'zon's savior?

Perhaps . . .

Lady Bretton's patience had reached its end. She grabbed hold of Vanessa's hand and tugged her toward the house.

"Come on, girl. If you're going to be on board that ship, you've still got half of England to cross. I have already packed your belongings and the coach is waiting as we speak."

Vanessa stared numbly at Lady Bretton's graying head as she allowed herself to be half-dragged across the lawn. She could not be sure that the decision she was making was the right one, but she did know one thing for a certainty: no longer would she be following her heart. It hurt too much.

Chapter Twenty-three

"Where is she?"

Daniel exploded past the footman into the foyer of Bretton Hall, then spun around to glare daggers at the startled servant.

"Where is Vanessa?"

The footman, one not familiar to Daniel, blinked stupidly and rubbed at his eyes. "Lord Bretton?"

Daniel's fingers curled, and he realized that the poor man thought the earl had miraculously reversed the aging process.

"Heywood," Daniel ground out. "The earl's one and only son."

"Oh, m'lord, my apologies. I—"

"Never matter," Daniel said, brusquely waving the man aside. "Where can I find my father?"

"The earl has been in London, m'lord. Though he is expected home today."

"Dammit, did he take the woman with him? Vanessa?"

The footman shook his head in a quivering motion. "No, m'lord, I—"

"Daniel?"

Whirling about, Daniel followed his mother's voice to the top of the curving staircase. Though he'd seen her less than a year earlier, recent months had not been kind to Lady Bretton. She looked aged and haggard, and much older than the earl, though, in reality, she was eleven years her husband's junior.

Daniel raced to the foot of the staircase. "Where is she, Mother? Where is Vanessa?"

"Goodness, Daniel, must you create such a scene?" she asked coldly, starting down the stairs.

"By Jove, Mother, I give you fair warning—If you want a scene, I'll happily oblige. Now where is she?"

Lady Bretton paused, her hand clutching the mahogany railing. "She's gone."

A deathly silence descended. Then a deep voice thundered from the doorway loud enough to set the crystals in the chandelier to swaying. "*What?*"

All eyes swung to the Earl Bretton, standing

red-faced on the threshold of Bretton Hall. In his peripheral vision, Daniel saw the footman, quite sensibly, slink into the shadows, taking refuge from the impending storm.

"Now, Bretton, you needn't act as if—"

"Constance, I am going to throttle you with my bare hands!"

His face purple and mottled with rage, the earl charged across the foyer, his intent clearly murder. Daniel caught him at the first riser.

"Damn you, let me go," Lord Bretton roared, his gaze fixed on his countess, cowering halfway up the stairs.

"You can't kill her, you old fool," Daniel shouted, holding on to his father with all his might, amazed by the older man's strength. "And if you do, we'll never find out where Vanessa is."

A muscle in the earl's cheek pulsed. He ceased his strugglings, then pushed past Daniel with a muttered oath, his gaze never leaving Lady Bretton. At the back of his mind, Daniel wondered at the reason for the earl's fury, surprised that his father cared so deeply—hell, that he cared at all—what became of Vanessa.

"Allow me to take care of this," Daniel said in a low tone of undeniable command. A voice that he'd learned from his father. Above him, Lady Bretton was watching them through eyes wide with not just fear but also a touch of vengeful satisfaction.

"Lady, I will give you one opportunity to explain what has happened to Vanessa. If I object to your explanation, I will invite Father to speak with you."

"Daniel!" she gasped.

He merely drummed his fingers on the side of his leg, struggling to keep his own temper under control.

"It's not as if I did anything wrong," she said defiantly. "The girl wanted to go back to her jungle and I helped her to do so. I saw no reason that she should have to remain at Bretton Hall against her will."

"She wasn't being kept against her will, Constance, and you damn well know it," the earl shouted. "She was waiting for the birth!"

The—?

Something inside Daniel dropped like a lead weight into his gut. Slowly, very slowly, he turned to the earl.

"The birth of . . . what?"

Across the earl's features flitted an odd mixture of contempt and compassion.

"The birth of your son."

Daniel inched backward until his spine was supported by the wall. He felt exactly as he had after taking that poison dart in his thigh. Dizzy, light-headed, and distant from the earthly plane.

"It cannot be," he whispered to himself. "We were together only once."

"That's all it takes," the earl wryly interjected.

"But the doctors said it was not possible and, after all these years, surely—"

"Oh, poppycock!" his father blustered. "I never did believe those damned doctors and their quackery. It was simply a matter of finding the right girl for the seed to take."

Daniel was having trouble breathing, an insidiously wondrous joy seeping into his veins. Could it be? Vanessa pregnant with his child? Without a doubt, he knew the babe could be no one else's but his. Vanessa valued herself too highly to have allowed another man to trespass upon her. She had integrity, pride. And, sweet miracle, his babe growing in her womb.

Swiftly, Daniel tried to calculate, although his brain was not functioning at its best. "S-Six months?"

"That's about right," the earl said. "And by the size of her, you're going to have yourself a strappin' young lad, boy. A real Heywood."

Daniel slanted his father a bemused, sidelong glance. Apparently Lord Bretton did not know that the Ama'zon bore only daughters.

"When?" Daniel whirled around to stare up at his mother, his thoughts chaotic, jumbled, his emotions in an equal state of turmoil. "When did Vanessa leave? And how?"

Lady Bretton sniffed, dabbing at her eyes with the tips of her white-gloved fingers. "I hired a private coach to take her to Bristol. Mind you, I sent the girl off with a tidy purse—she'll not want for anything."

"Bristol?" Daniel echoed.

His mother licked nervously at her lips. "The *Adventurer* was supposed to have set sail two days ago."

"I swear to you, Constance—" The earl lunged forward, but Daniel barred him with an outstretched arm.

"The sailing may have been delayed," Daniel argued, with more confidence than he felt. "Unfavorable weather, a problem with the ship . . ."

"Yes, of course, it happens all the time," Lord Bretton said. "I'll call for fresh horses and we can be on the road before dusk. There's not a moment to lose."

"We?" Daniel's brows slashed together. "I believe I can take care of this on my own."

The earl's answering scowl was darker than Daniel's. "See here, boy, so far I'd say you've done a lamentable job of 'taking care of it.' Besides, I've an important matter to discuss with you on the way to Bristol."

Irritated by that damned label *boy,* Daniel pushed away from the wall, eager to bid goodbye to Bretton Hall and its crazed occupants.

"Nothing," he asserted, "can be more important right now than finding Vanessa."

"Not even finding your . . . *wife?"*

On the staircase, Lady Bretton let out a cry of horror. "Bretton, you didn't!"

Daniel's wary gaze shuttled back and forth between his parents. "For the love of God, now what?"

The earl's jaw set at a belligerent angle. "You didn't actually believe I would permit my heir to be born on the wrong side of the sheets, did you? You'd made a sorry mess of it, boy, and I had to clean up that mess." He directed a gnarled finger at Daniel. "And do not think for a minute that you can overturn what I've done."

His patience long past spent, Daniel rubbed at his temples, his chin sinking wearily to his chest. "And just what have you done?"

"What you should have done in the first place. I've wedded you to Vanessa. By proxy."

A dismayed groan came from Lady Bretton.

A disbelieving chuckle came from Daniel. All his life, his father had outdone him, eclipsing him even now when it came to being a stubborn, manipulative bastard.

"How in the blazes did you manage that? You don't hold my power of attorney."

"Hmmph. Well, I may have circumvented a few legal stumbling blocks," Lord Bretton conceded, "but my London solicitors maintain that the marriage is sound. Provided it's not contested." His brown eyes narrowed threateningly. "And it won't be contested, will it?"

"Not by me," Daniel assured. He only hoped he'd be able to enjoy a wedding night someday.

"Not by Vanessa either. I'm sure the girl is smart enough to do what's right for the child."

"I hope so," Daniel said, thinking of the difficult trip across the Atlantic, only to be followed by the long, arduous trek through the danger-ridden Amazon.

"And let us hope that you are smart enough not to argue with me," the earl said, "for I *am* accompanying you to Bristol."

In dire need of fresh horses, Daniel didn't see how he had any choice in the matter, and shrugged in acceptance.

"As for you, Constance." The earl turned his merciless gaze on the countess. "You had better pray that your son and I return with Lady Heywood because, if we do not, you will be enjoying a prolonged and expansive tour of the continent."

Vanessa watched the English coastline fade away until only a cobalt blue ribbon of ocean bordered the horizon. She was exhausted both physically and emotionally after her hurried trip across England.

She had noticed of late how her pregnancy magnified feelings, amplified her worry, her sorrow, her doubts. Not only had her body reacted differently to events she might have met with strength before, but pregnancy had given her new *reasons* to worry.

It was difficult enough to leave Daniel, herself. But now that she was carrying his child, she had also to consider what was best for the baby. And that had not been easy for her to do.

Lady Bretton had persuasively argued that Daniel would not want a child who could never really belong to his world. A child who would only register as an oddity, an outcast. But Vanessa doubted Lady Bretton. She knew Daniel well enough to understand that he *would* want to keep his child near, to protect and educate him.

But Daniel would not want her. In fact, he would probably have difficulty conceiving of her as anything more important than the vessel for his heir. The fact that he considered her a barbarian, had planned to study her and write about her—both showed the low esteem in which he held her. Vanessa could not stand that. For her own self-respect, and for her child's, she could not be less than she was—a proud, Ama'zon woman.

Pressing both hands into the curve of her spine, Vanessa arched and tilted her face up to the sky, eyes closed, hoping the weak sunlight might warm her skin and, through it, her chilled soul.

"Pardon me, my dear. Do you need to sit down?"

Vanessa started at the starchy English matron's accent, which sounded uncomfortably similar to that of Lady Bretton.

"No. I am fine. Thank you," she said, turning to the woman who had spoken, a woman who, at first glance, did indeed resemble Daniel's mother.

To judge by the quality of her dress, the woman was of the upper classes, but there her similarity to Lady Bretton ended. This woman looked to be genuinely kind. Her blue eyes shone with intelligence, and her mouth was soft and good-natured. She wore her hair pulled back in a practical yet flattering style, not tortured into ringlets as the countess had worn hers. In her left hand, she clutched a pile of handwritten notes, in her right, a tattered copy of the *Westminster Review*.

"Bless me, my hands are so full, I cannot properly introduce myself. Forgive me, dear," she clucked, "I am Mrs. Edgar Longhorn."

"I am Vanessa." She curtseyed as she'd been taught.

"Child, excuse me for being direct, but you look frightful. You're tired, aren't you?"

Vanessa nodded, smiling.

"Is this your first?" Mrs. Longhorn asked, gesturing with her notes to Vanessa's stomach.

"Yes, it is."

"Well, I've delivered four of my own, and I can remember the need for a little kindness along the way, let me tell you. Come, dear, I insist you join me for a cup of tea in my quarters."

"Oh, that's very kind, but—"

"Now, now, none of that. Nothing would give me more pleasure than if you'd let me mother you a bit," the woman said wistfully. "Mine have all left the nest and I do miss fussing over someone."

"Mr. Longhorn won't allow you to fuss over him?" Vanessa asked shyly.

"Pooh. I may as well fuss over a potted plant as to get any notice from Edgar."

She laughed uproariously at her own joke, and Vanessa joined in.

"Come." Mrs. Longhorn waved her notes and periodical. "My friend is making an utter fool of himself in these essays he keeps publishing, and I need help in drafting a letter. You look like the kind of girl who could help me spot a stupid line."

Mrs. Longhorn looped her arm through Vanessa's as she began to explain why she needed Vanessa to come share her overly large cabin with her, and how it would ease her mind so much to not have to sleep alone, and how she couldn't bear Mr. Longhorn's snoring. . . .

For the first time in many months, Vanessa felt herself relax, suddenly all too eager to let the kindly Mrs. Longhorn mother her as much as she desired.

Chapter Twenty-four

Daniel wiped at his brow with the back of his hand as he walked back up the gangplank to the *Lion,* the unimpressive yet speedy three-master that had carried his father and himself across the wide Atlantic. The earl had leased the ship out of Bristol for an ungodly sum, promising its captain triple the standard fee if he could assemble a crew and ready the ship to sail within the week. Money had proven, yet again, to be the most powerful of incentives.

Throughout the nine-week voyage, they'd been hot on the trail of the *Adventurer,* though never quite able to overtake her. The passage, plagued by storms, had proved a rough one; so rough that, at one point, the earl had become convinced their demise was imminent. Summoning Daniel to him, Lord Bretton had tried to make peace with his son in his own pompous and domineering fashion. And, although the breach between father and son was far from mended, some healing had taken place. Enough healing to where the enmity Daniel had previously felt for his father had dulled to a prosaic acceptance. An acceptance of the fact that to despise his father was to despise himself, for their similarities were many, their faults the same.

On the *Lion*'s deck, Lord Bretton waited in a chair shaded by the foremast. He jumped up as soon as he saw Daniel come aboard.

"Well?" he demanded. His complexion was florid from the heat. "What have you learned?"

Daniel sighed, squinting into the sun as he tugged at the brim of his hat. "She's not in port."

"Damnation!" The earl stomped his boot to the deck. "What of the child?"

Daniel allowed himself a small half-smile. "By all accounts, Vanessa's health was excellent and she did not suffer unduly during the voyage. I was told that a woman by the name of Longhorn befriended her and attended to her like the proverbial mother hen."

"Thank heavens," the earl breathed. "But where has the girl gone off to?"

Daniel pulled at his hat again, feeling perspiration slide down his neck in a chilling stream. "Four days ago she was able to arrange for passage to Barra. Evidently, since I last visited the jungle, there's been a rush of interest in rubber. Some American has developed a method to process the stuff, and now people are pouring into the region by the boatload. Vanessa had no difficulty finding transport up the river."

"How far is Barra?"

"Roughly another eight hundred miles into the Amazon."

"Good God." The earl mopped at his forehead with his kerchief. "And from Barra, how much farther do you estimate it is to this Amazon village of hers?"

Daniel shrugged, that same uncertainty gnawing away at him. Throughout the voyage, he'd been praying that they'd be able to overtake Vanessa along the way, since he seriously questioned whether he'd be able to locate Eldra'to amid the jungle's never-ending maze of trees and brush. He had been unconscious on his arrival in the Ama'zon city and running for his life at his departure. Would he be able to find it again? Throughout centuries innumerable, Eldra'to had managed to remain hidden from the rest of the world. For him to find it again, he would need a miracle. An absolute miracle.

"I am not sure. The *Angela* never sailed as far as Barra; we veered south about fifty miles to the east of the settlement."

"Do you suppose we might catch up with her?"

Daniel quieted his inner uneasiness. "It's possible. Especially if we pull anchor tomorrow."

Lord Bretton snorted lightly. "I'll speak with the captain. We'll sail on the morrow."

As his father promised, the *Lion* left Belem the following day to wind its way up the sienna-colored waters of the great river. Despite the heat, Daniel clung to the ship's railing from dawn to dusk each day, searching for familiar landmarks. A sandy cove, a native village, an oddly shaped fork in the river. They all looked familiar, dammit, but none held the key to the lost city of Eldra'to.

"You cannot doubt," his father said, as they stood side by side on the evening of their fourth day out of Belem. "We must never doubt ourselves, Daniel. Never. To believe in oneself is power, the key to success."

Daniel nodded, determined not to surrender to his misgivings. He had found Vanessa before; he'd find her again.

Gripping the rail with white-knuckled force, he asked himself for the hundredth time, *why?* Why had he been such a damned fool? Why had it taken him so long to see that he had fallen in love with this woman, this unique and wonderful woman who epitomized strength and intelligence and beauty? And most importantly, humanity. The ability to care.

In retrospect, he realized that he had to have been in love with Vanessa long before that day at the zoo; yet would he have ever recognized it if she'd not flung those ugly accusations in his face? Absorbed in himself and his blasted career, he'd never stopped to examine his feelings for her—because he'd been afraid to.

Perhaps he'd been afraid to confess to his feelings, for then he'd have been forced to confront his unforgivable treatment of Vanessa. He'd set her up as a tool, a means of achieving his end. He'd not treated her with the dignity she deserved. And, by God, he was ashamed now.

With a consoling pat on his back, his father left to go read in his cabin, while Daniel remained at the railing, watching the sun fall away from the sky in a blaze of orange-red glory. It seemed like a lifetime ago that he'd stood like this onboard the *Angela,* desperate to find his own private redemption within the Amazon wilds. He had found it, all right. But it hadn't been the fame he'd been looking for. It hadn't been recognition from his peers. It had been the love of a woman.

As darkness fell, the jungle came alive with its nocturnal melody, mosquitoes humming, birds crying, palm fronds whispering in the breeze. Closing his eyes, Daniel allowed the sounds to carry him away to the past, to a time when—

He froze, a sense of urgency suddenly bringing his nerve endings to life. *That song. That rhythm of the wilds.* It was as he remembered it from almost a year earlier. It called to him.

He strained forward, leaning over the railing toward the shore. Though the black night revealed nothing, Daniel could not deny what he felt. It was the same excitement that had driven him into the jungle depths, driven him ultimately to Eldra'to and Vanessa.

Good Lord, was his imagination playing tricks upon him? Or were his instincts guiding him, the same instincts that had guided him nearly a year ago to his destiny?

He could not doubt himself. Whirling around, Daniel made straight for the captain's cabin. He knew he must go ashore.

"Are you sure about this?" his father questioned less than an hour later, as the moon hovered at its peak high in the velvet-soft sky. "Shouldn't you consider waiting until sunrise?"

Daniel, with no more than a pack of meager supplies, was preparing to climb into the ship's dinghy. "You were the one who told me not to doubt myself."

His father muttered something unintelligible, the swaying lanterns washing his worried face in an eerie, flickering white light.

"You go on to Barra," Daniel said. "I'll meet up with you there."

"Dammit, at least let one of us go with you," Lord Bretton insisted.

Daniel paused in setting the oars and glanced up. "I have to do this on my own. You know that."

The earl's jaw clenched in obvious frustration. "Daniel, you do not have to prove anything to me."

"No, Father, I don't." His mouth quirked to one side. "I think I have finally come to understand that."

The wind was ripe with the scent of grass and sea as Daniel turned to gaze into the impenetrable night. "But I do have to prove something to myself."

He gave his father a brief salute, then descended into the dinghy. The launch made a hollow, splashing sound as it hit the water, and then Daniel began, with long, firm strokes, to row toward shore. When the hull scraped the bank, Daniel jumped out and hauled the craft onto the marshy beach. He secured the dinghy well, hiding it behind a grouping of reeds, knowing that his life might well depend on whether he was able to locate it later.

Hauling his pack onto his back, he struck out, guided only by instinct and the welcome light of the moon. Traveling by night, he soon realized, was an altogether different experience than traveling by day. Cooler, as a result of the breeze, the night air was also filled with mosquitoes and gnats and chiggers who preyed on the few areas of bare flesh, like wrists and neck, that he'd foolishly left unprotected.

Nonetheless, Daniel found it easier to hack his way through the forest without the oppressive heat of the sun weighing upon him. He walked as his feet led him, trusting that whatever had called to him from the jungle would guide him in the direction he needed to go.

He walked until the sun rose too high for comfort, then slept away the afternoon. He ate some from his supplies, supplementing them with the native foods Vanessa had taught him were safe. He was ever vigilant of the dangers that lurked behind each tree, each bush, each deceptively lovely orchid spray.

After three long days of traveling in this manner, Daniel began to grow anxious. He was getting close; he could sense it. He could feel the tension beginning to draw taut his gut.

On the fourth day, however, he sensed that he had gone too far, and he spent that night backtracking, his hands raw from countless hours of wielding his machete. He also depleted the last of his fresh water supply.

The morning of the fifth day found Daniel hunched at the base of a rubber tree, just listening. Listening to the jungle, waiting for a sign. He knew he was where he should be. He knew it. But, while he'd searched every hollow, explored every gully, he could not find the trail to Eldra'to. He hoped that eventually he might be discovered by one of the Ama'zon, by a warrior party out on patrol or a healer who'd left the city to comb the forest for herbs.

Though he'd waited, and hunted hours on end for an access to the trail, he found nothing. Daniel was beginning to lose hope. Exhaustion, hunger and mental fatigue were beginning to drain him of the confidence that had driven him all these many months.

"A key," he muttered, crouched low against a tree. "There must be some kind of secret key." But what? What had been unique to Vanessa, unique to her people? What had allowed them to remain secluded when they should have been discovered ages ago?

Burying his face in his blistered hands, Daniel knew a desperation so piercing that he felt his eyes begin to ache with the unfamiliar burn of unshed tears. To have come so close . . . He could not lose her now.

He turned his face skyward. Only the smallest hint of cerulean blue showed between the thick overhead branches. *Who was it that Vanessa had prayed to? The Mother?*

"Show me," he whispered. "Show me."

A faint noise to his right jerked him alert, and he held his breath as a midnight-black jaguar prowled past him, so close that he could have reached out and touched her silky coat. Teats heavy and low, the animal appeared to have recently given birth. *She is probably out looking for nourishment to feed her young,* Daniel thought, his heart pounding in his ears.

He reached for the machete he'd dropped at his feet. The animal turned and looked directly at him with eyes golden and uncannily familiar.

Daniel's fingers faltered on the machete's handle. The big cat flicked her tail like a whip. *An invitation?* At the back of his mind, Daniel wondered whether he was approaching delirium. Did he honestly believe this animal was asking him to follow her?

The mother jaguar strolled with an almost human insouciance around a cluster of trees. Knowing himself to be thoroughly crazed, Daniel rose and, with careful and deliberate steps, trailed after her. He paused beside the trees, one hand clutching the cool bark of an elm, and watched as the cat hopped up onto a low, flat rock. She gave a seductive stretch, arching her back, then, without warning, let loose a ground-shaking, ear-shattering roar that puckered his arms into gooseflesh.

As the forest still echoed with her cry, the jaguar glanced back at him. He felt his mouth go dry. The innate intelligence in those hypnotically beautiful eyes was like nothing he'd ever experienced before. *Almost nothing.* With one more swish of her tail, the cat jumped down from her perch and ambled into the nearby underbrush.

Daniel stood beside the elm for a long moment, perspiration beading along his brow. Slowly, he advanced toward the rock, keeping a watchful eye on the dense wall of greenery that had enveloped the jaguar. He stepped atop the rock, careful to avoid the slippery moss at its base. Through the trees overhead sliced a ray of sunshine.

And then it happened. The path suddenly opened up before him like an illusionist's trick. How on earth had he not seen it before? It was there before him, clear as day. He struggled with indecision for a split second, realizing that he'd left his pack and machete back at the rubber tree. But he wasn't going to risk returning for them. The trail was open. And he took it.

He sped along the path as fast as he could in booted feet, his mind racing with thoughts of what might meet him at the gates of the Ama'zon city. Hell, for all he knew, he might very well be felled by an arrow before he even reached Eldra'to's walls. After all, he doubted that he'd be welcomed back to the village with open arms. Not after he had successfully thwarted their plans for him and the hopes of the next generation of Ama'zon.

Nonetheless, if Vanessa was at Eldra'to, he had to find her. He had to speak with her, no matter the risks.

Just when he had begun to believe the trail would never end, he spied the city's outer walls. He slowed from a run to a walk, expecting that a contingent of women warriors would soon appear to apprehend him, for he'd not been stealthy in his approach.

He edged to the side of the path. A cramp stabbed at his side. Ahead, Eldra'to's wooden gates were flung wide open, yet there looked to be no movement within. He crept closer, keeping low to the ground, until he was pressed against one of the wooden posts of the gate. He strained to hear any noise that would indicate activity inside the city. Nothing. A strangely unsettling quiet seemed to hover over the Ama'zon village.

Briefly, Daniel asked himself if he should try to find the gap in the wall that he and Vanessa had used for their escape. But he was too impatient, unable to delay any longer. Creeping around the gate, he peered inside. The central square was empty, with not a soul in sight. *Could they all be gathered for some ceremony in the amphitheater?* he wondered. His gaze alert, eyes moving furtively back and forth, he slipped into the village. A skin-prickling disquiet came over him. The silence was too complete.

Picking his way warily, Daniel headed first for the arena at the far end of the city. The sun on his back was punishing and he mentally kicked himself for leaving behind his pack. Even though he no longer had any water, a sugarcane stalk would have done much to relieve his thirst.

As he glided from tree to bush to rock, he felt almost irrational in his caution. It would appear the city was totally deserted, just as the stadium proved to be upon his arrival. Glancing at the floor of the arena, Daniel allowed himself a moment to remember Reeves, to remember the man whose life he'd taken there in the ocher-colored dust.

His uneasiness mounting, Daniel left the stadium, marching boldly through the heart of the city. *To hell with the risks.* Someone had to be here. Someone had to know Vanessa's whereabouts. Yet as he strode toward the healing chambers, it became clear to him that, if anyone was in the village, she had to be in hiding.

He pushed open the doors of the familiar clay huts. At a dead run, Daniel sprinted down the corridor to the stairs. He took the risers two at a time, bolting up to the tower, blinking as he hit the rush of warm air at the top. He felt lightheaded from lack of food and sleep and had to take a couple of steadying breaths, holding firmly to the wall.

Then, from his high perch, he looked out over the Ama'zon city. It was still as death. He staggered drunkenly to the other end of the lookout tower. Nothing. There was no denying it. He had to accept the truth: The village had been abandoned.

"Vanessa!"

Where was she? Could she still be in Barra? Would his father be able to find her?

Daniel leaned his forehead against a post and closed his eyes. The ache in his chest threatened to break him in two. He could remember no darker moment in his life; no other time when he'd felt the need to surrender, to give up. He had a half-crazed notion of throwing himself from the tower. He glanced down, knowing in his heart that he could not be so cowardly.

Yet as he looked out, a tiny speck of movement caught his attention. A bird? An animal?

He lifted a flat hand to his brow and squinted into the horizon. Someone approached on the trail. A lone figure.

An Ama'zon returning home?

His father following his trail?

Or . . . could it be . . . ?

Chapter Twenty-five

Vanessa pressed the heel of her hand into her back and sighed. She was so very tired.

Ten days ago, she'd left Barra, trading in her long-sleeved, high-necked, English-made gown for a plain square of cloth she'd fashioned into a wrap, like the pelts she'd worn of old. Although infinitely more comfortable, Vanessa had been surprised by how embarrassed she had felt in the simple garb. After months of wearing layers and layers of clothing, she'd been mortified to see her legs and arms exposed, and had thus waited until she'd left Barra to change into her traveling attire.

It *had* been much easier, however, navigating the jungle without the confines of petticoat, chemise, drawers, camisole and bustle. Stays she'd not worn in months due to her pregnancy. After a day or so of travel, as she'd moved deeper into the forest, Vanessa had readjusted to her freer style of dress, recalling what it was like to feel the moist earth between her toes, the sun and wind caressing her bare skin.

But, at the moment, she took little joy from nature's wonders, from the hummingbirds flitting past on lyrical wings and the lianas dancing, awakened by the forest breeze. At the moment, Vanessa could think only of reaching Eldra'to, of resting her weary feet.

Ahead of her, the city gates stood open like arms spread wide in welcome. She shifted her pack onto her shoulders, and sighed with relief, placing her hands atop the mound of her stomach, allowing herself a modest smile. She was pleased with herself. Pleased she had brought her child home.

It took no longer than a heartbeat for Vanessa to realize that something was amiss as soon as she passed through the gates. All about her hung a silence, a cold, lifeless silence that made the hairs at the back of her neck stiffen with foreboding. Where was everyone? Why did the buildings appear idle and unused, the paths untended and overgrown with grass?

She shrugged her burden from her shoulders and slowly walked into the central square, wincing as her belly tightened again, as it had been doing all morning. Bending her ear to the wind, she sought any sound of human life.

From afar, a parrot squawked, and water from the nearby stream whispered over moss-covered rocks. She listened and waited.

Then a muffled cry shattered the stillness. A cry that quickened her pulse.

"Sa-a-a-a-ah."

Vanessa spun around, honing in on the source. Was it coming from the healing chambers? Could one of her Ama'zon sisters be injured and in need of help? Or might it be an animal, wounded and crazed with pain?

Quickly, she reached into her pack, sliding the knife she'd purchased in Barra from its leather sheath. Although she had lost a large measure of her agility these last months, she was confident she could still defend herself. Defend her unborn child.

"Vanessa-a-a-a."

The blood that had been speeding anxiously through her veins seemed to freeze. A chill washed over her. *It is not possible. . . .*

Suddenly, the door of the healing chamber crashed open. Vanessa's knees weakened and she sank slowly to the ground. "Daniel."

Before she could gather another breath, he was there, kneeling beside her, brushing the hair away from her face.

"Vanessa. My God, are you all right?"

She nodded, then reached inside herself and found the strength to look at him, to look at him without tearing open her wounded heart. A gasp escaped her.

"Daniel, what has happened to you?" Impulsively, she reached out and cradled his jaw in her palm, shocked by the new sharpness of his features. "You are so thin."

He shrugged away her concern. "I have lost some weight," he said, his gaze lowering with purpose to her rounded stomach.

She laughed lightly, self-consciously. "And I have gained some."

Long brown fingers flattened on the side of her abdomen. "Our child."

Vanessa released a shaky breath. She could not lie to him. An Ama'zon did not lie.

"Yes."

"I wish you had told me."

She looked away, afraid she might lose herself in those reproachful cocoa-colored eyes. "I wish that I had felt as if I could."

A cloud skittered across the face of the sun, offering the respite of shade.

"Have you—" Daniel noticed her pack of supplies. "My God, Vanessa. Did you *walk* from Barra?"

"Do you know of another way?" She did not, although she supposed it was possible to approach Eldra'to via the smaller waterways.

Daniel stared at her as if he was seeing her for the first time.

"Come." He took her hand, indicating with a nod of his head a sheltered patio toward the center of the square. "We should both get out of the sun."

Not releasing his hold on her, he picked up her pack with his free hand and led her to the covered court. She sank onto a bench, biting into her lip as her abdominal muscles contracted once more.

Daniel moved from the bench to crouch at her feet, taking both of her hands in his. His palms, she noticed vaguely, felt rough to the touch. "Vanessa, do you know why I have come here? Why I have traveled half the world to find you again?"

Pain, both physical and emotional, lanced through her body. "Yes," she said, hiding her sorrow. "And I am sorry to tell you that you have come in vain."

"In vain? Won't you at least allow me to a chance to explain—"

"No, Daniel," she interrupted. "There is nothing that you can say. Nothing. Although I have been dressed in an Englishwoman's clothing and have been taught all that an Englishwoman is supposed to know, I am—and will forever be—at heart, an Ama'zon."

Vanessa closed and reopened her eyes, telling herself that she had to be strong. She had to be strong for the sake of her baby. "Your mother told me you would not care, but I suspected that, once you knew the truth, you would come after your child."

His fingers tightened on hers, his lashes flickering with surprise. "Is that what you think?

You think I've come to take our baby from you?"

"I am sorry, Daniel," she said, defiant and resolute. "I will not allow it."

He dropped his chin, shaking his head, so that his wavy chestnut hair parted to reveal the vulnerable nape of his neck. When he looked back at her, his eyes were glistening as if touched by dew.

"Vanessa, listen to me. Of course I am delighted to know that we are to be parents, but it is *you* whom I want. It is you whom I have been searching for like a madman these last five months."

"Five and a half," she corrected without thinking.

"Five and a half," he repeated with a small smile.

Dismayed by what she'd inadvertently revealed, she pulled her hands from his.

"Do not forget that I know you, Daniel" she said sadly, glancing away. "I know how determined you are, how you will do anything to achieve your purpose. In London I was yours for the asking, but you did not want me then, did you? You wanted a subject for your treatise. But now I am expected to believe that it is me you desire . . . not the child growing in my womb?"

Daniel rose to sit beside her, chasing her gaze as she tried to avoid his. "All I can say in my rather poor defense is that I am a fool. A self-involved and arrogant fool totally unworthy of you. Yes, I was blinded by ambition, blinded by the need to prove myself a man, to leave my mark on the world. But you, Vanessa, showed me that those were hollow goals. That I would never be strong, never really be a man, until I accepted all of me. Accepted my limitations and weaknesses."

Gently, he took hold of her chin, drawing her around to face him. "I love you, Vanessa. I first knew I loved you that day at London's zoo, but I didn't have the courage to confess it even to myself."

Confused as she'd never been before, Vanessa brushed his fingers aside and rose to walk away from him. She needed her distance; she could not think with Daniel so near.

"How am I to believe you?"

"I would ask you to trust in your instincts. You have always been able to see through me, Vanessa. What do you see now?"

She turned around and studied his handsome, emotion-ravaged face. "I see a man who feels deeply about what he wants."

"And that is you." He jumped to his feet, running a hand across the top of his head, sending one wayward lock of hair falling across his forehead. "How can I convince you? How can I convince you to return with me to England?"

"You cannot, because I cannot return. My child and I belong here, where we will not be scorned or mocked. Where we will be accepted."

"But there is no here." Daniel stretched his arms to his sides, indicating the deserted city. "Where are all the Ama'zon? You cannot think to stay here alone."

Worry furrowed Vanessa's brow. She had no idea what had happened to drive the Ama'zon from their home.

Daniel walked forward to grip her upper arms in a direct plea. "Please come back with me, Vanessa. It was my fault that you were viewed as some sort of curiosity. My fault alone. But I swear to you that when you return to England, all the rumors will be put to rest.

"Within hours of your disappearance, I burned every shred of evidence I brought back from Eldra'to, every drawing, every note I took on board the *Angela*. I also sent a formal apology to the Naturalists Society, informing them that I had jumped to false conclusions, that there is no society of Ama'zon, but for what my imagination had crafted."

"Daniel!" she cried, aghast. "How could you do such a thing? Your reputation will be destroyed!"

"Do you think it matters to me now?" he countered, almost angrily. "To hell with science. To hell with fame. Nothing means more to me than you, Vanessa. You and our child."

Thunder rumbled in the distance, and Vanessa realized that, while they had been talking, the sky had grown dark with rain clouds. A gust of wind rushed through the courtyard, fluttering a piece of cloth tacked to one of the arbor's posts. She and Daniel took notice of it at the same time. Frowning, he released her and walked across the patio to tear the cloth from its mooring.

"What is this? Symbols? An alphabet? The Ama'zon alphabet?"

She reached for the cloth as he handed it to her. She instantly made a low sound of surprise at the back of her throat.

"What?"

"It is a message." She quickly scanned the lines. "A message they left for me."

Daniel sidled closer, peering over her shoulder. His nearness brought a warmth into Vanessa's chest and neck.

"How in blazes did they know you would come back to Eldra'to?"

"They didn't. But in the event that I did return, they wanted to reassure me."

"Reassure you of what?"

Vanessa dipped her head to her shoulder, smiling slightly. "They wanted me to know that I had successfully fulfilled the Seer's vision."

"Vision?"

"Yes." Vanessa released a ragged breath, thinking it seemed a lifetime ago that she had sat beside the old woman, holding a hand so fragile and thin.

"On her deathbed, the Ama'zon Seer told me

that I would be responsible for the fate of our people, that I would ultimately save them. I had no idea how I was expected to do this. Nor did I fully believe that I was the right choice, that I was enough of an Ama'zon. But the Seer counseled me to follow my heart, and I did." Vanessa lifted her gaze to Daniel's. "I followed you."

"But you did not follow me, Vanessa; you led me. You led me to accept myself."

"Yes."

"And this is how you saved the Ama'zon?"

"According to their message. After you and I left, the Elders recognized that the Seer had prophesied this. Without another generation of Ama'zon to carry on, they knew they could no longer remain isolated and hope to survive. The world outside Eldra'to's walls was changing; they needed to join that world, to be part of those changes."

"Where would they have gone?"

"Anywhere. Everywhere."

"Well, I'll be damned," he murmured.

Vanessa glanced at the city's open gates, a sense of peace settling over her. Her people had chosen the right path; what they had to share with the world of men was too valuable to keep hidden here in the jungle.

And just as her people had chosen, now she must choose. Choose her destiny, her path.

Though born a child of the jungle, Vanessa knew herself to be a woman now. A woman who had successfully bridged two cultures, who had learned to accept the differences in those cultures—and the differences within herself. She had begun her journey a naive, untested girl; today she would leave the jungle at Daniel's side a woman both wiser and more confident.

Her decision made, Vanessa started to reach for Daniel's hand when she was taken off guard by another piercing spasm across her abdomen. She clutched for Daniel's fingers as the contraction continued for many long and painful seconds. When she again opened her eyes, she found Daniel staring at her, his expression wary.

"Are you . . . ? Now . . . ?"

With a resigned smile, she lifted a shoulder, accepting the inevitable.

"My God." Daniel huffed a nervous laugh. "Remind me to kiss my father's feet when we see him next, will you?"

Vanessa rubbed at her back with her fist, recovering her breath. "What do you mean?"

Daniel surprised her by leaning forward and kissing her full on the lips. A kiss so gentle, so sweet, she felt like weeping when he finally pulled away from her.

"I know this is going about the matter rather backwards, but . . . will you marry me, Vanessa?"

"Oh, Daniel, I—"

He pressed two fingers against her lips. "There's no use in saying 'no,'" he confessed ruefully, "since my father has already taken care of the matter and you are already legally my wife."

Vanessa's mouth formed a shocked *oh.* "Can he do that?"

Daniel shrugged. "As the saying goes, my love, the acorn does not fall far from the oak."

A sharp exhalation signaled the onset of another contraction as lightning cracked above them in a showy display of brilliant white. Vanessa gasped.

Daniel kissed her behind the ear. "Please, say yes."

"Oh, oh."

"Say, 'Yes, Daniel, I will be your wife.' "

"Yes," she managed between shallow pants. "Yes, Daniel, I will be your wife."

As if on cue, the skies opened their floodgates and rain began to fall in thick gray sheets all around their small shelter. Vanessa and Daniel shared a meaningful look as he reached for her other hand.

"I love you, Jaguar Eyes."

"I love you, too, Daniel."

Epilogue

Harold Thomas Heywood, the future Earl Bretton, was born in an abandoned village in the heart of the Amazon jungle during a thunderous lightning storm. Twenty-four hours after his birth he was strapped to his mother's back and carried for five long days through the forest to a moldy-smelling dinghy. At one month of age he was crossing the tempest-tossed seas of the Atlantic. By the time he was three months old he'd visited three different continents.

Young Harold settled with his parents at his father's baronial estate in Lincolnshire. As his father, Lord Heywood, worked to prepare himself to one day accept the duties of an earldom, his mother provided him three dark-haired, golden-eyed brothers with whom to play. His grandfather visited regularly. His grandmother he never knew, for she had died unexpectedly of a fever prior to his birth.

When Harold was old enough to ask about his mother's parents, she told him that she'd been an orphan, and had shared with him stories of her childhood, growing up in the jungle. Fascinated, Harold vowed to someday return to the site of his birth, to someday explore the very heart of the Amazon.

As for the fate of the Ama'zon, call it coincidence—or not—but in the decades following Harold's birth, the movement for women's suffrage gained strength in cities all over the world, as a new sense of female empowerment swept from London to New York to Paris. One John Stuart Mill, dear friend to women's rights advocate Mrs. Edgar Longhorn, wrote in his essay "On the Subjection of Women":

> If men had ever been found in society without women, or women without men, or if there had been a society of men and women in which the women were not under the control of the men, something might have been positively known about the mental and moral differences which may be inherent in the nature of each.

AUTHOR'S NOTE

As much as possible, I adhered to historical fact in the writing of this fantasy tale. I did, however, take the liberty of creating a cousin for Charles Darwin in the form of Samantha Perkins. I hope that he posed no objections.